Sam has his life after graduation figured out. Until then he has to deal with being terrorized for expressing his gender identity. His pleas for help have been ignored by the principal and most of the staff, and his time is spent moving quickly between classrooms and anticipating the freedom that will come with leaving high school behind.

Teacher Todd Keegan, at first, wonders if Amanda is on drugs and if he's underestimated her maturity. Between enabling his traumatized, dependent sister and hiding secrets of his own, Todd has no desire to waste time on a junkie teenager, but this one intrigues him. When Amanda shows up in his classroom, bleeding from a head wound, he decides to investigate further.

In order to survive senior year, Sam must convince Mr. Keegan that he's not a junkie teenager and decide if, unlike his family and school staff, this teacher can be trusted with the truth and become his only ally.

THE SIMPLICITY OF

BEING NORMAL

James Stryker

Published by
NineStar Press
PO Box 91792
Albuquerque, New Mexico, 87199
www.ninestarpress.com

Warning: This book contains bullying and violence specific to YA transgender character; mentions of past assault and sexual abuse.

Print ISBN # 978-1-947139-02-2
Cover by Natasha Snow
Edited by BJ Toth

For a young man who didn't have much faith that things could get better, Jane Watson Butterfield, Chris Weicks, and Penny Armstrong made a difference.

Acknowledgements:

While I'm now fortunate to have the support of multiple individuals—family, friends, and coworkers—this wasn't always the case. The three people to whom this book is dedicated were my champions when I felt I had no others. I am beyond grateful that they looked past my teenage strangeness to not only find value, but encourage me to develop confidence in myself.

Again, parts of this work were also written in memory of my grandmother, Elaine. The role she played in my life could span multiple volumes.

I'm always indebted to my wife, Jayme, for believing in my weird projects and supporting my endeavors to launch them into the world via continuous coffee supply, and not decapitating me.

I've continued to learn as a writer thanks to the editing counsel provided by BJ Toth. Thanks to her guidance, this and future works won't feature the unintentional migration of eyeballs.

And from the first idea to the last proof being sent, everything I write is created with you, the reader, in mind. *Simplicity* was a difficult book to bring to life, but the idea of you reading it saw me through the writing. Thank you.

Author's Note:

Respecting a person's chosen name, authentic gender, and terminology are critical pieces of accepting an individual for who they are. As language evolves, the terms people use to refer to themselves will continue to be fluid and largely dependent on preference.

In *The Simplicity of Being Normal*, Sam refers to himself as *transgendered* rather than *transgender*. Sam is based on a facet of the transgender community with whom I am personally acquainted and prefer this terminology. Sam feels that the connotation of *transgendered* being "something that happened" to him accurately describes his experience. For him, it's a circumstance that has occurred to an otherwise normal male identity—he doesn't view it as a permanent definition of himself.

The purpose of this Author's Note is to clarify that, while there are current recommendations on appropriate terminology, it's important to recognize diversity within transgender experiences. Allowing that someone's feelings about an experience may be different is an important part of the community pulling together to advance LGBT rights issues.

ONE

SAM PUSHED HIMSELF up from the tiles in the school hallway, and the back of his head throbbed. Though it seemed like he was walking on a waterbed, he managed to stagger into the bathroom. He leaned over the second in a line of sinks and, without looking into the rectangular mirror, threw up.

The memories returned as pain radiated down his neck. He saw it again in his mind. Felt it again. The hands on his shoulders, forcing him to the side. Bringing his body forward and then back. Whipping his head against the brick wall. Again, and again, and again. His eyes rolling and seeing the florescent lights pinging from one side of the hall to another.

"Say you're a girl! Come on, say it! Say it!" But their words had eventually melded into one long syllable. The last thing he'd heard was a crack before everything had fallen away.

Sam squeezed his eyes shut and grasped the sides of the sink to steady himself.

"What do you think you're doing in here?"

In the mirror, he met the eyes of a boy he didn't recognize. The stranger was shorter than Sam, and the round bottom of an inhaler extruding from his pocket indicated that an escape made at a sprint could be successful. But the pain that started in the back of Sam's head told him to be afraid.

"You'll get in trouble for being in here." The student curled his upper lip. "I'll get a teacher. It's against the law."

Being in the men's room wasn't against the law. It made people uneasy, which was why Sam didn't use public bathrooms and kept himself strategically dehydrated on weekdays. As far as dressing for gym went, he'd been using the vacant handicapped bathroom, but that had ceased to be safe a few weeks ago. Now he just hoped his movement to the next secure location would be fast enough.

That's all school was—a constant migration to the next safety zone. He pined for the fifty-five minutes spent in trigonometry and United States history. In trig, the comically rotund teacher never rolled out of the room, and US history was wonderful because of Mr. Keegan. Among other things, Mr. K also didn't leave his classroom unattended.

"Are you deaf? You don't belong in here! Get out!"

Sam glanced at his own reflection, the cause of the student's demand for his immediate departure. He patted the back of his head, and a jolt spiked through his brain. When he withdrew his hand, blood stained his fingertips. But it wouldn't matter if he was bleeding out his eyes, he'd still have to go. He stuck his hand under the running water.

"I'm sorry." Sam turned to face the young man, who appeared to be compressing and decompressing like an image in a funhouse mirror. "My mistake."

He stumbled from the bathroom. The empty hallways and the clock above the lockers confirmed that dismissal had been fifteen minutes prior. Had the sound of the buzzer woken him?

I should go to the hospital. Sam pulled his hand back from the tender spot every few seconds to rub his thumb and pointer finger together. To feel that the blood was smooth, but that it was only blood. That his brain wasn't starting to protrude through his skull.

But I can't. There's no point in doing anything or telling anyone.

"Kids get hurt in gym class," Principal Smith had said when the boys had taken Sam's wrist and slammed it against the gymnasium's brick wall. He'd then ordered Sam to leave the office. His time was very valuable.

The memory of Mr. Smith's reaction to his "accident" was short-lived. Sam heard a door close, and the wall clock became a timer. He was alone. And he heard footsteps echoing up the adjacent hall. His muscles tensed as he primed himself to run.

It'd be foolish to try to make it out of the building. Even if he did, it was more dangerous on the outside. Sam didn't want to vanish and be found twenty years later when construction workers excavated a field for a strip mall. The school was filled with tigers, but the walls of the cage were defined.

There was a bathroom behind the deserted main office. It was along the outer wall and had windows facing the street. If he could make it there, he could barricade himself and watch the windows for them to give up and leave.

The footsteps quickened, and he heard boys laughing. Sam didn't look as the group rounded the corner behind him. He began to run. And as he started to run, so did the pack.

Their sneakers pounded in unison against the vinyl tiles, and he knew he wouldn't make it to the bathroom. He was no match for a herd of teenage boys when the floor persisted in tilting. He lost precious milliseconds weaving to keep on the teetering lower side.

"There it goes!" one of them shouted.

Sam almost gave up. But he heard music from a classroom to his right and saw an open door. He dodged into the room, grabbing the door behind him as the harmonica solo wailed, and a soccer ball rolled down the hallway.

Forty-five pairs of eyes stared at him as he caught his breath. The room swirled, and each set of eyes seemed to move, though only one actually did.

"Are you okay?"

The sound of four chair legs dragging across the tiles made him wince. He raked his watery vision along the presidential posters that bordered the left side and back of the classroom. Sam focused on the face of Mr. Keegan, but he had to blink several times to interpret the man's expression. His brow wrinkled, and the skin underneath his eyes was pinched.

When was the last time someone worried about me? That someone looked at me with concern not originating out of self-interest? Probably when his grandmother had died a couple of years ago. *But they "cared" about me in the same way a person rubbernecks past a car accident, or outside a building on fire. That's all I am, first-class entertainment for morbid assholes.*

Mr. Keegan didn't look at him like that. He had nothing to gain. And Sam hesitated. For the first time, he considered telling someone his secret.

"Are you okay?" Mr. Keegan repeated. Although Sam had watched his approach, it seemed as if the teacher had materialized before him.

"Yes. Well, no. I—" Sam tried to form a smile. It felt lopsided and he considered tilting his head to counter it. "I just have a migraine."

"I'm sorry to hear that."

Sam didn't reply. He stared at the man now sitting on one of the student desktops. Mr. Keegan wore a yellow button-up shirt with a gold-striped tie. The sleeves of the shirt were rolled, and with his arms straight and his hands curled around the sides of the desk, Sam could see the winged "A" logo tattooed on his inner elbow. He wore the same tan slacks and leather shoes he always did. And his auburn hair was immaculately combed, his glasses straight and tight to his face.

Last year, when Sam had been in Mr. K's AP US History class, his mother had been convinced that he'd had a crush on his teacher. Sam denied it. Mr. Keegan was young—no more than thirty, and he wasn't bad-looking. But Sam didn't want to be with him.

"Then you want me to be with him, I guess," Scarlet had said without sarcasm. "Is he single?"

"No," Sam had replied. *God, no. Even if he was, I'd tell you he wasn't. You don't deserve him.*

Mrs. Keegan actually taught freshman English at the same school. She'd never been Sam's teacher, and he'd said less than two words to her. But every year when Mr. K took his AP US class on a week-long tour to Washington, DC, she accompanied as a chaperone. Sam had expected the best part of the trip would be studying Mr. Keegan outside of school; however, he hadn't anticipated how Mrs. K's presence would elevate the entire experience. He'd loved watching them together. She looked nice with Mr. K and completed the fantasy that his mother would've destroyed.

Sam didn't want Scarlet to be with Mr. Keegan, and he didn't want to be with him himself.

I want to be *you. So badly, you have no idea...*

"Do you have a ride home? Can I call someone for you?" After waiting several awkward seconds for a response, Mr. Keegan spoke again. He tried to hold Sam's eye contact, but Sam could only see him clearly through one eye at a time.

"Yes, I'm fine." As Sam nodded, the room made a giant dip forward, then back. The action brought to mind the image of a drinking bird toy.

What also occurred to him was that the coast was likely clear. There were never guarantees, but he doubted anyone would wait after he'd sought asylum in a teacher's classroom. If they thought their bullying was being reported, they'd scatter like a group of dirty pigeons and pretend to have never been pursuing him.

"I'll see you tomorrow, Mr. K." He clapped a hand over the back of his head and inched toward the door in reverse.

"Ms. Porter, are you sure you're okay?"

The heart must be made of something like snakeskin, in that pieces of it were continually being sloughed off. Only, once detached, they ceased to be dead cell fragments. They became baseball-sized hailstones falling from his chest and pelting his stomach, dent after dent. Crater after fucking crater.

"Yes, thank you."

Sam slipped out the door so quickly that upon turning he ran into a woman. The collision sent her sprawling to the floor, the books and papers she'd been carrying falling around her. Customarily, Sam would eagerly retrieve the articles as he apologized, but he had to clasp his hands at either side of his spinning head to keep upright. When he'd regained his center enough to focus, he paused.

Mrs. Keegan hadn't moved.

I only bumped into you. You aren't hurt.

But she remained on the floor, her arms curled above her head and her breaths panicked. She didn't even look at him until he said her name and fumbled an apology. Only at the sound of his voice had she relaxed.

"Amanda." Mrs. Keegan turned onto her knees to collect the scattered books and papers. "I didn't see you."

Sam didn't know which was worse. The name his teachers, classmates, and family used, or what Mr. K called him. The former hurt the most. When his mental faculties weren't impaired and he was called "Ms. Porter," he could pretend the title wasn't part of it. And he liked how Mr. Keegan pronounced his last name.

Mr. K wasn't from Idaho—something else that set him apart from the other teachers and drew Sam's desire to emulate him. He wasn't a born-and-raised Mormon. A good old boy with a CTR ring on his finger and magic underwear beneath his clothes. He was from New Orleans.

He says N'walins.

Sam further felt a camaraderie toward him, because he thought that *if* Mr. Keegan ever *did* know his secret, he wouldn't turn Sam away and say something like "Kids get hurt in gym class." Mr. Keegan wasn't one of them. He didn't pander to the asswipes that filled his classroom.

"I could try to persuade you that what you could learn inside these walls could have an impact on your life," Mr. K had said to an obnoxious student he'd held after class while Sam watched from the back desk. The teacher had folded his arms with an easy air. "But I care as much about encouraging you as you care about being here.

"I didn't become a teacher to inspire anyone. I like to hear myself talk about something I enjoy. It means nothing to me if you take anything from my classes. But don't disrupt my lectures. I paid a lot of money, and spent a lot of time, listening to other people pontificate to have the pleasure of doing so myself."

Sam liked how he was cool and put together. Mr. Keegan hadn't been poisoned by Idaho yet. He put the dumb fucks in their places. He had an Aerosmith tattoo on his arm. He had a beautiful wife and spent every day doing what he loved. He was perfect and proof there could be a life beyond. And he had an accent where he didn't pronounce the "r" on words that ended in "r."

So, Sam could tolerate "Ms. Porter" better, though it still stung.

"Amanda." Mrs. Keegan snapped her fingers in front of his face and brought him back to the present. "Do you need help with something?"

"No." Sam scrambled for an explanation. "I was checking with Mr. K when we're meeting on Thursday."

"The parking lot at five in the morning," she answered.

There was no way Sam needed to be reminded of this information. Since he'd secured permission to go on the Washington, DC, trip again, he'd practically been counting the hours until departure.

Safety for a week. Getting free of this shit hole and being around him. Watching and imagining I'll be like him someday. Sam took a deep breath. *And I'll take the opportunity to be myself. I'm going to go back to The Attic.*

There were many reasons he was reluctant to disclose his secret to Mr. Keegan or reveal that anything was amiss, but the possibility of being barred from Washington, DC, had the strongest pull. He needed that mini liberation.

"Thanks, Mrs. K. I'll see you then."

Sam had covered his injury and walked down the hall. No one could know, not yet. He wasn't ready for anything official with the trip on the line.

The rest was fuzzy, but somehow Sam had made it home.

The next morning, he woke in his bedroom and held his breath to quell the nausea. When he turned, he saw the dried blood that stained his pillowcase. Putting his hand to the back of his head, he felt parts of his hair were crispy and stuck together.

Despite the fact he'd had no interaction with her, Scarlet hadn't checked on him. She'd come home the night before and gone about her usual routine. By the time he got up in the morning, she was usually gone for work. His brain could've swollen and perforated his skull. He could have never woken up. If he told her about the students beating his head into a wall until he lost consciousness, she'd ask if any of their fathers were single.

I could be dead a hundred times. Tears rolled down Sam's cheeks, and he brought his knees to his chest. *If that fucking teacher wouldn't leave the room unattended and do her damn job. If everyone would do their job. The principal. The parents of those motherfuckers. If my mother would do her fucking job!*

Sam swallowed and unfolded his legs. *But I'm not going to hide at home. I won't be afraid. Well, I'll be afraid. But I'll just be more careful. And I can't afford any more absences.*

He took his cell phone from the nightstand and flipped it open to silence the alarm.

It can't go on like this forever. Three months until I graduate, and they can kiss my ass. I'll be able to do something about my situation. I'll make it out.

Sam stood, but unfortunately, misjudged the dizziness he thought had left him. The room churned. He put his hand to the nightstand and snapped his eyes shut to keep from crashing to the floor. The phone wasn't as lucky.

The hard plastic cracked, reminding him of the sound his skull had made against the brick wall. When he reopened his eyes, there were three pieces of the phone at his feet, but in his mind, he saw himself. Limp and broken in the hallway with blood pouring from his head. His confidence almost evaporated.

If I make it out. If they let me.

He crossed the room to get dressed.

TWO

THREE YEARS AGO, Todd Keegan's sister had given him an Aerosmith video slot machine. It'd become one of his mind-numbing activities to sit on a barstool in his library and cycle quarters through it for hours when he couldn't sleep or when something was bothering him.

At first, he hadn't known what to do with it. He wasn't fond of gambling, though neither was his sister. She was mechanically inclined and enjoyed refurbishing old casino games. Before they moved to Idaho, she'd been on the verge of starting what may have been a lucrative business repairing and reselling machines.

And you were only nineteen—far ahead of the game with everything in line and ready to go. You made me look like a slacker. He frowned and slipped a few more quarters into the machine. *Sometimes the person you used to be makes a brief appearance, but not often.*

"Come on, Todd. You can put it in your library," Julie had said.

"Sure, a library is a great place for a slot machine. Will you get me a neon beer sign for my birthday? I'll read David McCullough by flickering florescent lights to the beat of pinball machines."

"Give it a chance."

Todd had to admit the game had grown on him. He loaded it with eight hundred quarters from the animal cracker bucket and hit Max Bet until he lost it all. Then he'd unlock the cover to run through the change again. There was something about watching the seven reels spin, the flashing lights, and getting a bonus game or jackpot that he enjoyed.

Instant gratification. That desire for payout with little effort given.

Todd was used to putting a lot of effort into anything he received fulfillment from. He had a habit of worrying and thinking continuously, which made him feel somewhat like a rock tumbler.

And that gets old when it's everything.

A good example was the situation with his sister. It shouldn't be something he mulled over four years later. But Julie was another fucking river rock he couldn't pull from the barrel. He felt like an asshole for even wanting to.

Really, this is therapy for me, Todd thought as he hit Max Bet and watched the reels. All seven whirled at the same speed for a blissful ten seconds before slowing. *No prep, consequences, skills, or emotional strings. Hit the button, and hope for the jackpot. If you get it, awesome. If not, hit Max Bet again.*

The combination of symbols yielded a bonus game. Twelve mystery boxes appeared on the screen; each hiding items to fight the New World Order, the organization who'd abducted Aerosmith with the intention of destroying rock and roll. He could make three selections to accrue objects with enough value to free a member of the band.

I will rescue you, Joe Perry. Todd selected the box in the upper-right corner. It revealed a machine gun, a moderately good choice. He touched the box in the lower-left corner. A ticket stub, also a respectable pick. His finger hovered over the center.

"Don't do it." Julie stood at the doorframe, her smile illuminated by the neon beer sign she'd given him for his twenty-seventh birthday. "I told you. Pick from the inner circle."

"That's your strategy. And there is no strategy. It's random, and I'm fine on my own."

"You should take your responsibilities seriously, Todd. The future of rock and roll rests on your shoulders." She sat on the barstool beside him. "If the New World Order succeeds—"

"Shut up." Todd pushed the center mystery box. The image of an electric guitar filled the screen followed by an LCD graphic of Joe Perry being released from the evil headquarters. Joe appeared disheveled and emaciated, but he was free, all thanks to the strongest weapon of all— music. Todd glanced at his sister. "If I didn't know any better, I might think you're a member of the NWO yourself."

"Holding a rock band hostage is a full-time occupation. When do I have time for it? Between grading papers? Working on machines? Taking care of you?"

Todd turned to the machine and scooped his payout from the latest liberation into the animal cracker bucket. He wasn't the one who needed constant care and reassurance. While he might be attached to the leash, he held the loop. When he cared enough to lead, *he* led.

"You're up late," Julie said.

"Yep. Hope I didn't wake you."

"I could sense the forces of darkness. The impending doom of Steven Tyler. That you might require my assistance in saving the—"

Todd pulled the slot machine's cord from the electrical outlet. He held it in his hand, the plug ticking back and forth.

Complete and indifferent control.

"It's a game, Julie." He folded his arms. "Is something wrong? What do you need?"

"I wanted to make sure you were okay."

He imagined her bolting up at the slight creak the stairs made when he'd descended. She would've spent fifteen minutes clutching the comforter to her chest and panicking. Had it been him, or someone else? Was he coming or going? If going, where to? Was he leaving the house? Should she check? Follow?

Tag me like I'm a criminal. Put me on GPS so you can track my proximity. How long did you stand outside the door calming yourself before you came in? Look at you, trying to play it cool. You wanted to make sure I was okay? Wrong. You wanted to make sure I was still here, and you *could be okay.*

"Really, are you okay?" Julie asked again.

Todd crossed the room to a mini-fridge set on a long table.

You're turning my library into a man cave. He pulled two emerald beer bottles from the fridge. *Someday you'll replace my Newton's cradle with a dish of corn nuts.*

"I find myself worrying over things I don't customarily care about."

There wasn't anyone else he could talk to, and for all the ways she irritated him, she usually gave decent counsel. He handed one of the bottles to her and twisted off his own cap.

"Things would be much easier if all our cares were focused on the New World Order." Julie took two swallows from her beer bottle. "What's your problem?"

"Remember Amanda Porter? She went to DC last year."

"Popular girl. Hangs around with the goody-goody clique. I ran into her as she was leaving your room today. Or rather, she ran into me." She rocked her beer bottle by the neck and gave him a narrow look. "If you have a jones for her, Todd, I don't want to know."

"You're a sick bitch."

"No, you're a sick bitch if that's your issue."

"It's not." Todd leaned on the desk he'd once used to grade papers. To arrange lesson plans and packets. He'd unfold a map on the desk and plot coordinates or use his magnifying glass to examine the smallest details. Now the surface of his desk was home to Julie's lava lamp, an open jar of olives, and fanned-out arcade game manuals. He pushed them aside and sat on the desktop. "I think she's on drugs."

"And you care?" His sister raised an eyebrow.

"Yes."

She grasped her chest and swallowed, speaking slowly. "'And what happened, then? Well, in Whoville they say—that 'the Grinch's small heart grew three sizes—'"

"Can you manage thinking before you speak?" Todd snapped. "If it won't be amusing to anyone else but you, say it in your head, laugh to yourself, and move the fuck on."

"Well, there's no fun in that. I like to hear myself talk as much as you do."

Todd had no illusions of grandeur, and he didn't pine for *Dead Poets* or *Emperor's Club* glory. He talked a good game in an interview, but he didn't care much about his students. Since a person couldn't be forced to absorb something against their will, why put massive amounts of energy toward futile attempts at cramming information into thick skulls?

The only person worth that effort is the only person you can completely depend on. The bottom line is I only have complete control over myself. Occasionally one of the lemmings turns around and runs into the wood chipper. When the choice is cliff or wood chipper, and I can't influence either, I take a third option. I don't give a shit and do what I want.

What he wanted to do was lecture—it was one of his favorite things. To be the focal point and hold all the aces. Before deciding on teaching, he'd considered pushing this narcissistic propensity into some kind of performing. But audiences came and went. Fads shifted. If he was lucky enough to achieve popularity, he'd fall out of it. But what never changed was the endless parade of teenagers filling twenty-five desks six times a day. And while a *captivated* audience was ideal, a *captive* one was also gratifying.

It was the perfect job, and he got most of what he needed from it. He liked history and enjoyed sharing what he knew even though few, if any, of the little idiots grasped the finer nuances of the subject. Their brains were too saturated with designer clothes, boy bands, Japanese animation, and whatever else they were into. The neural pathways for drawing patterns and deriving pleasure from dates, facts, and historical figures had been eroded with cheeseburgers.

However, there was a more important knowledge that he found easier to impart. Based on his disinterest and his refusal to negotiate or empathize, he could coax a vital life lesson to grow in the shamrock shake mush of the teenage brain.

You aren't entitled to anyone else's understanding or sympathy. When you're microwaving burgers at McDonald's, your boss won't give a shit if you're sleepy or if your hamster died. Outside the high school doors, there's no more "cut poor little Snoochie a break." Fuck little Snoochie. That's the most valuable thing I could teach you.

On principle then, he didn't care what the little Snoochies did if they weren't disrupting his classes. They could space out. There could be tears behind their doe eyes because they broke up with their boyfriend, or they didn't make the swim team, or any other meaningless teenager problem. They could be shooting up with cat piss or breathing feces from balloons. Just shut the hell up while he was talking and pay him the respect he'd earned and deserved. That's why it'd been hysterical when a group of them had been caught in The Attic on last year's Washington, DC, trip. They'd been easy to convince that he'd care about their fake IDs, drugging their chaperones, or sneaking into a club.

Oh, the debauchery.

Todd had been in the bathroom at the time, but Julie told him how the students came giggling through the door. They didn't have the magic alcohol-securing bracelets, but were tickled at having made it past the bouncer and into another dimension. Until they saw Julie. He could imagine how the color must've drained from their faces.

She told them he was in the bathroom. And not that it mattered, since they were responsible adults, but they were stopping for a drink on the way to dinner. Why at The Attic? The same reason their group had chosen this club to saunter into. Curiosity. Did they know misrepresenting age was a misdemeanor in Washington, DC? They'd better get their asses to the hotel before Mr. Keegan returned. If *he* caught them there'd be hell to pay. She was more willing to forgive and forget.

They were gone before Todd came back to the table. And while Julie had urged him to take the situation seriously, he'd only been entertained. So, what? If they didn't overdose, commit murder, or have sex with anyone but each other, what did it matter? How hilarious that they believed he would've done anything. It wasn't his job to coddle and keep them innocent. They needed to make it on their own.

That's what bothers you about Julie. She made you bend your standards. And that's what also bugs you about caring that Amanda Porter is on drugs. She's also making you bend your standards.

Julie set her empty bottle on the floor of Todd's library. "What's the big deal? You're supposed to care about your students. That's good. Feeling something for someone else."

I'm incapable of feeling, yep. That's why I let you use me.

"She's a smart girl. She shouldn't be so stupid," he said.

"What makes you think she's on drugs? She was weird when she knocked me down in the hallway, but you know how these girls are. Moody. Irritable. Pull your eyelids over your head infuriating."

"She's been different this year."

Todd's beer bottle was half-full, but he went to the fridge and took another, which he walked to his sister.

Julie had been accurate in her rundown of who Amanda Porter *had been*. A popular girl in the sanctimonious clique, one of the high school breeds Todd had the least patience for. But she hadn't annoyed him like the others. On the contrary, Amanda seemed to understand their specific and only functions. As the teacher, he was there to lecture. As the student, she was there to hang on his every word. Which she did, but not in the brown-nosing way. And also, not in the pitiable puppy-dog fashion that meant she didn't get enough love at home and was desperately trying to bond with anyone. Amanda took things seriously. She had a genuine interest and showed initiative—two things he highly valued.

So, after serious consideration, he'd broken his longstanding rule about letting students spend a class period being his "assistant." Sure, since her presence didn't irritate him, she could waste her time grading tests or stapling packets. Todd cared as much about that as he did if she wanted to huff glue behind the school parking lot. But now that she might be huffing glue, he was concerned.

Amanda's senior year began differently. At first, she wasn't hanging around the same crowd, and she looked depressed. She stopped wearing makeup and tight-fitting clothes. All things Todd noted, though of themselves they didn't set off any warning flags. It was the typical teenage identity crisis. But then her grades started to dip. She was absent for days at a time, and when she returned, she looked exhausted. She lost a lot of weight. And she was silent.

"She came into my room twenty minutes after dismissal." Todd inadvertently placed his palm in a wet beer ring on his desk. He knew it belonged to Julie, and he wiped his hand on his pants with a scowl. "She was still wearing her gym clothes, she looked panicked, and she couldn't focus on me."

"No one can possibly focus any more on you than *you* do." Julie set her second empty bottle beside the first.

Sometimes he wanted to staple his sister's mouth shut. He might as well be talking to a brick wall. An annoying, emotionally dependent brick wall. A brick wall that didn't use coasters. He was better off resolving the Amanda problem solo while saving Aerosmith from the New World Order.

"I mean literally focus. She couldn't keep eye contact with me. Her pupils were unequal. She said she had a migraine. She was shaking. That's coke, Julie."

"You've stared into the dilated eyes of how many other teenage drug addicts and shrugged it off?"

Todd knew she wouldn't be persuaded by "I care and don't know why." Even if *that* was the real problem. She obviously wasn't in the mood to be helpful, and he wasn't in the frame of mind to deal with her shit. Yes, there had to be a reason the Grinch's heart grew. Grinch hearts didn't spontaneously enlarge. He had some form of Grinch heart disease. That's what it felt like. A disease.

"I don't want someone to overdose while they're on my watch. They can sneak into any clubs they want. But no OD'ing," he said.

"Tell her she can't go if she doesn't take a drug test. Report it to the counselor. Todd, you can't go back to The Attic."

The rush of power from such a simple manipulation.

"I'll do whatever I want." Todd again hopped off the desk. "Same as last year. We babysit while Janet and Doug have dinner on Wednesday in Pennsylvania. And they assume the watch tower with their sniper rifles on Friday."

"Some watch tower. They're such morons."

As many idiots were, Janet and Doug were old and college educated. Somewhere in the thirty-five years they'd spent teaching wild baboons, one of them had had the misfortune to get a paper cut and become infected with the "teenage stupid." The pathogen had been passed to the other via denture or arthritis cream. How else did two adult people get drugged every year on a school field trip? How did they not know you couldn't trust any student as far as you could throw them?

You never eat or drink anything that isn't factory sealed. If you open it and set it down, you assume it's been contaminated. Never take anything they offer you, no matter how innocent. Sleep with one eye open.

The couple was elevated above the students due to their usefulness, but they weren't worth brooding over. Todd gathered Julie's two empty bottles with his own and tossed them in the garbage can.

"Whether you come is immaterial to me, Julie, but I'm going."

"It's fucking stupid. You were inches from getting caught last year."

"So? What are they going to do?"

"Get you fired."

"Let them try. Let them succeed." He shrugged.

Todd did care about being fired or being strong armed into resigning. Despite his motivations for the career choice, and even if he wasn't a weepy "every child is someone's baby" teacher, he enjoyed what he did.

But the only reason you care about me being fired is that would mean relocation. Where would you find another sweet setup like this? You never have to be more than fifty yards away from me. Todd considered jamming a fork into the electrical outlet instead of plugging his slot machine in. He was a dick to think such things, let alone mean them at times, but he didn't have a fork on him.

Julie sighed as the LCD screen illuminated.

"I'll go with you."

Thought you might.

"You should talk to Amanda Porter tomorrow." His sister stood for a second in the doorway.

"Good night, Julie." He kept his eyes on the screen.

"Good luck with the New World Order." Her voice faded.

"Don't need it." Todd finished the rest of his thought under his breath. "Although, thanks to you, Joe Perry is once more being held captive. We'll fix that though. It's only two in the morning, and I have DayQuil. Time waits for no man when the future of rock and roll is on the line."

He deposited a reasonable amount of quarters from the animal cracker bucket and resumed pressing Max Bet. And thinking about his student, Amanda Porter, and why he gave a shit if she was on cocaine.

THREE

IT WAS BAD enough that Sam's mother had blown up at him that morning, but to have the looming expectation of a talk with Mr. Keegan after school?

And it's always bad. I only get spoken to when it's—

His thoughts broke off as he heard footsteps outside the handicapped bathroom door. This time, he didn't panic. As rehearsed, he slipped his backpack over the hook on the stall door. He then stepped onto the toilet seat and balanced on the right side, his fingertips pressed against the wall to steady himself.

Why are you tempting fate, Sam? Trading discomfort and feeling like a pervert for safety. Not that he was sure of being any safer in the girls' locker room. For all he knew, they might be anxious to start the harassment. He couldn't accurately predict potential allies or enemies. The only person he could rely on was himself.

The footsteps stopped. The bathroom door opened, and Sam held his breath. Behind closed eyelids, he saw the bathroom stall as it'd looked three weeks ago. Threats scrawled across the door and walls in black marker. It took him forty-five minutes after school to scrub them away.

The door closed. He waited a few more seconds before opening his eyes. The entire bathroom was dark, but he balanced on the toilet seat in silence. He imagined one of them standing in the darkness by the sink, waiting for him to breathe and give his presence away.

What is he holding? A knife to pare the skin from your muscles? A hammer to break your bones? Ropes to strangle you? To tie you down and rape you? Sam shook his head. *You're paranoid. They may have come in, but once they saw the bathroom deserted they left. They aren't so—*

"Fuck." A disappointed voice. And a kick to the door. A slice of light cut into the bathroom. "She's gone. Bitch."

The footsteps faded.

Sweat poured from Sam's brow, but he stepped down from the toilet seat and felt for his backpack. Reaching inside, he found the ribbed collar of his polo and pulled it free.

It's only three more months. I should suck it up and go back to the locker room.

Sam had been surprised that his request to use the unisex bathroom across from the gymnasium had been granted at all. There hadn't been cause for it to be denied; he had a reputation as a good student and wasn't a troublemaker. But who knew how far that status would carry him, especially if the rumors reached the gym teacher? He'd been worrying over the gym problem since the class reared its ugly head on his schedule.

"You won't like gym any more as a senior than you will as a sophomore. Get it done now," the guidance counselor had advised when Sam had been selecting his class schedule as a freshman.

He'd learned long ago that most adult suggestions could be taken with a grain of salt; however, he should've heeded the guidance counselor's recommendation. But how was he supposed to anticipate that the feelings he'd had for years and been shoving aside—the feelings of not being Amanda, and of really being Sam—how could he have foreseen that the true part of him that was Sam would refuse to be silenced during his senior year?

And how could I have also known that the bathroom would be my undoing? I never thought it would go this far. I knew I'd be shunned, but I never thought they'd physically hurt me. They used to be my friends.

Sam pulled his polo on in the darkness and fumbled through the backpack for a comb.

If he had the option again, he would've taken the required gym credits two years ago. And if he couldn't rewind that far, he might've forgone using the handicapped bathroom to change in. But not having the knowledge of how bad things would get, at the beginning of the trimester he'd asked the teacher about the unisex bathroom. The worst she could say was no.

"I have a problem with people watching me change."

"Everyone thinks everyone else is looking at them." The teacher had rolled her eyes. "No one is looking at you, twenty-three. You all have the same stuff."

That burned. One of those hailstones the size of a car. It was so big it crushed him. A pestle grinding him into its mortar. But he'd shoved aside the hurt. His cause wasn't dead. He still had an ace. A shameful ace, but one nonetheless.

"I used to be okay with it, but I have this thing about privacy. I'll get you a note from my psych if you want." Sam had leveled his eyes with the gym teacher and tried to look unhinged around the edges.

He was fully aware that the school had flagged him as "emotionally disturbed." Anyone discovered to be seeing a therapist received this identifier. When Sam's parents divorced seven years prior, he'd met with a psychologist provided free of charge by the school for a few sessions.

But Sam couldn't get an excuse from the doctor. He hadn't seen the man in years, and there was no way his mother would pay for a therapist. Not while there were Time Life music sets to purchase. He crossed his fingers that the teacher wouldn't demand one, but would instead remember the warning tag on his file.

And it'd worked! Maybe he looked crazy enough that she didn't see the point in fighting with him. Or he was a senior, and teachers cut seniors a break, especially in the third trimester. They seemed torn between being excited to be rid of them and clinging to them with a pity born from their imminent departure to the "real world." Except Mr. Keegan. He gave no one a break.

That's what gave me the courage to ask about the bathroom.

Sam had remembered one of his classmates standing before Mr. K's desk pleading at the end of the second trimester. The student wasn't a member of the bullying pack, but even if he had been, Sam would've been safe in the corner of the room, stapling packets. "Come on, Mr. Keegan. Give me some extra credit, or take that last paper for partial."

"I don't give extra credit, Mr. Stuart. Or accept late work."

This was his policy without exceptions. Even for his favorites, which Sam liked to imagine he might be. The year before, Sam had attempted to hand in a paper the day after it was due. It'd been promptly returned with a note at the top: "Better late than never, but better never late." And a big, fat zero. But Sam had been amazed by this maintaining of principles and the unbiased dealing of consequences. Holding his late paper with the red zero at the top could've been when he'd started to hold Mr. Keegan in worshipful esteem. Sam wanted to be a man of unwavering ethics too. And as he listened to the conversation between his classmate and the teacher, he'd waited for another display of this quality he admired.

"My counselor says I need to pass your class though," the boy had whined.

"I'm sure she's mentioned that numerous times." Mr. Keegan hadn't looked away from the paper he was grading.

"But I need to pass, or I won't graduate."

He set down his pen and looked at the now smug-faced Mr. Stuart. Sam couldn't help but peek. "That's quite unfortunate for you."

"Come on, man. I've had all this stuff going on. A string of bad luck—"

"Bad luck and bad decisions are two different things. Though even if your situation weren't the latter, the results don't change. But cheer up, Mr. Stuart." The teacher tapped his stack of papers on the desk. "There are plenty of occupations that don't require a high school diploma."

Mr. K never disappointed. But he did occasionally surprise, as he had after Mr. Stuart left the room in a huff. Sam had hidden his smile and continued stapling. They usually spent the period working in silence, so he snapped to attention when Mr. K spoke.

"'When we are no longer able to change a situation, we are challenged to change ourselves.'" Mr. Keegan hadn't looked at Sam and folded another page onto a secondary pile. "Do you agree with that, Ms. Porter?"

Sam wanted to say "Yes." But from his careful observations, he knew this wasn't what Mr. Keegan wanted to hear. Immediate and simple agreement wasn't what had endeared him to the man.

I think endeared anyway. Maybe.

"Is it wrong to want to change the situation first, or try to change it, sir?"

"Trying to make the world accommodate you is the best route to try initially, depending on the circumstance. But if that doesn't pan out, you must be prepared to use your only completely reliable resource, yourself. And sometimes you have to change in ways you didn't imagine." An infrequent grin escaped him. "You have to put on the Burger King uniform. Lower the fry basket into the grease."

"Or pay for a GED."

"Pay from your minimum-wage job when you could've had a diploma for free. What a valuable lesson Mr. Stuart will learn from facing the 'challenge to change himself.'"

"'If you want to make enemies, try to change something.'" Sam had swallowed. Every day more of his previous "friends" looked at him with anger and disgust. "I'd imagine that could apply to changes made to one's self."

The effort Sam had made to remember this quote from one of Mr. Keegan's lectures was rewarded by the even rarer direct eye contact with smile.

"That's very good, Ms. Porter. But when it's about you and to your benefit, you are worth the enemies you create." He'd returned to his papers.

Sam frequently remembered that conversation. Many times, a part gave him the strength to do what he needed. Though his request to use the handicapped bathroom had been granted, he'd been prepared for the "challenge to change."

"Fine, twenty-three. Use the bathroom. But when we do two weeks in the pool, you'll need to use the locker room there. No exceptions."

It'd been a relief until the violence began, and it was nice not to feel like a dirty Peeping Tom. And while the two weeks in the pool were drawing closer, Sam pretended they were far away. He'd worry about changing then.

The dismissal bell sounded, and Sam opened the stall door. Using his cell phone to illuminate the bathroom, he set his backpack on the sink counter. He unzipped the front pocket and dug out a pill bottle. In addition to strain from the panic, pulling a shirt on and off four times in the past hour with the fabric rubbing across the wound at the back of his head had restarted the pounding. He was maxed on ibuprofen for the day, but he had to do something about the pain.

That's what Mr. K wants to discuss. Calm down. Sam shook four tabs into his palm and swallowed them dry. *He could be worried. He did ask about my migraine this morning.*

He stuck his head out the bathroom door to confirm that the hallway was empty. Sam slung the backpack over his shoulder and walked fast. He knew he wouldn't be safe until he was in Mr. Keegan's classroom.

Even though I'm not anxious to hear what he has to say.

He hadn't wanted to sit through his mother's talk that morning either, but in a similar way he'd felt trapped. He couldn't not go to Mr. K's room. And he hadn't been able to jump out of the vehicle Scarlet had been driving.

"Mom, you remember I'm leaving in a couple of days, right?" Sam had ventured, since she'd probably forgotten. It'd take her a day or so to notice his absence, but eventually she would. "I'm going to DC with the AP US class."

"Oh, I remember. Your getaway is why I can't have mine."

Scarlet's boyfriend of the week, Gary, wanted to take her to Wendover for three days. But someone had to babysit Sam's younger brother. Stevie was thirteen. When Sam was thirteen, he'd been expected to care for eight-year-old Stevie, even after the school psychologist had warned Scarlet that she needed to stop shoving her parental responsibilities onto Sam. It was one of the reasons for Sam's depression and why he'd wanted to kill himself, the doctor said. It was all too much.

It'd been too much for years, though having to be Stevie's pseudo-parent hadn't been the biggest issue. He hadn't confessed his true gender identity to the doctor, but keeping his family from falling apart was a contributing factor.

"I'm sorry. Can't Gary reschedule?"

"I can't ask him to do that, Amanda. What would he think?" Scarlet had paused, waiting for him to cave and keep the peace. Quickly relenting was his first instinct and not giving in to her requests felt uncomfortable. But not this time.

I'm going to forget you for a few days and just hang around with Mr. K. For the first time ever, I'll go someplace as the real me. I'm going to The Attic as myself. I'll be around people who are open-minded and don't give a shit about catering to anyone else. The type of people you can't find in Idaho. That's why I'm leaving after I graduate. And you can grow up and take care of Stevie yourself.

"Go right ahead." His mother puffed out her cheeks. "Have your vacation. You're young and have no responsibilities. You don't know what it's like to be a single parent. To never be able to get away."

But Scarlet got away at every opportunity. She had a built-in babysitter.

When my friend Mike committed suicide, you refused to go to the graveside service with me. Don was taking you to Colorado.

Scarlet couldn't ask Don to change his plans. What would Don think?

A vicious part of Sam hoped that Scarlet's priorities being out of whack was the reason Don had dumped Scarlet. Why Robert dumped her. Why Martin dumped her. Why Frank dumped her. Why Gary was eventually *going to* dump her. Scarlet thought she was clever and manipulative, but her true nature could only be concealed for so long. There was a difference between the unyielding principles of Mr. Keegan and Scarlet's brand of parenting.

I will never treat my children the way you treat me, Sam had thought more than once.

"You have fun on your vacation, Amanda." Scarlet pulled alongside the school curb. "With your teacher, and your friends, and your *girlfriends.*"

Sam waited for her favorite catch phrase.

"You're ruining my life!"

He'd heard it so often that the accusation now just made him angry.

I'm your teenage child. You're forty-one. Shouldn't I be saying this to you?

Sam unbuckled his seat belt and opened the car door without replying. When he slammed the door, the noise resounded painfully inside his skull.

Fuck your life. I'll go to DC. And soon I'm going to move out, start hormone therapy, and change my name. That will really piss her off. What will Gary think of that? And she'll say it: "Amanda, you're ruining my life!"

Sam had grinned as he walked into school that morning. And he felt the same smile as he pulled open the door of Mr. Keegan's classroom. He thought about Mr. K looking from his papers at poor, failing Mr. Stuart with that uninterested look on his face. The look that read: "Are you really under the impression I give a flying fuck about anything you have to say? You're not worth a grounded fuck, let alone an airborne one."

And I'll say to her: "When we are no longer able to change a situation, we are challenged to change ourselves." It's time for you to be the adult, Mom, and take care of Stevie.

FOUR

TODD THOUGHT AMANDA Porter looked better, which was a relief. He didn't relish having a heartfelt conversation or barring her from DC

The field trip was primarily for his AP US History class, comprised of juniors, but he opened a few spots to previous students. A specific body count unlocked a host of special pricing for airfare, vehicle rentals, and hotels. Not to mention that he charged each plane ticket to his SkyMiles account, which earned him free miles. And he spared the little bastards half a thought when he went home to New Orleans for two weeks every summer.

But he didn't need Amanda Porter to cross into group rate territory or to accrue enough mileage for his personal vacation. It was within his authority to cut her without any explanation. Above all, he didn't want to have a fuzzy-wuzzy talk with Amanda. That wasn't his thing. Regrettably, immediate expulsion also wasn't his style.

You are an asshole, Todd, but not an unfair asshole. Give her the chance to explain. Keep it strictly business. If the conversation crosses into too much personal, put a stop to it, and refer her to the guidance counselor. Those idiots have nothing to do anyway.

To his great fortune, though, Amanda seemed okay and had been her shy, polite self. She spent the class period in silence making copies, assembling and stapling packets, and grading quizzes. He noticed nothing amiss.

"So, I'll let it go." Todd twisted an old light bulb out of his overhead projector and glared at Julie. She was eating a sandwich with her feet on his desk. "Get your feet off my desk."

"My feet, your ass. What's the difference?"

"Besides the obvious, *my*. *Mine*. That's the difference." He exchanged the light bulb for a new one, replacing the old in the packaging.

"You should still say something." His sister removed her feet, but in leaning above the desk, she made no attempt to prevent bread crumbs from scattering liberally across its surface. "Even if she appears better, you need to let her know she can't pull one over on you."

And while he didn't feel he was asking for her guidance, or had said anything to incite another unfounded, snarky remark: "Did you know that even three-month-old infants can mimic facial expressions? Think of what a nice, caring person would say. Channel Mr. Holland, Todd. You can do it."

He tried to let it roll, though his skin prickled. Julie had been more antagonistic toward him lately, but it went in cycles like this. His sister had been an independent woman, and he imagined the jabs stemmed from the Julie within straining for freedom. Was this where she imagined herself at twenty-five? It certainly wasn't where he thought he'd be at twenty-eight. He understood the bitterness of an unplanned, restrained situation. His resentment traveled in the same orbit. But as they reached their breaking points—when she was going to leave of her own accord, or he was on the verge of decapitating her—something happened. She was pushed backward, and his mighty principles and bitterness collapsed. That rewind scenario was only a few days off.

It'll happen Wednesday. I'd put money on it.

"At any minute, Julie, a student could walk in." Todd tossed the light bulb box to the corner of the room. It bounced off the wall and into the garbage. "If they saw me throttling you, that wouldn't bode well for either of us retaining employment."

Julie grinned. She balled the rest of her sandwich in its wrapper and pitched it toward the same garbage can. It flapped against the wall before falling to the floor, leaving skid marks of peanut butter on both.

Todd considered her advice. He supposed it was the right thing to mention his knowledge of the situation. The responsible adultish thing. He could warn her without getting personal and let Amanda know he was aware. She'd take the hint and straighten up or hide it better. He'd be okay with either option.

When he'd seen Amanda in the hallway, he tapped her shoulder to catch her attention. He asked her to stop by after school and said they "needed to talk," thereby obligating himself to say something.

Though, as it happened, he needn't have made the commitment. Julie was in his classroom when Amanda Porter walked in, and per the usual, she couldn't keep her damn mouth shut.

"Amanda." His sister waved the girl in. "We were just talking about you."

He gave Amanda a nod when she hesitated at the door. Her cheeks were red, but she shuffled in.

"Are you excited for the trip? Probably not as much as you were last year, but it's nice to go places." Julie smiled.

"I enjoyed the museums and landmarks. I might move there after I graduate."

"That's good." Todd was pleased to hear her plans. In his experience, junkies were not goal-oriented individuals. "I think you'd do well there, Ms. Porter."

"Did you know that drug possession is only a misdemeanor in Washington, DC?" Julie blurted out. "In Idaho, depending on how much cocaine you're caught with, it could be a second- or third-degree felony."

Exactly how Mr. Holland would've broached the subject, Julie. Exactly.

But he watched Amanda's face carefully. Her eyes didn't go to the floor. She looked between the two of them and answered without delay.

"It's good I don't have a problem with that. Wherever I decide to live."

Amanda's reaction was enough for Todd. Based on the number of teenagers who tried to blatantly lie to his face, he could evaluate honesty. Whatever had happened yesterday, Amanda wasn't a drug addict. As such, Julie's presence was no longer necessary. Not that it had been in the first place.

"Didn't you say you were leaving?" Todd turned to his sister.

"No."

"I could swear we were finished with our conversation. You were saying you had papers to finish before tomorrow, Mrs. Keegan." He placed no emphasis on the title. He didn't need to.

"Oh, *those* papers. Yes, you're right." When Julie reached the door, she glanced back at him. For the first time in days, her eyes didn't hold that cocky edge. "See you at home?"

"I'll be there."

Where else am I going? Todd thought as he heard the door close. *I'll go back to the house and wait while you peer through the peep hole to make sure it's me. While you draw back the three dead bolts and two chains to open the door. Unless you can't bear to go in the house without me. That's the usual. God, I long for the days when I had to* stand outside my own house waiting to be approved for entry. That meant I'd been somewhere unaccompanied. And you could be alone.

Tonight would be like most nights. He'd be locking the door to his classroom and hear her behind him. She never gave him the chance to come to her room, as if she didn't trust him to not leave her. Each time he thought about how her suspicions were completely unfounded, his anger surged.

I've never left you. I'm not heartless. I'd help you for a while. Not for four years. I'd tell you it's time to move on. It's a shit thing that happened to you, but you should pull your life together. I've never said that to you or given you no reason to worry I'd leave you. I'm the one who came to your rescue, for God's sake.

The next scene of their familiar act featured Todd driving Julie home because, though it was close enough to walk, she preferred the car with its locks and pepper spray in the glove box.

He'd exit the car, shut the door, and hear the locks click.

I don't want any prospects currently, but that could change. And this façade that you feel keeps you safe and distanced from the world? There's no one for whom this wouldn't be considered an insane arrangement.

He'd open the door and start a lackluster tour of the house, meandering through all three levels, ensuring the rooms were empty. He didn't check the closets in every room, though he assured Julie he did.

Even if we're so close to Utah that I could have a harem, I don't want one. And I don't want a live-in maid, or a cook, or whatever the new fucking thing you'd want to pass as if I found someone.

Todd would stand in the front doorway and nod to confirm the location was safe. *I want my sister in a separate house from me. Working in a separate building. With a separate life from mine. Not posing as anything. Just being my sister, like how it used to be.*

Julie would make a beeline to the house, and he'd go in after her. He'd walk down the hall to his library. As he loosened his tie, he'd hear her at the door. Sliding the three dead bolts and two chains. Jerking on the doorknob a couple of times to ensure that it was locked. And then replaying the same precaution on the back door. And the door to the garage.

You did me favors when I was a kid. Covered for me. Made excuses. Helped me not feel alone. I'm grateful for that. But I'm not a teenager anymore. I'm almost thirty. I'm okay with who I am, and what I do. I don't owe you my life for making my childhood easier. If I knew you'd blackmail me, I might've told you to go fuck yourself then. I could've made it alone.

Todd wouldn't see his sister until dinner. She worked on her casino games, or whatever else, and he had a few precious hours to himself. They'd have dinner together and go to bed in their separate rooms. And if he couldn't sleep, or something was bothering him, he'd stay awake most of the night rescuing Aerosmith from the New World Order. The last bit had been happening with increasing regularity.

Maybe I'm so tired of everything that I'm even too tired to sleep anymore. Thank God for DayQuil and strong coffee.

"Mr. Keegan, I'm not a drug addict."

Todd blinked and refocused on the student standing at his desk. "I didn't accuse you of taking drugs."

"Mrs. Keegan seemed to insinuate I might be." Amanda's brow furrowed in confusion.

"Her comments were in reference to something we were talking about previously. It was inappropriate for her to continue a discussion not concerning you, I apologize."

Todd sighed. He shouldn't chicken out in this way. There was value in making her aware that he knew something had been up. He was the teacher, and Amanda was the peon student. She should know he had the upper hand. *Always.*

He folded his arms on his desk. "But you've seemed off lately, Ms. Porter. Yesterday something was wrong."

"I told you that I had a migraine," Amanda replied, but her coloring paled, and her gaze drifted to her shoes.

Goddamn it. Now Todd knew she was lying. He should've left it alone. And he was capable of ignoring a lot of things to make his life easier, but he couldn't pretend to be ignorant when he knew he was right.

"I've had migraines and seen people have migraines. Your pupils aren't unequal when you have a migraine," he said.

He waited for a lie. A microexpression of distress passed across her face, and her shoulders trembled. Seconds passed in silence before he got tired of waiting.

"Ms. Porter, this trip is usually reserved for my AP class." Todd removed his glasses, untucked a corner of his shirt, and began to clean the lenses. "I have my hands full corralling thirty juniors two thousand miles from home. I offered you a spot since I didn't think I had to babysit you. I thought I could trust you." He put his glasses on and met her eyes. She looked like she was about to cry, but he pushed past caring. "Has my confidence in you been misplaced?"

"No. Absolutely not."

"Then do you want to tell me what happened yesterday?"

"I hit my head, Mr. K. It wasn't a lie. I had a headache because I fell and hit my head." Amanda spoke too fast.

The disbelief verging on annoyance must've come through on his face, since upon not receiving a response, she turned and pulled a section of her hair to the side. A large elevated lump rose on the back of her head. The skin stretched from the swelling and a jagged red laceration marred an otherwise white surface. The edges around the gash puckered and a bloody, clotted gap showed in the middle.

"Jesus Christ, Amanda." Todd stood so quickly that his chair fell to the side. She needed stitches. Several. "You need to see a doctor."

"I'm fine now." Amanda let her hair fall into place and faced him as he came around his desk. "It's not that bad. I just fell yesterday."

"When? On what?"

"In the hallway at the end of the day. I tripped."

"What really happened?" Tripping in a school hallway wouldn't cause that amount of damage. It took repeated blows to break the skin and create that much swelling.

"I tripped and fell."

"What *really* happened, Ms. Porter?"

"I tripped. And then I fell." She shoved both hands in her pockets. "That's all."

"It's insulting you think I'm that stupid."

Todd knew what had happened. He didn't know why or necessarily care why. The reason behind teenagers falling in and out of the popularity clique were many and perpetually trivial. Amanda may have been caught buying jeans at the wrong mall boutique. Perhaps she'd flirted with someone's two-minute boyfriend. Or she gave one of them a dirty look. What was the word they used? Scuz. Christ, kids were stupid, but they were also mean. He'd suffered his share of high school bullying, though never to this extent.

"I don't think you're stupid, Mr. K. But you don't treat us like kids. You have respect for us."

It was interesting to hear his disdain interpreted differently. Sure, he respected them. Todd respected karaoke singers, screaming babies, and gnats too.

"I think you'll understand that I don't want to talk about it," Amanda continued. "I appreciate your concern, but I want to handle things on my own."

The epiphany that hadn't revealed itself during his night-long quest to rescue Aerosmith hit him now.

Todd remembered the time Julie found him in the lower corridor of lockers by the auditorium at their high school almost a decade ago. His knuckles had been raw from knocking on the inside of the locker door, but he hadn't panicked. The bell rang to dismiss the middle school a half hour before the high school, and his sister waited for him by the car. If he didn't show, she knew to look, and if he made his location known, Julie would find him. So, when the nerve endings in his fingers felt stubbed from tapping, he twisted his body to keep signaling with his elbow. He'd only been locked in for an hour before being freed.

Julie had removed the duct tape from his wrists, and he pulled off the piece that'd covered his mouth with one biting rip.

"Someday. I swear to God. They will listen to every fucking word I have to say." Todd had leaned against the lockers and bent to unwind the tape that bound his ankles.

"That's not what pisses them off." She searched the locker.

"They can kiss my ass. I'll be untouchable. In their faces and fucking untouchable."

"Where are your clothes?"

"Well, my head was in a toilet, and I was shoved in a locker." He removed a jacket that didn't belong to him. "If they stuck with the cliché, I'd imagine they're up a flagpole somewhere."

"This has to stop, Todd." Julie said. "We're going to the principal and Mom."

"No, that'd make things worse. You keep pulling me from lockers before I starve to death. I can take care of it myself." Todd held the jacket in front of him. It was a cropped, tapered-fit jacket made of black polyester with one hot-pink sleeve.

"Besides, the joke is on them. And whichever of their sisters they stole this from. Check it out, Julie." He turned a piece of the fabric. "Satin lining, standing collar. This is slick. I'm keeping it. I have the perfect cocktail blouse to go underneath it. Idiots."

Somewhere in his closet, Todd still had that jacket.

I should take it with me to DC. I love that jacket. I would've spent another hour in the locker for it. Another two hours. Oh, you sick, stupid bitches. Thinking you scarred me, when you only added to my wardrobe.

So, Todd smiled at Amanda Porter for multiple reasons.

He liked to think of the obstacles he'd overcome and reflect on how he'd enacted his revenge by forcing teenagers to listen to "every fucking word he had to say." He loved when one of the nosey pricks asked what he did outside of school. He'd answered that like every teacher, he spent each waking minute that he wasn't making them miserable, devising new ways to make them miserable. They always laughed, even though it was an honest answer. Well, not completely honest. "Every waking minute" was a bit much. He did have other interests, but he'd be lying if he didn't admit that finding joy in making most of them wretched didn't occupy some of his time.

He was also happy to remember his sister before she'd eroded into this insecure, anxious person who aggravated the hell out of him. When all the saving consisted of Julie pulling him free of a locker, or Todd giving her a ride home. When they had lives with the right degree of separation. Before she became his shadow and fake spouse. He missed that person—the real Julie.

But primarily, Amanda's comment spurred the realization he'd been looking for. It lay the pieces into place. On an intellectual and personal level, Todd genuinely respected someone wanting to solve their own problems.

"If you do find yourself in over your head, I hope you feel comfortable talking to me."

"I will. Thank you, sir."

When Amanda smiled, Todd was glad he hadn't blackballed her from DC and that he'd persisted in questioning her behavior. No wonder she'd been absent so often.

He'd make sure she wouldn't have to worry about being bullied during their travels. Except Friday night, when he left the pack of hyenas with the geriatric nimrods.

"Did you have anything else for me?" Amanda shifted her backpack.

"You blew through everything this afternoon. Thank you for your help."

Todd considered his torture chamber complete. There were stacks of papers and packets meticulously divided by day and class period covering his desk. These were his whips and thumbscrews. The video he required them to watch was the rack. Or the wheel. And God help them if they were successful in convincing an inexperienced substitute he didn't seriously want every ounce of the work finished, or if they misbehaved.

"I'm good at pressing the copy button."

"And you're the fastest stapler in the West."

She grinned and walked toward the door.

"Ms. Porter," he called. When she looked over her shoulder, he went on. "I truly mean that. If you need help, don't hesitate. Anytime. Even if I'm in the middle of a lecture. I don't consider you an interruption."

Amanda paused before replying. He'd expected a shy smile in gratitude, but when she turned to him, her cheeks were red. She cleared her throat, but her voice came out like a rusty hinge. "Thanks. The offer does help."

"My pleasure. And put some ice on that." He would've advised her to do what she should've done yesterday—go to the hospital, ensure she didn't have a skull fracture, and get that damn gaping wound stitched shut. But he said nothing else. Even if his bullies had tried to crack his skull open like an egg, would he have revealed it or willingly sought medical treatment? Probably not. Amanda was confident she could handle it herself, so he'd let her.

"Yes, sir."

After she left, Todd righted his fallen chair and sank into it, letting his arms hang loose at his sides. He closed his eyes. Crisis forestalled. Mystery solved. One less thing to worry about. Maybe he could get some sleep.

The size of the "Grinch's heart" is measured on a case-by-case basis. Most Whos are dickheads. He kicked his feet up on his desk and leaned the chair back. *But I suppose that occasionally you come across one that reminds you of yourself, and you have to give a shit.*

Todd heard his classroom door open, but he didn't need to look over. His sister had been alone for twenty minutes outside the house. He imagined there might be a bald spot on one side of her head.

"So you can have your feet up on the desk, but I can't?" she said. "What's the difference?"

"I told you, Julie. It's *my* desk. Mine. That's the difference."

FIVE

IF HER BROTHER thought Julie was happy with the current situation and that she didn't care what she was doing to him, he was mistaken.

I didn't mean for it to go this far. Or for this long. She tried to take deep, quiet breaths. She didn't want to disturb the six teenage girls asleep in the room. *I thought I'd need you for only a while. That I could get it together. In a few weeks. In a few months. But I can barely stand this.*

Julie couldn't stop fixating on her location. Far from home. In a strange hotel. Who knew how many people had keys to this room? There hadn't been anyone inside other than herself and the girls when she'd locked the door, but they could've let someone in while she'd been in the shower. No one could be trusted.

Perhaps one of them opened the window to admit some fresh air, and an intruder had climbed in. She'd been this naïve once. Gullible enough at nineteen to believe danger made itself known with flashing lights and sirens. She had thought it was like hovering a hand above a stove burner. She'd be able to feel the heat and know to not touch. But evil didn't bare its teeth so you'd back away like it did in the movies. It invited you in. With innocence. With kind words and friendly smiles. With pink stargazer lilies.

Wednesday night was the worst when it was more economical to split the students into four rooms instead of two. At least that's what Todd told her.

She shook her head. *No. If I can't trust him, there's no one left. I know I frustrate him, but he'd never do this on purpose or lie to me.*

Sharing a room with decrepit Janet Farr and fifteen girls on the other nights helped somewhat. But she knew the sleep deprivation played into her obsessive terror. Until Friday, when she and Todd shared a room, she'd be lucky to get two hours a night. But by Friday, her nerves would already be fried.

Why can't you create an itinerary where Washington, DC, is in the middle? Maybe it wouldn't be as horrible if I had six hours midweek.

"This trip isn't about you, Julie," Todd would respond. "I'm not zigzagging across multiple states to feed your insanity. Don't you think you ask enough of me as it is?"

He wouldn't say that. We pick at each other, but he's never been nasty. The answer would be no, but he'd be genteel. He'd tell me it's more economical to fly into Philadelphia and out of Baltimore.

But even if Julie asked her brother to reroute travel plans for next year, that was of no present help. She would spend the night with her eyes following every shadow. Waiting. Anticipating. Listening for the breath of someone who didn't belong. The scent or movement of a stranger. With her arms folded under her pillow and one hand clasped around a bottle of pepper spray. Hopefully none of the other girls needed to use the bathroom. Amanda Porter didn't even realize how lucky she was.

Julie wasn't sure where her paranoia had been headed. Her anxiety didn't escalate higher and higher until it broke through the ceiling like the Great Glass Elevator. Her elevator only rose to a certain point, before the cable snapped, and the cab went into a free fall down the shaft. It was somewhere during this drop that she felt a hand on her shoulder.

And she froze. Her brain urged her hand to start shooting the pepper spray into the face of her assailant. Like she'd prepared and practiced. But every muscle in her body went limp, and she was powerless—a prey animal trying to play dead.

"Mrs. Keegan, are you all right?"

Hearing the voice caused the shadows in the room to reposition. Instead of staring at a thug, the dim lighting curved around the contours of a familiar face.

Amanda. Julie released her held breath and tried to drudge up the cocky teacher persona that'd been shoved to the pit of her stomach in the anxiety drop. This was the second time the girl had caught her off guard and seen her weakness. It couldn't be allowed to—

"You were breathing fast and shaking. I was worried something might be wrong." More light swept across Amanda's face, allowing Julie to read her expression. The girl was genuinely concerned. "Did you have a nightmare?"

Every fragment of my life for the past four years has been a nightmare, whether I'm awake or asleep. It's an absolute lie that things get easier with time. Time isn't a healer. It's a countdown to the next terrible thing.

"Yes, a nightmare. I'm fine."

"Can I get you anything? A glass of water? A cold washcloth? Or if you need to talk..."

"No, thank you, Amanda. Go back to bed." Julie managed a smile as the girl stood there hesitating. "I'm fine. I promise." She waited for a lightning bolt to strike her, but avoided swift, divine justice again. "Please, go to sleep."

"I'll use the restroom first, if that's okay?"

"Yes, I'd prefer if you didn't wet the carpet as the hotel has Mr. Keegan's credit card on file."

Amanda paused a moment longer before smiling and turning away. Julie then listened to her maneuver around the baggage and five other sleeping girls on the floor. The bathroom light came on, but was quickly extinguished by the closed door.

You're a complete fucking wreck, Julie. You're such a liability. You should give up now. Find yourself a padded room to live out the rest of your days. You almost maced a seventeen-year-old girl for God's sake.

Everyone would be better off if she committed herself. Maybe she wouldn't be terrified constantly if enough locked doors and hospital personnel separated her from the outside world. Todd would be happier without her. And some fortunate student in the future would avoid being pepper sprayed in the face.

But I didn't use the spray—either time she scared me. The thought wasted no time in changing from comfort to further fear. *Why didn't I? I should have. I must not be as prepared as I thought I was. To freeze like that. Not even once but—*

"Mrs. K." Julie recognized Amanda's voice this time, so she only jumped a little. She heard the alarm clock on the nightstand being pushed aside, and two objects were set on its surface. "Here's the water and washcloth if you change your mind. And if you need anything, don't hesitate to wake me." There was a pause. "I know how it is."

You have no fucking clue. You're seventeen. If I need help selecting pizza toppings or designer jeans, I'll let you know.

"Thank you, Amanda. Get some sleep."

Blankets rustled as the girl settled into her position on the floor. Julie focused on every sound from that quadrant until she was sure Amanda had fallen back to sleep. She then released her brain into the wild.

Amanda Porter. Julie didn't know what transpired between the student and Todd after she'd been driven from the classroom by his veiled threat. Her brother had only confirmed that she wasn't a drug addict. There'd been a misunderstanding. They were all the same—big, sloppy packs of children shoved into adult bodies and going stir-crazy because they lacked the maturity to control their hormones. She shouldn't worry about Amanda. After all, he wasn't going to.

But Todd had lied; he was still thinking of Amanda. Julie had observed him scrutinizing the girl as he never did with any other student. Pinpointing her in the group and keeping her within his line of sight. It made Julie nervous. Very nervous.

Please don't have a thing for her, Todd. You said you didn't, but you also said the issue with her was resolved. Obviously, it's not. I could care less who you like or what you do. You know I've never judged you. But you'll destroy yourself and your career. For your own good, tell me you don't have a thing for Amanda Porter.

Of course, he wasn't there to answer. That was the major issue.

The only *positive about you getting fired, whether for being caught at The Attic or having a relationship with a student, is I wouldn't have to go on this stupid trip.* She rubbed her hands over her face and tried to erase the image of her brother and Amanda.

During the day, it was tolerable. Being in a cluster with three other adults made her feel somewhat safe. But with bigger cities the danger ratio increased. She couldn't stop the statistics from entering her mind.

With one hundred being the safest, Philadelphia is a nine on the crime index. Chances of being a casualty in a violent crime—1 in 86. Washington, DC? Five. 1 in 80. And Baltimore is only a four. A fucking four. A 1 in 71 chance of being a victim. And we're staying there overnight. I won't make it.

She tried to remember that she wasn't in Baltimore. Furthermore, she'd stayed in Baltimore several times and lived to tell the tale.

How much longer can I beat those odds though?

She was in Gettysburg now. For fuck's sake, there were only seven-and-a-half-thousand people in this hole. It was a twenty-nine. Only 1 in 283. It wasn't as safe as where they lived in Idaho—

Sixty-three and 1 in 840.

But statistically speaking, Gettysburg was three times as safe as New Orleans, where she'd lived without a traumatic event for years. But her logic only went one way after dark.

I'm more of a target here. I'm a tourist. There might as well be a blinking sign outside the damn door. How many people have keys to this room? The manager, the lobby, housekeeping, maintenance. They all have keys.

And Todd was at the other end of the building. If she screamed, he wouldn't hear her.

Twelve doors away is better than two thousand miles, Julie. He knows where I am. He could be here in less than two seconds.

No one made her feel safe like Todd did. He'd never hurt her or allow anyone else to. She didn't mean to make him miserable or stifle him in any way, but she could only function when he was around.

Todd liked being able to talk about what he enjoyed and got some sadistic pleasure from boring teenagers, but Julie didn't care for teaching. All it did was keep her close to her brother.

And I like the metal detectors. And the three security officers who roam the halls with their guns, pepper spray, electroshock weapons, and hydrochloric acid. But mostly that Todd is two doors down. Fifteen steps away.

If Julie could do anything, she would've liked to spend her time working on the casino machines and arcade games. She had a passion for taking things apart, figuring out how they worked, and putting them together. It was how she imagined a surgeon might feel, without the pressure of a life on the line. She could pull together CPU board parts, LEDs, and fuses to build whatever she wanted. And then change it. Construction and deconstruction. Somewhat like art, but there was a definite right and wrong with mechanics. The device either worked or it didn't. No critique, taste level, or preference as far as operation went.

You get the creativity, but also the satisfaction of your efforts being universally justified.

And she'd been on her way to making her side hobby a full-time occupation. Five years ago, she drove with Todd and a couple other friends from New Orleans to Las Vegas. It'd been before she kept neurotic track of things like the crime index—

Las Vegas is a fourteen.

Or the odds of becoming a victim of a violent crime in a particular location—

1 in 124.

It was before Julie's world had fallen apart.

She went to the electronics exposition and returned with a box truck of twelve slots, six arcade games, three pinball machines—

"And a partridge in a fucking pear tree." Todd had needed the help of both their friends to load a jukebox into the trailer.

"Don't break a nail, cher."

Julie thought of herself, standing confidently by the U-Haul and flipping through the schematics pages of the Arcade Legends operation manual. Her plan was to Tetris the machines in her garage and work on them one by one. Pushing the newly acquired games out the door in a couple of months would be her start into full-time repair and refurbishing of electronics.

She'd quit her job at the call center as soon as the small business loan came through. Talking to idiots about miniblinds was superfluous, but it covered bills at the house where she lived alone.

After she left that job behind, she had her eye on the perfect space in a nearby strip mall. She'd sell and repair machines at that location as well as online. It'd be fantastic.

But I'm not that woman anymore. Her stomach rolled at thoughts of being in a store alone or living alone. Being this strong, independent person who only required her brother when something heavy needed to be moved... Never again. She could never be that woman ever again.

The only thing that'd gone as she'd envisioned after Las Vegas was that she'd quit the call center. There was no way she could go back. She couldn't return to her house either. Even to pack her belongings.

Julie had asked Todd to stop the car before he made the right turn onto her old block.

"Asked" probably isn't the right word.

Her eyes locked on the green street sign when it came into view. It loomed before her, as if instead of them approaching it, it was coming to her. Pursuing her in ravenous leaps, its jaws gaping open—

"Stop! Stop the fucking car!" She seized Todd's arm. He slammed the brakes and a couple cardboard boxes in the backseat catapulted into the front.

"Christ! What the—"

Todd stopped midsentence because she was crying. Which was also doubtlessly the wrong verb. She was sobbing. She brought her knees to her chest and tightened her arms around them as she hyperventilated. She could see the green sign behind her closed eyes. And then her house. Her safe, secure house. The unfamiliar white car on the curb. It probably belonged to a neighbor. No big deal. It's not like it was blocking the driveway. She just had to run in to grab her cell phone.

"I can't! I can't go back! I can't!" Julie gasped.

"You're not going back, cher. We're getting your things." His hand touched her shoulder, and his voice was soft. But she couldn't relax.

"Turn off the car! Turn off the car!"

Julie hadn't given him a chance to complete the order. She snapped from the fetal position and reached across the gearshift, jerking the keys from the ignition. They fell to the floor as she turned and pressed the automatic door lock. She heard all four doors latch at once.

She pressed the button again. Four clicks confirmed all doors were locked.

She pressed the button three more times in rapid succession.

And then, she caught her breath.

"Julie, I'm not dropping you off. You're going to stay with me, remember? It won't be bad." Todd tried making eye contact with her, but she avoided it. Something new materialized in her mind, and she was having difficulty breathing. "Everything is clean. They even ripped the carpet and—"

"Turn it on! Start the engine now! Hurry! Drive! Drive!" Julie darted her hand to the floor and retrieved the keys. She desperately jabbed the key toward the ignition, but the tears blurred her vision, and she continued to miss until Todd took the keys from her.

She hadn't regained composure until they'd been blocks away. And then she asked her brother the first of the long string of favors he'd yet to refuse. She asked him to go to the house without her and pack her things. She couldn't go down that street, let alone be in the house. Even if the carpet had been replaced. Was the drywall up? Were the support beams behind the drywall there? Had the earth beneath the house been scorched and purified? Even if it had, she'd stay with a friend while he filled the boxes with the few things she wanted. But he had to come back as soon as possible. She couldn't be without him for very long.

"Very long" had only escalated. Julie quickly put together that the anxiety was not as severe when Todd was there. If he was in the same building and not separated by too many doors or too much distance, she could pull herself together. That realization had led her into education. She accepted a job at the school office where Todd had been teaching in New Orleans until she got her own certificate.

Then, around the time Julie began obsessing over crime rates, she convinced Todd they should move. His apartment was miles from her old house, but she felt the dark pull from it. She swore when she looked from the balcony, she could discern a greenish smog encroaching from its direction. They needed teachers in Idaho, and what could be safer than a place full of Mormons and potato farmers?

He thought I'd get better here. I thought I might too. Maybe it would be enough of a new beginning that I could forget.

But she'd been too daring. She'd gone for that jog around the high school track alone, and a man had approached her.

He'd come beside her and kept pace for too long.

"I'm Charlie Smith." He smiled.

Julie scanned him. He wore a loose T-shirt and athletic shorts. His hands were empty, but he had a green CTR ring on one hand. Every indication of being a harmless, popcorn-necklace-stringing Mormon. And sweat dripped down his red face. He was already tired, giving her the advantage. It was a risk she wasn't willing to take though. She ignored his introduction and picked up speed.

"You're...the. New teacher." Gasps punctuated Charlie's sentences as he reached her again. "Just...moved...here, right?"

She ran faster.

"Woah, slow...down."

He caught her sleeve.

Julie thought about screaming. It hadn't helped before, but could it now? She looked around. No one was there. Why had she come alone? Why had she let herself believe everything would be okay if she went out of range? Now she'd be the 1 in 840.

However, the stranger was weak. He held her sleeve, but he bent over, puffing heavily. She could grind her shoe into his shin and flee, yet she felt frozen.

"I know...what...it's like. To be new." Charlie had squinted. "And I used...to teach here. Maybe I could...give you...a few pointers. At dinner sometime. What was...your name?"

"Julie Keegan." She expelled the breath she'd been holding as an idea burst into her mind. A great idea. A brilliant idea. "Mrs. Julie Keegan."

"Mrs.?"

"Yes." Suddenly, Julie was stronger. More in control. She pulled back her sleeve. "My husband will be teaching here as well."

Charlie had raised an eyebrow. "Really? I was in on Todd's interview, and he didn't mention he was married."

"I thought you said you *used* to teach here?"

"I did. But I've been the assistant principal for the last couple of years."

Fuck. Why didn't she pour the amount of research her brother did into these things? Todd probably knew who the last eleven assistant principals had been, while Julie had sat in the lobby before her interview trying to remember the school's mascot. If they asked the area crime rates, *that* she could answer in detail.

But she hadn't been quizzed on the number of homicides, assaults, or reported rapes. The principal hadn't been interested in useful information. He did ask about the mascot, but there'd been a dozen plush eagles in his office. And thank God they were desperate, since the principal was patriotic, and the school mascot was a wombat.

When Todd found out, he hadn't been as irate as Julie expected. Picking at him and teasing was one thing, but she knew her emotional dependence was something he opposed, yet had taken in stride. So far anyway. In addition to her relief that he didn't completely hate her, when she'd gotten past the initial panic over the lie, the idea had again taken on the attractive sheen that compelled her to make it in the first place.

Being married. Now that was an excellent safeguard. And a better role to the rest of the world than the pathetic, paranoid sister living with her brother. As Charlie Smith had, men would be more likely to respect her boundaries if she was clearly unavailable. With a ring on her finger, everyone would leave her alone. She was taken and protected. A person might think twice before attacking her or holding her captive. No longer would she be a young, single woman who could be murdered in a basement, her body left to rot in a ditch. Her absence would be noticed. She'd be missed. By her husband.

Julie wouldn't force Todd to do anything; it was all in the title. She only had to go by "Mrs." instead of "Ms." And it was temporary. When she got better, she'd leave. Or if Todd got tired of it, he'd ask her to go.

No matter how paralyzed with fear she might be, if Todd wanted a relationship with someone, she'd back off.

Even if the someone is Amanda Porter. I swear to God, I won't stand in your way. I'll just tell you to wait until she's not a minor. Again, Julie shook the more recent issue from her mind and traced to where her thoughts had ended.

An additional realization that had occurred to her was that, until her brother found a companion, the arrangement could be mutually beneficial.

Being married is a good image. It's what people want to see. They'll be less likely to give credence to anything else they might discover if you're a happily married man. They might forgive you for not being Mormon if you're married. And if you stop saying the F word.

"Oh, Julie, it's you," Todd had been reading in the living room when she entered a couple of days later. By the tone of his voice, she knew he'd found out. "I was taking some of my books to the school this afternoon and ran into Charlie. He informed me that he'd met my wife a few days ago. Funny, I don't remember getting married. I was waiting for her to come home." He brought his book up and carefully turned a page. "Apparently, her name is Julie too. What are the odds?"

She hadn't been able to interpret what he was thinking from his expression—her punishment for not immediately divulging her actions. She had to fly blind and, without having an inkling of what she was in for, she couldn't pace herself. Everything spewed out, including the calculated reasoning she'd been recently confident in. Todd kept the book hiding his face and turned the pages so slowly she couldn't tell if he was listening. But when the deluge of excuses dried, he closed his book and glared at her.

"What the fuck is wrong with you?" It was as close to calling her a delusional lunatic as he'd come.

"I'm sorry. I really am. This is why I shouldn't go anywhere alone. I panic." Julie lowered the grocery bag she'd been holding.

"I see. Did you panic and bring home a couple of kids from the supermarket this afternoon? Are they in that bag? You shouldn't put a baby in a plastic bag, Julie. It says that right on the fucking bag!"

Of course, she'd started to cry.

I'm so scared, Todd. Julie stared at the dark hotel ceiling. All the rationalization aside, her fear had been the only explanation she could give him. At the time, she then worked herself into the manic hysteria where she ceased to be coherent. *I'm scared to be cornered and alone. That's the thing about corners. You can't be cornered and recornered and recornered. It's not some fucking Russian nesting doll. You're just cornered. And if I'm cornered with you, I'm safe.*

Not that she felt safe currently, though the gentle breathing of six girls should've put her at ease. She tried to isolate each soft wheeze with one individual and end with only six. But she kept hearing seven. Or eight. Or nine different people breathing in the room.

Any number of people could have a key to this room. It's only a swipe card. Julie tightened her grip on the pepper spray. *Anyone could put in a fresh card and program it to this room. Anyone. They don't even lock the front doors of this place. They never lock the front doors in any hotel! Someone could be programming the card right now. Climbing the stairs right now.*

Her cell phone vibrated on the mattress, and she nearly screamed. With one hand on the spray bottle, she turned the phone and squinted at the screen.

—*Calm the fuck down. I can feel you panicking from here.*

Julie smiled and her pulse slowed. Another text message came through.

—*Do you need me?*

She tapped in and sent a response. Seconds later, she received her reply.

—*It's fine. I've got Dayquil. Ten min elapse?*

After Julie confirmed, she was able to relax. If ten minutes went by without a message from her, Todd would leave his room and come to her rescue. In her personal experience, a lot couldn't happen in ten minutes. She held the phone and waited until it buzzed.

—*Sure you're okay? I know how it is.*

She glanced toward the spot where Amanda Porter was sleeping and considered her harsh censure of the girl for making the same statement. Julie was still certain Amanda didn't "know how it is," but she seemed like a good kid. One of those empathetic and insightful types. After all, no one else had woken to check on her. And even if they had, how many would've brought her a glass of water or washcloth?

Julie moved her hand along the nightstand until she found the bowl Amanda had placed the damp cloth in. She folded and placed it on her forehead. It helped. Todd helped most of all. Ninety-nine percent was him, but one percent could be the washcloth. Maybe two percent.

Holding the phone up, she dashed the same assurance of her well-being to her brother as she'd given to Amanda. She considered broaching the topic of the student now. They had the rest of the night to get into a deep discussion via text.

For what you've done and continue to do for me, you deserve every happiness in the world. But she's a girl. You need a woman. Or a man. Or whatever. An emu. I just don't want to see you on a talk show, or in a newspaper, or behind bars. You can't bring that tacky pink jacket with you to jail, Todd. You know that, right? Yes, that's what I'll say. That will get him.

Julie was punching in the question about Amanda when the next text came through. She allocated the accusation to her draft folder and viewed his message.

—*You think the NWO will gain much ground while we're gone?*

She grinned. Amanda Porter could wait. Julie replied that she was sure Aerosmith, and rock and roll in general, would survive until they returned.

SIX

SAM HATED WHAT he'd have to do to get into The Attic, but it was worth the discomfort. He'd never entered a room without the preconception of Amanda being present. There'd never been the fresh opportunity to walk up to someone, put out his hand and simply say, "Hi, my name is Sam."

I'll be smooth. Make eye contact. I'll offer my hand first, palm to the left. Take his hand. Or her hand. Firm. Strong. Two or three pumps and release. "Sam Porter. Nice to meet you."

However, to gain access, he had to put on the old skin. It was temporary, but terrifying. When he even thought of regressing, his stomach pinched itself into the size of a marble.

But I'll change in the bathroom once I'm in, Sam reminded himself as he removed two outfits from his bag. *I'll focus on that.*

It was Friday night, and from behind the door of the hotel bathroom, he could hear Mrs. Farr snoring. In the room on the opposite side of the hallway, he imagined Mr. Farr had also succumbed to the Sonata slipped into their evening tea. And Sam hadn't seen either of the Keegans after they dropped the group off and drove away.

"Be careful, Ms. Porter." Mr. K had caught his attention in the rearview mirror as Sam opened the car door.

He said it as if he was aware that the remaining chaperones would shortly be out of commission. His knowledge of the coming events and disinclination to intervene weren't surprising. What Sam found stranger was the look Mrs. Keegan shot him after the words of caution were given.

Sam was aware that Mr. Keegan had been keeping a close watch on him. Nothing more had been said about his bullying problem, but Sam could feel his presence nearby. It was an alien, yet comforting, feeling to be looked after. He didn't understand why Mrs. K would be offended though.

All he did was tell me to be careful. Sam grimaced when a negative parallel between Mrs. Keegan and his mother jumped out at him.

Since the incident of the previous night, he'd been thinking how she reminded him of Scarlet. The night terror combined with her unnecessary panic when he'd bumped into her in the hallway made it clear that something beneath the surface was bothering her. Mrs. Keegan was sensitive, like his mother. It wasn't necessarily a bad thing; he liked vulnerability. Not as far gone as Scarlet, of course.

Scarlet wore her victimhood on her sleeve, and while she'd never been much of a mother, she often deteriorated to not being much of a person. Mrs. K wasn't like that. She wasn't a succubus. Whatever haunted her, she only needed someone to care for her. Someone to tell her they understood and bring her a washcloth and glass of water. Sam was sure this was what Mr. K would've done had he been present, and he was proud of himself for filling in.

Mrs. Keegan's controlled frailty played further into the fantasy. Not only was Mr. Keegan the type of man he was striving to be, but the more he learned about Mrs. Keegan, she seemed to fit what he imagined as his ideal woman. Until she'd glared at him.

I don't want someone like Mom. I want and like to be needed, but I'm tired of being used.

Sam put Mrs. K aside and moved his bag to the bathroom floor. He looked at the two sets of clothes he'd placed on the counter. He had to steel himself and gather the courage to put on the mask.

You can do this. It won't hurt. It's clothes. Just—

A loud knock sounded on the hotel room door. The chattering of the girls outside the bathroom stopped short as they all shared the same fear: the Keegans were back.

Fortunately, the knock only hung in the air for a few tense seconds before it was followed by "shave and a haircut." The gaiety resumed as the girls responded "two bits" confirming that, yes, Mrs. Farr was out cold as well.

It was too simple to drug them. So easy that last year, when Sam had been part of the popular crowd, the idea was proposed to drug the Keegans. But the scheme had been abandoned. The argument that ultimately swayed the circle? What the fuck was there to do in Gettysburg? They didn't come two thousand miles to tip cows or hijack tractors. DC was full of bars and clubs. It had a nightlife, and there were fascinating people around every corner. As a result of Pennsylvania's dullness, the Farrs were victims year after year.

Mr. K is too smart for it anyway, Sam had thought but not said. Admitting that an adult couldn't be defeated was one way to get ousted from the group. And at the time, Sam cared very much to remain within the upper crust of high school society. *The only way you'd get him is if you shot him in the neck with a tranquilizer. Maybe not even then. He might sense the trigger being pulled and rip a mirror from a wall to deflect the dart.*

Was Sam alone in noticing that Mr. Keegan only drank bottled water? That he just ate things that were sealed or had been handled exclusively by him? Even if the vote had been to try to drug him, they would've failed. Mr. K trusted no one.

I need to be like that. Trust and depend on no one.

He pulled a fitted red blouse over his head. The sleeves came to his elbows and the neckline was cut in a V. The blouse seemed like a corset, and the pressure from the laces prevented him from getting enough air. Instinct urged him to tear the garment from his body.

But my fake ID says I'm a nineteen-year-old woman named Amanda Porter. I need to look like the girl in that picture so I can get in. Sam pulled a pair of black skinny ankle pants from his bag and hesitated. *Maybe it's not worth it. With this type of club, I could get away with wearing anything.*

If he hadn't cut his hair, he might've talked himself into that logic. After he'd done it a few days ago, it occurred to him that the outwardly small change would make things worse. The bullying would increase, his mother would be pissed off and take it personally, and he wouldn't bear as much resemblance to the photo on the fake ID.

But those considerations came after the ecstasy of looking in a mirror and not seeing the mop of snarled brown hair that branded him as female from every angle. The curves and smooth face were still there for now, but at a distance, he was convinced a person would think twice which side of the fence he was on.

Tonight I don't want to give the bouncer any reason to swipe my ID though. Last year the gang had paid extra for the holographic image on their IDs, but not to have the magnetic strip encoded. Sam would be sunk if the bouncer swiped the card. If the man compared the picture of Amanda with the new Sam, he might be suspicious. *All I can do is take the utmost precaution to ensure that doesn't happen.* He took a full breath and exhaled slowly. *It's just clothes. Don't be dramatic, Sam.*

Outside the bathroom, the door closed as the girls left. He heard more footsteps in the hallway when the boys joined them, and the herd stampeded into the night.

At the beginning of the trip, the junior class's ringleader had pulled Sam aside in the Denver airport to inform him that they'd be carrying out the traditional drugging.

"We're only telling you so you won't rat us out. You're not coming with us. But you can do your own thing."

Like I couldn't. He turned away to hide a contemptuous eye roll. Who were they to tell him what to do? To give him permission—

The young man clapped his hand on Sam's shoulder.

"It's shit like that."

He wasn't part of the group that harassed Sam—just a wisp who never broke the Mormon dress code and wore his CTR ring like a medal. But being zealots hadn't prevented the others from hurting him. Jesus didn't enter their heads while they were beating Sam's into a wall.

"It's not only that you're a freak. You're a cocky freak. You think you can go against everyone else and Heavenly Father's plan. That *you* know better than *Him*. Satan has so clouded your mind that you *think* you're right and can do whatever you want without consequence."

Sam felt torn between fright and amusement at this double standard. This sanctimonious douchebag would forget all his godly principles when he led the others in drugging the Farrs. And when he punched Sam. Or kicked him. Or whatever he was planning as punishment for being "cocky."

Do it, motherfucker. There were security guards and cameras in the airport. Somewhere nearby were four teachers, including Mr. Keegan. Sam locked eyes with him. *Hit me. Then let the school try to ignore it. Go ahead.*

The defiance seemed to melt the leader rather than provoke him. At first, Sam was comforted since he didn't really want to be punched in the face.

"It's wrong of me to be harsh with you. You're confused and have been led astray."

He took Sam's arm and swung his bag to the side, removing a thick leather book with gold leaf pages. Using one hand, he flipped it open and smoothed several pages back until reaching the desired section.

"It can be difficult, but you need to remember the teachings of the prophets and let them guide you. This is one of my favorite scriptures, 'And it came to pass that I, Nephi, said unto my father: I will go and do the things which the Lord hath commanded, for I know that the Lord giveth no commandments unto the children of men, save he shall prepare a way for them that they may accomplish the thing which he commandeth them.'"

The leader shut his book and met Sam's eyes. "Your commandment is to be a female, Amanda. Obviously. You have an important role in Heavenly Father's plan as a woman that's—"

"It's shit. As such, you can flush it." Sam hadn't cared if it urged him to violence. The pious crap was too much to bear.

"It's not shit. They're the words and will of the Lord."

"They're the words of a fraudulent jackass read out of a fucking hat."

"I *know* the scriptures are true. I *feel* the Holy Spirit. You want your evil words to fill me with anger, but all I'm feeling right now is the Holy Spirit."

"Is 'Holy Spirit' a euphemism for your dick? You really shouldn't be doing that in a public place." Sam winced as the leader squeezed his arm tighter. "I think it's illegal to—"

"I don't agree with what the others have done to you, but you need to have some respect for—"

And then he'd appeared like an angel—any type of angel, from any messed-up religion.

"Is there a problem here?" Mr. Keegan gave a fleeting look to Sam, but subsequently turned all attention to the other, who released Sam's arm. "Mr. Johnson?"

"No, Mr. Keegan. I was sharing some words of scripture—"

"This isn't a holy mission. Save it for Guatemala or Zimbabwe."

"When Heavenly Father's wisdom is needed—"

"There were many things that the First Great Awakening led to, Mr. Johnson. We discussed them last week. Name two of them."

The proselyte was unable to give an answer.

"Try for two out of three. The main purpose of Alexander Hamilton's economic program, what was that?" Mr. K folded his arms and waited a few seconds. "How about, tell me what statement declared the United States to be the 'policeman' of the Western Hemisphere? Even a guess?"

"The Constitution?" Mr. Johnson shrugged.

"It sounds like you need to focus on another book. The Lord's wisdom won't help you pass the AP test. If I see any beams of light around your chair, I'll flunk you." He cleared his throat. "And if you cause any trouble on this trip, I'll ship you and your holy books straight home. And then I'll flunk you. You can see if the Lord's wisdom will help you get a GED. Understood?"

"Yes, sir."

Once the Book of Mormon had been repacked, Mr. Keegan threw one glance to Sam and walked away. Sam gazed after him, observing his movements with the usual awe. In comparison to everyone else Sam had ever known, Mr. K was from another planet. The teacher stopped in front of his wife and—

"'He shall prepare a way for them that they may accomplish the thing which he commandeth them.'" Mr. Johnson zipped his bag. "You like euphemisms, sister. Think about that one. A righteous man *will* prepare a way for you to accomplish what is commanded by the Lord." He smiled. "I know *several* men who'd prepare a way. Who *will*. It's only a matter of opportunity."

Sam had never experienced fear that caused his heart to crystallize so quickly that it separated from his aorta and dropped into his stomach. The group leader turned and walked away whistling "Nephi's Courage."

Back in the bathroom, Sam dropped the black pants to the floor and shook his head to clear the memory. There wouldn't be an opportunity. He was being far too careful since the head injury, and the only chance they'd have on the trip had been lost. The group had chosen a night on the town instead of ganging up on him. And he wasn't worried about crossing their path.

They weren't heading to The Attic. Sam's classmates wouldn't have gone last year if he hadn't suggested it. He'd been surprised how easily they'd been persuaded.

Goes to show how much influence I used to have. He retrieved the pants from the floor. *And another example of Mormon hypocrisy. Not a single scripture-toting bitch had the balls to question me. Oh, you'll "go and do" when people are watching or it's convenient. When there's no better, more exciting, option. What does it say about your "true scriptures" or "courage" when you fold at going to a drag club? Fuck Nephi. Fuck all of you.*

Sam buttoned the pants and they conformed to his body. He smoothed his palms down his thighs with a grimace. He used to love this outfit. Or he loved how other people loved the outfit. His mother had said it was flattering and showed off his curves. The girls had asked where he got the blouse, and the pants met envious approval as well— they had a great cut and were paired equally well with heels or sneakers. His boyfriend had lifted his eyebrows when Sam wore the outfit.

Making other people happy used to be very important. It mattered so much that I washed this blouse nightly and wore it every day for two weeks. Like I was a fucking cartoon character. Sam brought out the round compact, eye shadow palette, and pencils he'd tucked in his suitcase. *But I'm not a character anymore. I'm not here for anyone else's entertainment. This is the last time I'm putting on the mask.*

His plan was to get into the club and go straight to the bathroom.

The men's room. No one will say a damn thing, no matter how much shit I cake on my face. He'd lock himself in a stall and peel off the choking layers of this skin. He'd use the makeup-removing wipes and put on the binder he'd made by sewing four three-inch elastic bands together.

Sam had developed the binder idea himself. While he could use an actual binder manufactured specifically for transgender men, how would he explain that to his mother? Scarlet hadn't taken note about his change of appearance the last few months, but if he received a package in the mail, she'd notice and open it. And he wasn't ready for her to find out yet. He wanted to be in the position where he could leave if the news was taken too poorly.

He remembered Scarlet's reaction when he'd told her he was gay. He'd hoped homosexuality explained the problem since, at the time, he wasn't aware of anything else he could be, besides insane. He reasoned that expressing his attraction to women openly would cause the masculine feelings to go away. Maybe he was a super-butch lesbian and coming out would fix everything. His first step had been to tell his mother. Strategically, he made the declaration in the presence of her boyfriend of the week.

Martin. Sam thought back as he concentrated on not stabbing himself in the eye with the pencil.

Martin had been a religious dickhead. While Sam didn't understand what men saw in his mother, he'd been especially confused by Martin's motivations. He eventually decided that Martin saw Scarlet as a pet project. The man liked that she and her kids were a mess. Sam was sure that somewhere in his fifty-odd years, a woman had castrated Martin and hung his balls around her rearview mirror. He got off on being in control as the strong patriarch.

Martin did things like urge Scarlet to go to church even though she hated it. He pushed her to have regular scripture study with Sam and Stevie, and they needed to have family prayers multiple times a day. Though they barely made ends meet, Scarlet had to contribute as much as possible to the church. Tithing. Fast offering. Missionary Fund. Every dime counted.

And Scarlet needed to encourage Sam that the right path for a young woman was preparation to be a helpmate to her husband. To be occupied with becoming temple-worthy and readying herself to raise a family. Less time on applying for scholarships. More time on the hope chest. Martin was a traditionalist—a Mormon girl put in a year or two to prove she wasn't an idiot before marrying her return missionary and settling down.

Then Martin would brag what a good man he was. He'd beaten his children with belts instead of coat hangers unlike his father before him. And he only used the buckle end when they *really* deserved it. He was "breaking the chain of violence." When it came to women, Martin proudly declared that he could care less what a woman's face looked like so long as there were paper bags in the world. This was "resourcefulness."

Sam had told Scarlet he didn't like Martin or feel comfortable around him. But Scarlet bulldozed his concerns and said Sam was trying to ruin her life, as usual. She invited the man to their house and played "happy Mormon mother" by fixing disgusting food and praying over pats of butter. Martin was her world. She even had the audacity to bring him to Sam's paternal grandmother's funeral. The two of them sat outside the viewing room giggling and snuggling on a couch.

But Sam had been through the boyfriend merry-go-round enough times to figure out how to turn whatever he could to his advantage. Martin was a jackass. But being a religious Mormon jackass, one of his primary tirades was on the supreme importance of family. Of a mother unconditionally and foremost loving her children. As with all her boyfriends, Scarlet was different when Martin was around. She always put on a show. She'd never say "you're ruining my life" or storm out in a tantrum.

His best hope for a reaction without theatrics would be to tell her in front of Martin, where she'd rather die than throw a fit. Scarlet had sat calmly beside Martin as Sam confessed he was a lesbian. She hadn't screamed or cried. She hadn't bemoaned the cruel fate of being cursed with a difficult, ungrateful, embarrassing child. Sam knew she was thinking these things, but it'd been nice to pretend he didn't know her as well as he did. Scarlet nodded along with the self-righteous nutcase, who urged Sam to "pray about it."

I've been praying about it. You don't know how much I've prayed, you fat fuck.

No one knew how often or earnestly from a young age he'd prayed to be a complete person. God created the world in seven days, didn't He? Was it really that much to grant one small child a body and mind that synced together? He made an entire man out of dust. Surely creating a penis could be done in a quarter of the time. A fucking sixteenth! And with less dust too. It shouldn't be a big deal. Or if God *insisted* that He'd give babies two heads but a boy couldn't have a penis, at least grant him the strength to endure. Sam prayed for Jesus to enter his heart, to ease his burden, to carry him across some fucking sandy beach. He prayed for peace.

But he'd figured it all out years ago. Instead of listening to him, the Lord was too busy talking to the Mormon prophet, inspiring a quarterback to win a football game, or playing cornhole. All He had time to give Sam was His middle finger. Flip him the divine bird. Prayer didn't work if God was the beer-swilling couch fungus He appeared to be.

However, Sam's tactic partially paid off. Scarlet gave him the silent treatment for two weeks, and there was only the occasional time in which she rolled her eyes as if she were on the verge of fainting from the weight of Sam's betrayal. He'd expected those melodramatic reactions, but what he hadn't anticipated was the bonus of Martin dumping her.

His mother degenerated into a basket case—volleying between rage at Sam for ruining her life and wailing hysterics. And Sam went through the motions of responding to a Scarlet crisis. He made things easy. He tried to do anything she might want or need in advance. He hid the knives and sleeping pills. Eventually Scarlet's emotional state leveled off as much as it ever did. But she'd never forgiven Sam. Even when he still wore the outfits she liked and tried to be the perfect, albeit homosexual, daughter.

I wonder how long I'll get the silent treatment when I tell you I'm not a lesbian; Sam took a dark-green-striped shirt from his bag. He shook it out and refolded it, smoothing the collar. *When I tell you I'm not your daughter. I'm your son. And I'm going to move out, change my name, and start hormones, and there's not a Goddamn thing you can do about it.*

Until that happy day in the future, to balance his sanity with a relatively peaceful home life, Sam had to be careful. Hence the homemade binder. He'd tried the Ace bandages other transgender men suggested online, but it didn't yield the results he wanted. He couldn't get it tight enough, and he stuck himself with the safety pins. It also never lasted and slipped all day at school. So, he created a better solution. The elastic binder was quick to use, more effective and comfortable than the Ace bandage, and it was easy to hide.

I'll put it on, and then the green shirt. And the jeans that are cut straight so they don't hug my hips or knees. And the sneakers. Sam placed each piece of clothing in the purse.

When he looked at himself in the mirror, his cheeks flushed. He felt like a prostitute. A whore painted for the pleasure of someone else.

It's a means to an end. I'll throw this fucking outfit in the garbage, scrub this shit off my face, and I'll never be Amanda again. I'll walk into that club and bathroom as her. But I'll walk out as Sam. I am no one's whore.

SEVEN

THE BOUNCER AT The Attic was the same man who'd been at the door last year, and Sam presented his ID with what he hoped came across as an air of nonchalance.

"Idaho, eh?" The man touched the edges and bent the card slightly.

"Yep."

"I'm marking today on my calendar." He shined his flashlight over the hologram.

"Why?" Sam's mouth went dry, and he tried not to swallow.

Keep his eye contact. Stay calm. Do not look suspicious.

"This is probably the last Idaho ID I'll see until this time next year. Seems like there's one day a year I get a crowd of you. Is it some kind of holiday?"

"You said you get a crowd of us?" *Damn it.*

"A few." The bouncer returned the ID with a smile. "Go on through. But no bracelet, sweetie." The man nodded to his colleague, who was holding a bucket of green neon strips. "Your friends were in the upstairs lounge when I walked through a bit ago."

"Thanks."

Sam paid the cover and walked through the door into another dimension.

It sounded like the walls were made of speakers and each thump of the music caused them to flex in and out. This rhythmic motion seemed to slosh the dance floor crowd together in large clumps, and Sam felt seasick as he watched. Violet and pink lights cast over hundreds of heads and hands periodically thrusting toward the ceiling, while most eyes focused on the stage or video screens plastered around the room. Sam's eardrums stung, and the floor vibrations rattled him to his core. His brain hummed with the electricity of the atmosphere.

I'll go to the second-floor bathroom. Sam took a deep breath as the ocean of movement swallowed him. *It was less packed.*

Last year his boyfriend found the first-floor bathroom and led him there. The line had been out the door.

"There's another one upstairs!" A six-foot-tall man in stilettos and a blond wig had shouted in Sam's ear when he'd noticed the hallmark shuffling.

"Thank you, sir—erhm..." he yelled, and his eyes followed the man's long red fingernail to a fluorescent sign by the staircase.

"It doesn't matter, honey! Get your ass up there before you wet yourself!"

Sam balanced on his tiptoes to find the sign he'd been pointed to a year ago. When he spotted it, he forged his way across the room through the glittering swirls of beautiful, but tightly jammed, sardines. He didn't have any interest in bobbing around, hooting with these prima donnas. He wanted to socialize with like-minded people in an area where he could use his normal speaking voice. In addition to the bathroom, this less crowded and quieter environment could be found upstairs.

A year ago he'd been the only one of the group to make it to the second floor. He went alone although his boyfriend had cautioned him to wait for the rest of the troops. Sam had called him a dumbass. It wasn't a football game; it was taking a piss. He was capable of independent movement outside the unit. To him, the menagerie was far from intimidating.

Sam received the text message from his boyfriend as he left the bathroom: —*Get the fuck out now!*

He raced out the door and discovered his friends pale-faced and shaking behind The Attic's dumpster.

"What's wrong?" Sam had asked.

"You'll never believe who we saw in there, Mandy."

"Who?"

"Mrs. Keegan."

"No way." His jaw dropped.

"For real. She was sitting at the bar."

"Did she catch you?"

"She reamed us out. Told us to get our asses to the hotel. She said 'ass' to Brody. Isn't that balls?"

"What was she doing there?" Teachers didn't do that kind of thing. And she wasn't just any teacher—she was Mr. K's wife. What did this information say about her? About him? His mind reeled with all the things this could mean.

"She said it was 'none of our damn business.' She's probably lez. We took a vote and decided she's lez. Which is awesome, since she's hot as shit."

"Where was Mr. K?" Maybe he wasn't there. After all, if Sam hadn't been who he was, would he have any interest in a gay nightclub? Not really. Did Mr. Keegan know his wife was there? Was she a closet lesbian? What if she was cheating on him or—

"She said he was only in the bathroom, so we had to move quick. Can you imagine what he'd do if he found us?"

He didn't think Mr. Keegan would do anything. Sam had observed him walk by students smoking outside the auditorium or inhaling aerosol fumes behind the cafeteria and pretend to not notice. This indifferent behavior had initially bothered him.

Something doesn't affect you, so you don't care? He'd briefly questioned if his idolization was mislaid. Did he want to be the type of man who didn't care about anyone but himself? No one knew better than Sam that the most important aspect defining a man was his character. How he looked, his knowledge, and his power were an amazing glaze; however, Sam wanted to be more than a donut topping.

But despite the displayed antipathy, Mr. Keegan had continued to be kind to him. He worried if Sam was late and welcomed him back when he returned from an absence. And he'd complimented Sam's writing abilities, praising him for his clarity and for drawing creative parallels in essays. Flattery didn't come easily or often from Mr. K, but it was more frequent and genuine than from Scarlet.

You're not like Mom. You do care. Other people's self-destruction just isn't worth your time, since you can't do anything about it. I can support that position. I need to take that attitude when it comes to my mom.

Sam had doubted Mr. K would flip. He'd have kicked them out but wouldn't have escorted them to the hotel. Their secure imprisonment wouldn't have been equivalent to the effort it would take. Mr. K considered himself "off the clock" Friday night and made it clear he was only to be called in the event of death or loss of limb. And only major limbs. Losing a finger in an elevator door didn't necessitate disturbing his evening.

"We have to promise we'll never talk about this," his boyfriend had said. The other heads had nodded rapidly. "If Mr. K finds out, he'll kill us, Mandy. Even if he is officially the coolest son of a bitch in the world. Do you think he watches? I bet he does. He's that badass."

Even among the group, they hadn't discussed seeing Mrs. Keegan in a gay nightclub again. Sam might've thought the incident forgotten if the group hadn't spent the rest of the year looking at the Keegans in a new light. Mrs. K had been declared a hot lez, and Mr. K was unanimously voted to have baller status.

What made them tell? Sam wondered as he climbed the staircase. *Or is there someone in this group that is curious? Not exactly like me; that's too much to hope for.*

He stepped through the beaded door at the top of the stairs and walked down the hallway, the thudding music fading behind him. Lines of rainbow lights in the corners of the ceiling led his way to the other end. He braced himself before pushing through the door into the lounge.

Sam prepared to see a terrified cockroach cluster of students, but a sweep of the dim lit room yielded no creepy teenage huddle. Although, he was only able to give the scene a quick scan before he dashed to the bathrooms.

I've got to get out of these clothes. If he didn't change the red blouse it would burn into his flesh.

He went straight into the men's room, though his choice wouldn't have mattered. The men's bathroom was exactly how he remembered the women's had been.

They might as well take the damn signs off the doors.

A blast of flowery perfume made his eyes water. It seemed part bathroom part women's dressing room, as the antechamber contained three round banquette sofas upholstered in gaudy red velvet, and a wall of adjacent full-length mirrors. Past this staging area were five urinals, two in use by tall figures in high heels. When he walked by the line of stalls, he noticed only ankles in the open space underneath. Whether the toes pointed toward or away from the door, it was ankle after ankle.

I'm the only person in the men's room wearing pants, he chuckled to himself.

None of the eyes he met were unkind, and no one looked at him like he didn't belong. Instead of feeling pulled by a horse cart through a dirty medieval street, he was walking through a butterfly house. Despite the overwhelming department store musk, there was a light friendliness to the air. God, he loved DC and hated Idaho.

Sam shut himself in a stall and opened the purse he'd brought. He began his transformation by removing the awful red blouse. As he held it, he was inspired with the urge to not just discard, but destroy it. He wanted to rip it to shreds and flush it down the toilet. Or burn it.

The garbage will have to do. He shoved it into the purse.

Sam buttoned his fresh shirt and pulled on the acid-washed jeans followed by his sneakers. He listened to the boisterous laughter that filled the bathroom as he cleaned the disgusting makeup from his face. They were calling each other "honey" and "girlfriend" and "sweetie" in fluttering voices.

Everyone outside that state is so nice. Why does anyone live in Idaho? He thought of Mr. Keegan. Why had he left Louisiana for such a horrible place? Sam imagined New Orleans was like Washington, DC— exciting and full of people who didn't bash each other's skulls in due to their differences. *When I graduate, I'm gone.*

He was prepared to leave everything. The pain. The school. Stevie. His mother. At present, he didn't feel he cared to see Scarlet again. After all, it wasn't like she'd ever seen him. And the more time that passed without her forgiving him for saying he was gay, the more convinced he was she'd never see him as her son.

Even when I wear shirts and ties all the time, or when I have a deep voice and facial hair. You won't see it; you won't accept it.

Sam imagined standing with Scarlet in a grocery store checkout after he'd been on testosterone a few months. She'd address him as Amanda and call him her daughter.

And the cashier will look at you like you're nuts, Mom. Like you've been smoking crack. You care so much what everyone else thinks. What will they think then? That you're a fucking tweaker.

Sam squirted some gel into his palm and ran it through his hair. Thinking of the perplexed look on the fictional cashier's face filled him with confidence. Yes, the tables would turn. Instead of the public having to find the boy, they'd have to hunt for a glimmer of the girl. She'd disappear like the phantom she was, and Scarlet could do nothing but look like a fool in insisting he was anything but a normal young man.

When I change my name, you'll have a conniption. And when I tell you it's Sam, you'll erupt.

The careful selection of his name had been explained multiple, agonizing times. It was in honor of his family, particularly Scarlet, that he'd been named. "Amanda" was a traditional family name on Scarlet's side. For generations, the girls in his mother's line had carried "Amanda" as either a first or middle name.

"I had three miscarriages before you, and we were sure you'd be it. We named you after both of us. Amanda, for me. But we also had to get your jackass father in there."

That's how it'd come to be. Amanda Michelle: the name meant to define him for the rest of his life was an amalgamation of his parents' vanity. A mobile monument to them. But that's all he'd ever been. An expensive bauble. A miniature dog in a zebra-striped fucking bag.

Stevie has his own name. Of course, he's a boy, and it's okay to regurgitate a name if it's for another baby factory. Amanda 7.1. But a boy is completely different. He looped the dark-green tie around his collar and paused before adjusting the wide end. *Maybe I'm a hypocrite then. For choosing "Sam."*

Sam's paternal grandmother, at whose funeral Scarlet embarrassed him with Martin, had been the closest to a real parent that he'd known. He hadn't been her fashion accessory. She never asked him to do anything one wouldn't normally expect of a young child. She spent time with him. She wore how much she loved him and what a priority he was on her sleeve. She'd been proud of him without taking ownership of his achievements. She'd never blamed him for anything or made him feel ashamed for wanting to be loved. And she'd apologized, profusely, for the behavior of both his parents.

He cleared his throat. *She was my champion. The only one I had.*

Scarlet wouldn't support him at the graveside service of his friend who'd committed suicide, but Sam's grandmother had sat in the front row in the school gymnasium when he received his letterman sweater. And she'd been dying with cancer when she pulled herself out of bed and drove across town to pick Sam up in the rain outside a Target.

He'd been at the store with his father, Stevie, and his father's new family. As frequently happened, there'd been a fight where Sam was called a worthless mistake and ordered to "walk the fuck home!" He watched the happy family leave without him, Stevie's nose mashed against the window in glee.

Sam first called Scarlet, who refused to come. It was his father's turn with them. She needed time to herself. She deserved it. Why should her weekend be ruined? She *served* her sentence with them during the week. There was no way she was driving thirty minutes to get him. Frank could call at any moment.

So, although wracked with guilt, Sam called his grandmother. And from a distance as far, she'd been there in twenty minutes. Without having to beg, cry, or even explain. Just "I'll be right there."

He'd slid into the passenger seat of the green van, and she handed him a towel. Sopping from the rain, he'd collapsed into her arms and cried. It wasn't fair. It wasn't right that his parents treated him this way. He tried to not let their cruel words bother him, tried to focus his fifteen-year-old mind, and remember he couldn't be held accountable for everything they blamed him for. He tried to separate from the things they said and did, but it hurt so badly.

His grandmother cried with him. She was the only person who hurt when he hurt. Who gave a shit. She bashed her own son. She assured Sam his parents were wrong, and he didn't need them.

"You're my heart," she'd said. "I'm proud of you, and I love you."

It was wonderful to hear. But as Sam hugged her, he thought of the cancer. Of the doctors opening her, only to close her again. They couldn't take it out—it was everywhere. All that could be done was to alleviate the pain and wait for the inevitable.

Having been raised in such a religious environment, Sam had found it difficult to abandon the prayers and hope that his gender identity would magically resolve itself. Though the optimism declined, he'd continued to ask. Except for the period between his grandmother's diagnosis and her death. His prayers shifted then, and he desperately bargained with God.

"Please, don't take her from me. I swear, whatever is going on, I'll stop. I'll forget feeling like a boy. I'll go to church and be the best Mormon girl I can. I'll do whatever You ask of me. Go on a mission. Marry a man in the temple. Pop out kids. I promise. Just please don't take my grandma from me."

But He'd killed her. Another divine fucking middle finger. He kept alive murderers, child molesters, and rapists. God kept Scarlet and his father. He kept billions of people on the fucking planet who didn't mean anything to anyone. But He took a young boy's grandmother when she was all he had. Some benevolent, loving God.

Fuck you. Above everyone else, FUCK YOU. Sam took several breaths to calm himself. He needed to concentrate. He should be excited. What prompted this rabbit hole had been something thrilling.

Ah, yes. He smiled and folded his tie. His face was cooling off, and the clamor in the bathroom returned. *My name. And how Mom will throw a fucking fit when she finds out.*

His grandmother's name had been Samara. And Scarlet hated many things and many people, but Samara had been near the top of the list. When Sam described his grandmother as a "second mother" in her eulogy, Scarlet blew a gasket and gave him the silent treatment for a week.

If there's anyone I want to be named after, anyone I want to be reminded of and commemorate, it's not you. And you can be damn sure that after I legally change it, I'm never letting you call me Amanda again. Ever.

He crammed the purse of women's clothes and makeup into the bathroom stall's garbage can.

But you may not have the chance to look like a stoner in a grocery store. If you can't accept me as Sam, I won't be around you. I'll leave and never come back. There's no shortage of people who'll care about me.

Sam snuck a glimpse at his reflection in the rectangular mirror above the sinks as he walked by. It wasn't perfect, but it also wasn't Amanda looking at him. Maybe he should go this far in dressing at school—ditch the unisex polos and wear button-ups and ties all the time. Perhaps he wouldn't be ejected from the boy's bathroom if he dared to enter it.

And someday, I won't have to worry about something as simple as walking into the right bathroom. Outside school I'll do what I want. He plunged one hand into his pocket and pushed open the bathroom door. *In a place like this, I can be me. In a place like Washington, DC, or New Orleans. No, N'walins. That's so fucking cool.*

Sam reentered the lounge feeling like a different person. He felt like himself. He felt free. But then his stomach dropped as he found himself face-to-face with someone he hadn't expected.

Mr. K.

Kind of.

EIGHT

TODD HAD BEEN adamant that he was going to The Attic on Friday, even though Julie had hinted strongly twice more that *they* shouldn't. She could come if she liked or do something else.

"You know I can't do that," she'd whispered as they hung behind the tour group of students being led through Gettysburg.

"I guess you've made your decision."

"Compromise with me then. Go in your normal clothes."

"That defeats the purpose, doesn't it?" Todd shrugged and kept walking. He knew his detachment aggravated her as much as his refusal to give in. "Besides, they recognized you, not me. Maybe *you* should dress up."

"It was only because you were in the bathroom."

"Who's to say they would've recognized me at all? They're teenagers. They're idiots."

He'd motioned to a couple straggling from the flock a few yards ahead. The boy's arm was around the girl, and his hand was on her ass. Todd considered approaching silently and tapping them on the shoulders.

Maybe he'd accidentally bite her tongue off. But then I'd never be able to stop laughing, and they'd fire me for sure. Todd figured he was doing the world a favor by staying with his sister and allowing the behavior to continue. *I can't have much empathy for self-imposed stupidity. We need a new generation to wash dishes and deep-fry chicken. This country would collapse if there wasn't anyone to run the drive-thru windows. There'd be riots in the street if people couldn't get breakfast burritos at two in the morning. I should get the Nobel Peace Prize. I at least deserve a nomination.*

"They would have. You don't look that different."

"Ouch, Julie. Ouch."

"I don't mean it like that. I'm sorry."

"No worries. That isn't the point anyway." Todd laughed. It was too bad she didn't express the same concerns when she said things that actually offended him.

Being a completely different person was the objective for many people, and he didn't fault them for it. Expression was unique for everyone. But he wasn't gay. And he didn't feel he was a woman. He didn't even have a separate persona like some drag queens did. Ultimately, for him, trying to be another person spoiled it. He didn't want to cover anything—he was releasing.

I have a feminine side I'm not afraid to show, and I'm comfortable being a man in a dress. I like myself too much to not want to be me, whatever I'm wearing.

"I know. But I'm still sorry." Julie had shoved her hands into the pocket of her sweatshirt and kicked a stone with her tennis shoe.

Todd looked to the troop of students led by Janet and Doug Farr walking side by side. Janet wore a baggy cat T-shirt and olive stretch pants. Doug had on a silk Hawaiian shirt, cargo shorts, and brown sandals with tall, white socks. They also modeled matching fanny packs.

I have no casual mode. He hooked his thumbs in the belt loops of his slacks. *Even when walking around a dusty old battlefield. No wonder these kids think I have a stick up my ass, but I just like to look nice. Do I even own a sweatshirt? A T-shirt?* He smiled. *I have two Aerosmith T-shirts in my dresser that I never wear. I should.*

His eyes skimmed the adolescent crowd until he spotted Amanda Porter. She was near the front and appeared to be paying attention to the tour guide. Like him, she was also wearing what she usually wore, or what'd been the norm this year—a solid-colored polo and corduroy pants.

Even I wouldn't wear corduroys in this weather, but whatever floats your boat, cher.

There was something else different about her now. Amanda used to have dark hair that hung halfway down her back in a tangled mane. But when she'd arrived at the bus stop two days prior, the hair was gone. Not completely, but cropped above her shoulders. He wondered why, though hadn't asked. And he'd been curious as to the excuse she'd given a stylist to account for her head laceration. Had she learned from her failed lie to him and invented something new, or stuck with the same story? But he hadn't questioned that either. He gave her an offhand compliment on the new look and hadn't spoken to her since.

Todd had been watching though. He was keeping an eye on Amanda. Possibly closer than the guarded observation he kept over his sister. Whether Julie believed it or not, she didn't have anything major to fear; however, Amanda Porter was vulnerable.

The past several days, he'd been kicking himself for not doing more. He respected and identified with her desire for independence, but she wasn't just being shoved in lockers. From his surveillance, he saw how the students looked at her. With cruelty.

As of yet, he'd only had to physically intervene at the Denver airport when the Johnson boy took her wrist. For half a second he considered hanging back and observing. He would've loved an excuse to expel Johnson. What a pleasure to tell the boy's missionary president father that his self-righteous son had hit a girl. Don't believe the non-Mormon from New Orleans? Airports have cameras, bitch. And if Johnson was one of the douchebags bullying Amanda, it'd be great to get him out of the picture.

But Amanda being hurt wasn't worth it, and he stepped in to shut the situation down. His interference hadn't met resistance, and Amanda gave him a look so saturated with gratitude and awe that it made him self-conscious. As he walked away, he sensed her staring at him and almost expected her to come trailing after.

Don't go puppy on me. I have my limits.

She hadn't, thank God. Which led him to believe that the dewy-eyed thankful gaze was an indication he'd interrupted at the right time. Who knew where it could've escalated? And that yielded another question—why? What inspired violence out of a scripture-toting geek?

What did you do? What do they think you did?

Pairing the bullying with Amanda's change of appearance had occurred to him. Had she come out of the closet? That would've caused her to lose her popular friends; however, it didn't explain the level of hostility. The few openly gay students hung around together. They were looked at strangely and regarded with caution, but no one physically assaulted them. If she was a lesbian, there was something else as well.

Todd had considered pulling one of the punks aside and demanding to know what their fucking problem with Amanda was. But in addition to this being another venture beyond his standards, it was dangerous. And not only for Amanda.

He imagined the dickhead teenager spouting something incredibly stupid: "Dude, we were at Fat Joey's a few weeks ago, and she, like, scuzzed off my girlfriend and stuff. And then she ate all the fucking chips, man. You can't forgive a bitch for hogging all the Doritos. They were Cool Ranch, Mr. Keegan." And then Todd would be forced to kill the little bastard, which didn't bode well for retaining his employment.

"Todd, I really am sorry," Julie said.

He broke his line of sight from Amanda Porter and looked at his sister.

"Relax. I'm not some frail flower." Todd laughed again, but then his smile disappeared. He knew how manipulative she could be. He got so fucking tired of her trying to control him. "I'm going. I brought my pink-and-black jacket; remember that one?"

"Why would you wear that? It was dated when you got it."

"There it is." He stopped walking.

"What?" Julie halted. She looked behind her shoulder, and he saw and heard her breaths come quicker. "Where? What? There what is?" Lighting her panic fuse made him feel almost guilty. Almost.

"Your jealousy. Rearing its ugly head." Todd chuckled and resumed his pace. He didn't look back, but heard her following him. Always following him. There'd been a time when she'd been in front, blazing a different path. Now she was too afraid to place a toe outside his footsteps. "I told you, Julie. If you want to wear my clothes, just ask."

"I'll wear your clothes when you have something worth wearing. But it doesn't matter; you shouldn't go to the club."

"Fortunately, I don't need you to approve my decisions."

Todd jogged to the group, leaving his sister behind. As he'd been fighting the impulse to do, he clapped a hand on the shoulder of the young man who'd become increasingly distracted by the inside of his girlfriend's mouth.

"Mr. Thompson, does this look like a pond to you? A river?"

"No, Mr. Keegan."

"A stream then? A tributary?"

"No." The boy hesitated. "It's a battlefield?"

"That's right. More than fifty thousand men lost their lives here. Their bodies fell where you and I are walking. So, whatever you're trying to *fish* out of Ms. Cook's mouth, save it for a lake, not hallowed ground."

"Yes, sir."

Todd watched Mr. Thompson hurry to catch his classmates and folded his arms with a smile. Reprimands made in a crisp shirt and tie were more effective than rebukes from an old woman in a cat sweatshirt and purple sun visor. The admonishments were also taken more seriously than if he'd been wearing his hot pink-and-black jacket, no matter how awesome it was.

PERHAPS BECAUSE TODD had prevented her from having a panic attack on Wednesday, Julie hadn't bothered Todd again about The Attic. Despite her snide comments about his selfishness, she'd been flooded with appreciation for him. He could feel the gratitude.

It's well-placed. Few people would stay awake all night texting you every ten minutes.

Todd knew her paranoia well enough to anticipate the freak-out. But he'd delayed sending the first message.

Sometimes I feel like I'm an enabler. Maybe you'd be more secure if I let you deal with your apprehensions alone. Isn't that what you're supposed to do with crying babies when they get to a certain age? Stop picking them up at every whimper. Close the door and let them scream? His finger hovered over the cell phone's send button. *You're twenty-five years old, Julie. You're not a baby.*

He deleted the message and stared at the ceiling. He had no idea what she'd been through, so he had no right to judge her. But he did feel she was being a child at times.

I'm your father. I'm your husband. I'm your brother. I'm not even thirty, and I shouldn't have to be this fucking responsible. Goddamn it.

But Todd swiped the screen and punched in the text message to think over. He pictured her lying in bed and working into a fit. Each terrifying scenario escalating to higher degrees of horror and immediacy. It was like a coiled spring pushed into a box. Compressing and condensing until the pressure became too much.

He erased the message. *You fight with me and try to keep me from doing what I want. Then you act like I'm the one dependent on you. Why do you even think me being around makes a difference? What good would I be in a fight, Julie? I'm not a three-hundred-pound taekwondo master. I could take him in history trivia. I sincerely doubt an attacker would pause stabbing or raping to play Jeopardy to the death. However—*

"Alex, I'll take 'FUCKED UP SHIT THAT HAPPENED TO JULIE' for six hundred, please."

"All right, Mr. Keegan: 'Machine guns, brute strength, and skills of any kind beyond turning a doorknob.'"

"What are things not needed to rescue Julie from the sociopath who shot himself after torturing her for a week?"

"Correct, for five hundred."

Applause from the live studio audience.

Four years ago, Todd and Julie had their separate lives. They were close and spoke frequently, but she didn't want to be constantly attached to him. And they'd shared many of the same friends, so it wasn't unusual to meet on a regular basis. However, Todd hadn't heard from Julie in days.

"No Julie? She must be super pissed at me. She hasn't returned my calls or messages." He'd stood when a couple of their friends approached the bar. He pointed at a woman who worked with his sister. "I blame you, Suze."

"Why me?"

"You said that eye shadow looked better on me than on her."

"It did. I can't help that." Suze slipped onto a barstool. "Don't worry. She's off on a romantic week with her new boyfriend."

"New boyfriend?" He raised an eyebrow. Julie hadn't mentioned a boyfriend. Not that he was under any delusion that she told him everything, but someone she was dating seriously enough to go away with?

"The client who's been calling for the past few months? The big account? He was *really* impressed with her professionalism and customer service."

"She's queen of the bullshit." Todd laughed.

"No, *I'm* queen of the bullshit. Julie is emperor of the bullshit."

"All hail Caesar."

"Anyway." She cracked a peanut shell in half. "He's been talking to her exclusively. He won't let anyone else handle his orders, and he sent her flowers earlier this week."

"I can't believe she didn't tell me this." He looked away from her and into his glass.

Suze pried the peanut out with a fingernail. "And she hasn't been to work since. I can only assume she rode off into the sunset with her Prince Charming. That fucking bitch. No one ever sends me flowers." She grinned and shoved his shoulder. "Don't give it a second thought."

But Todd had given the idea many thoughts. Julie told him about men she casually dated. He knew she thought her garbage man was worth waking at 5:00 a.m. to ogle. She might not disclose everything, but she'd have mentioned someone she was interested in when he'd seen her last week.

He questioned Suze further and with rising panic. Had Julie been out with this guy before? No. Was he from around here? She didn't think so. Did anyone know him? No.

"But I talked to him once before he latched onto her. He sounds handsome. Has this deep—"

Had anyone *seen* this man? No. Had *Julie* even seen him? Not to her knowledge. Did Julie call into work? Give an excuse for her absence? Suze wasn't the supervisor; how would she know that? Todd turned to their other friends at the bar. Had anyone at all heard from Julie in the past few days? No.

"Will you reeeelllllax, cher? He sent her flowers! Creeps don't sent flowers," Suze protested when he pushed his credit card across the counter and jumped off the barstool.

Alex Trebek cleared his throat.

"Excuse me, Mr. Keegan. It's your category again."

"Thanks. Let's go for 'STUPID-ASS WOMEN' for three hundred."

"And this is our Daily Double! We have six hundred on the line. Your answer: 'Creeps don't send flowers.'"

"What are things stupid-ass women say?"

"Correct for six hundred."

More applause from the studio audience.

Creeps did send flowers. They sent flowers if they knew where a young woman they'd been speaking with worked, but not what she looked like. Creeps sent flowers when they wanted to know more, but were too awkward to ask for a date. They sent flowers so they could sit in a white car outside the office at five o'clock to watch the workers leave.

He'd found out later that Julie had been the young woman wearing the yellow summer dress and carrying a ribbed vase of a dozen pink stargazer lilies. The creep who sent them picked her out. And he'd followed her home.

Todd had raced to his sister's house. He lost track of the red lights he ran and hoped the police would tail him. He knew. Just had this gut feeling. When he heard sirens, he floored the accelerator.

There'd been a strange vehicle on the curb, and Todd slammed the brakes to avoid hitting it. He thrust his car in park, not bothering to turn off the engine before he was out the door.

"Ma'am! I need you to stay in your vehicle!" an officer shouted as Todd grabbed the doorknob. "Ma'am!"

"Julie! Julie!" He hadn't cared if the police had a sniper rifle trained on his head or if the man in Julie's house had a gun.

Todd pushed open the unlocked door. There was blood. Everywhere.

"Now it's time for Final Jeopardy, ladies and gentleman." Mr. Trebek waved his hand toward the blue screen. "Let me remind you that the category is 'ASSHOLES.' That's a broad category, but we have a specific question we're looking for our contestants to match: 'Ignoring your deeply traumatized sister when she's terrified.' Mr. Keegan, you're in the lead, and you've wagered how much?"

"I bet it all, Alex. I've got this."

"Nice to see that confidence. What do you have written there?"

Todd imagined he hit the podium button to illuminate his handwriting.

"What is something a good brother wouldn't do?"

There was a rumble across the studio.

"Our judges have decided to give it to you, Mr. Keegan. Though we'd have accepted, 'Something that would send a person to Hell' or 'Something an asshole *would* do.' Any synonym of 'asshole' would also have been satisfactory. Jackass. Dickhead. Son of a bitch. Mother—"

"Point taken. I win. Hurray for me," he answered dryly.

Wild applause from the live studio audience.

NINE

"THANK YOU, TODD." Julie had met him in the hotel hallway at five o'clock the next morning. She wrapped her arms around his neck and hugged him tightly.

Remember this the next time you feel like being a jerk, he thought as he held her. *I get so angry when she's cocky and tries to control me. But I need to stop grouping her with my students.* Todd patted her back. *You're not little Snoochie, who didn't get a kazoo for his sixteenth birthday. You've been hurt. Horribly.*

Part of him still waited for Julie to bring up The Attic though. The brash attitude was overcompensating, but it was closer to who she used to be than the anxiety-ridden stranger. He wouldn't have given in, but it was nicer to argue than for her to be "puppy."

There'd been nothing though. Friday night rolled around. They split the herd between Mr. and Mrs. Farr and left. Of course, the look Julie shot toward Amanda Porter when they dropped the students off hadn't eluded him. It was the only fire his sister had shown in the past two days.

"Be careful, Ms. Porter." He adjusted the rearview mirror as Amanda unbuckled her seat belt.

Amid his worries about Julie, he'd been considering the dilemma of leaving his student unprotected. Not that there was much of an impasse. He rationalized that Amanda would've prepared to keep herself safe, since she knew what would happen.

Still, if they beat the shit out of her, will you be able to live with yourself, Todd? It could be like finding Julie again. He regarded Amanda in the mirror. *Will you be okay without me?*

The girl smiled, but it evaporated when Julie whipped around and gave her a fierce glare. This reaction surprised him, as she'd never given indication of having a problem with Amanda. Or any student.

Todd chose to ignore Julie and proceeded with a compromise to ease his conscience. He took a business card he'd collected earlier from his shirt pocket and handed it to Amanda. He'd written his cell number on the back. "Call me for any reason."

"Thank you, sir. I'll be fine."

But she took the card—putting her hand forward as if Julie were a viper that would spring if she moved too quickly. He watched her tuck the card in her bag and slide cautiously from the car. She fell into the group beside Janet Farr, who wrapped an arm around her shoulders. The combination of Amanda's cringe at the touch, and the skin of Janet's arm wobbling in the breeze as she waved made him laugh.

"Christ, it's like a flag. Like wash blowing in the fucking breeze." Todd pulled away from the curb and flipped on the radio. "Holy mother of—"

"Todd, what the hell was that?" Julie cut him off, as expected.

"What was what?" He kept hitting the seek button since he knew his disinterest would fuel her irritation. "There's never anything on. Commercial after—"

"What you said to Amanda! And you gave her your phone number!"

"How else is she supposed to contact me? Telepathy? Carrier pigeon? Pony express?"

"She shouldn't need to contact you!"

"I guess she could go Bogart and whistle, right? 'You know how to whistle, don't you, Steve? You just put—'"

Julie turned off the radio. He felt her looking at him, but kept his eyes on the road. "I need you to tell me. Right now. Do you have a thing for Amanda?"

Ah, so you're pissed it could destroy your nice setup. Like why you're worried about going to the club. Nothing whatsoever to do with me.

"Do you know how vast the definition of 'thing' is? Couldn't the word 'thing' substitute any noun? I don't have a troupe of dancing poodles for her, Julie. Or the key to a large city. Even a medium-sized city—"

"Todd, stop being an asshole. I need you to tell me the truth. Are you attracted to her?"

He left the question unanswered as they sat at a red light. Yes, it was shameful to bait her, but after two days of clinging timidity, any assertiveness was refreshing.

"I won't even dignify that with a response," he said.

From the corner of his eye, Todd saw Julie put her hand to her face and rub her eyebrows with her thumb and forefinger.

"You'll ruin yourself. Absolutely, irrevocably ruin yourself. Why? I know she doesn't bug you, but—"

He couldn't maintain the farce and laughed.

"Chill, cher. Freeze fucking solid." Todd put his hand on her arm and shook it until she looked in his direction. When she did, he smiled and turned to the road. "No, she doesn't bother me; however, if I only wanted to date people by *that* criteria... Well, granted it would be a small pool, but lack of irritation does not a romance make."

"Then tell me what that was. What's been going on the entire trip? You've been watching her. You've made certain she's been with *our* group, in *our* car, sitting at *our* table. You won't let her out of your sight."

He'd decided from the beginning that if anyone questioned his attentions, he'd be perfectly honest. "A bunch of those fucks have been bullying her, so I've wanted to keep an eye on her. That's all."

"Bullying her, why?"

"How should I know? Maybe she took the last enchilada in the lunch line." Todd parked in the hotel lot and pulled his keys from the ignition. "Nimrods shoved a boy's head in the toilet for liking to wear dresses and makeup, no matter *how* good he looked in them. You can't derive logic from cave dwellers, Julie. And they'll never evolve from beating their clubs, swinging on vines, or eating lice off each other."

Without waiting for a response, Todd opened the door and walked behind the car to retrieve his bag.

"These aren't your bullies." Julie followed him and lifted the trunk as he unlocked it.

"Fully aware of that. *My* bullies are pumping gas." He pulled out their luggage. "Or rather, since this isn't the 1950s, they're in a gutter somewhere. Or a halfway house. Or being used to test shampoo. Can you imagine? What lucky son of a bitch gets to squirt them in the eyes with shampoo every day? Now *that* is a job to be envied."

I don't get angry about the douchebags who shoved me in lockers very often, but when I do that's what I dream of. Todd rolled his bag across the parking lot, hearing Julie's footsteps beside his. *Shooting all kinds of bathroom products into their eyes. And—*

He almost tripped over the threshold of the automatic doors when his sister grabbed the side handle of his suitcase. When he turned to snap at her she released the bag and spoke first.

"I know what it's like to have demons. If you need to—"

"In no way is my past vaguely relatable to what you went through." He used his most serious tone. The grim pitch he employed when he told a student they were going to fail his class, and he didn't have a gram of sympathy for them. Except there was no underlying amusement. Few experiences could match Julie's horror. Being shoved in a locker? Ludicrous. Even what Amanda was going through. No comparison.

And you'll never recover. We're both fooling ourselves. Two additional sobering realities. He swallowed and forced a smile.

"Besides, real demons are omnipresent, aren't they? I empathize with a kid going through something similar." Todd pulled the retractable handle from his bag. "I can't believe you thought I wanted to be involved with a student. You're one twisted bitch."

"Anyone would've come to that conclusion from how you've been acting." They went through a second set of doors, and he felt relieved she was willing to drop into another subject.

"I won't find the love of my life in Podunk-fucking Idaho, Julie. I'll find her scantily clad in the history section of a library. Or scantily clad in the American History Museum. Or scantily clad and draped provocatively over the steps of the Lincoln Memorial. You get the picture. Occupying the visible reality of space while insufficiently clothed."

The last bit of tension in Todd slipped away when Julie smiled at him. Perhaps she was back to that plateau of "normal" anxiety.

He removed the ID and credit card from his wallet and slid both across the counter. "But we should find you a nice, Mormon husband that you can castrate and ride off into the sunset. And by 'ride off into the sunset' I don't mean *with*, or *alongside*. I'm thinking a saddle, spurs, a bit. I mean—"

"I know what you mean, Todd."

WITH THE VARIOUS mini-crises behind, Todd looked forward to a relaxing evening. Essentially his only reprieve aside from going home at summer vacation. Sure, could he come home from work and put on a skirt with a nice blouse? Absolutely. He could get fully dressed as if he was going out. But it wasn't the same.

For this, I don't need the spotlight, but general acknowledgement? Yes. He slipped a black stretch-knit dress over his head and smoothed it along his hips. *It's true of anything. "I think; therefore, I am"? Part bullshit. Proof of my own thought but not of existence. In some measure, who we are is based on the dickholes out there and the culture standards and expectations they've established. If I don't have recognition from the world, I'm not as real. I'm a ghost.*

He wasn't ostentatious. For him, drag shows weren't necessary, nor were stereotypes. This was only part of his identity, and he wanted to let it breathe. Cross-dressing was also a compulsion that he enjoyed and had given up fighting many years ago. There was an entire subculture dedicated to all the Idaho rednecks who loved to shoot animals. Instead of hiding what they enjoyed, there were hunting lodges, for God's sake. Where they went to show their trophies, their skins, and their various racks.

No pun intended.

He was only displaying a piece of the individuality that made him who he was and that he took pride in. It was more than nice. It was relief. Long coming after months of being stifled.

Todd unzipped Julie's luggage and brought out his makeup carrier. It was a large silver train case with multiple foldout and stacking trays. In the bottom sat his sister's dinky zippered cosmetic bag.

"Those girls will never believe that circus wagon belongs to me," she'd said when he placed it in her suitcase. It occupied a quarter of the space.

"First, they won't notice. Second, even if they do, why is it *my* fault they wouldn't think it belonged to you?"

"Have you considered what it says that it takes all that equipment to make you look presentable?"

"Have *you* considered what it says that your brother can get more phone numbers than you?" Todd had proceeded to fill another fourth of her suitcase, feeling less bad for monopolizing the space due to her spitefulness. "Don't resurrect that competition. It doesn't matter the effort I put in. The end justifies the means. The end being that I win. *Every* time."

"No, the end being that you look exactly how you look now, but with makeup."

No matter how many times Julie made these digs to get under his skin, he didn't believe he was *that* easily identifiable by strangers. How often did people pay as close attention as they'd need to discern him from such a well-constructed disguise?

He actually thought he was less likely to be recognized by the Mormon community they lived in. That was a plus of living in small-town Idaho and being "married." Women ignored him, and he was no longer in competition with the men. The only people who paid him any mind were those who saw him as another potential conquest for the church. He was just a positive number with a dollar sign around his neck. Their spawn looked at him in class, but it was behind the hazy film of video games and nacho cheese. He put too much effort into his transformation, and they put nil into knowing him daily. The scales were forever slanted in his favor.

Todd had laughed at Julie. "I can't regard you with any seriousness when shit is dripping out both sides of your mouth. You say it takes a lot to make me look okay, and then two seconds later you say I look the same as I do now. So, I'm left once more with the truth of your overwhelming jealousy for my natural gorgeousness. It's a pity you're falling prey to immature teenage girl syndrome."

"That's—"

"Shh, it's okay." He'd used his most patronizing voice and walked past her. He pursed his lips and nodded his head before leaving the room. "*I* think you're very pretty, cher. Don't worry."

Julie appeared in the bathroom doorway as he finished contouring his face. "My God, there's a piece of Africa right here in a DC hotel room, Todd."

He brought the mascara brush away from his eye. "Is there a football-sized bug you want me to kill? Or did an eighties band crash through the wall and I need to shush them with a broom?"

"You know those birds that sit on top of hippos?" She tipped two extended fingers toward her makeup pouch on his cosmetic case.

"Don't disparage those birds, Julie. They serve a noble purpose." He turned to his reflection in the mirror. "They're *miracle* workers."

His sister snatched the homely bag and rolled her eyes. "I'd like to leave soon, Madonna."

"Then get out."

After she left, Todd briefly set aside his makeup to lock the door. He then unfolded the left tray inside the train case to ponder through a dozen shades of lipstick.

There'd been a time when their banter had been good-natured

heckling without self-serving paranoia. He hadn't had to lead such a restrained double life.

Well, I've always had one in a way. Even before everything happened, most people didn't know. I was good with that. It was on my terms.

In New Orleans, he could go to any bar in full dress any night he wanted. If he ran into someone from work, who cared? Even should one of his students' parents recognized him, so what?

"Yes, Mrs. So and So, I'm your son's homeroom teacher. I'm also a transvestite."

Pause.

"Yes, I did get this blouse in the Lower Garden District."

Pause.

"I believe they did have it in yellow. That color would look great on you!"

Todd hadn't been excited to move and leave his friends, his way of life, and his home. But he wanted Julie to get better. To come back.

He pulled a bundle of hairpins from a side compartment before shutting the cosmetic case and exchanging it for a small, pink fire chest.

"And if I'm asked why I brought a fire safe? What excuse do I give, smart-ass?" Julie had demanded the first year they'd gone to Washington, DC.

"Say you don't trust hotel security, and you keep your valuables locked away. I don't care. It's not my problem."

"Well, it's not *my* problem."

"*Yes.*" Todd had pointed a finger at her. "Yes, it *is* your problem."

It'd taken a while before the anger about the marriage lie settled into resentment. At that time, he'd been on the edge of boiling. To his knowledge, no one had ever questioned Julie regarding the large makeup case and fire chest.

Todd turned the combination dials on the pink safe and opened the lid. He lifted out a wig cap and shoulder-length, auburn monofilament wig. After pulling the cap over his short hair, he placed the wig at his hairline and slid it on. It only took a few seconds before he flipped the hair back and was looking in the mirror to strategically pin it.

It's been years since I wore this one.

He usually went with something longer. Long and blond, or a dark brown. It didn't have to match his eyebrows or look natural with his skin tone. But tonight he wanted to be normal.

The last time was when Julie and I took that picture together. Todd pushed a lock of the wavy hair behind his ear.

He remembered years ago, when they'd stood side by side in front of the large rectangular mirror at his sister's house. They were going out with friends, and Todd had convinced her to scrap the jeans and T-shirt to dress up with him.

They'd been shopping earlier that day, and he'd chosen a yellow, sleeveless summer dress for her. The dress fit perfectly. Julie wasn't one for fashion, or dressing in anything more feminine than a denim skirt if forced, but even she admitted that the dress was exceptional. And after she let him style her hair and do her makeup, she looked amazing.

Even I was jealous, and that's saying something.

The chances of his sister looking that nice again by choice weren't high, so she'd been coaxed into taking a picture with him. There were two pictures actually. One in which they had their arms around each other's shoulders, and the other where he'd turned his head and kissed her cheek. It had caught her by surprise, and in the photo, her eyes were squeezed shut with laughter.

Todd sighed as he pressed the final pin into his wig and ran a hand through the hair.

Julie had worn that yellow dress one more time—for a morning meeting about her small business loan. Two weeks later she'd asked him to burn it. And seeing the photos of herself in the dress had sent her into a panic attack. She demanded he burn them as well. However, he hid the pictures in the pink fire chest when he wasn't using it for wig storage. They were some of the last memories he had of her as herself, and he couldn't bear to destroy them.

"Are you done?"

A fist pounding twice on the bathroom door erased the image of his sister in the yellow dress. Todd took a last glance in the mirror before unlocking the door. When he opened it, Julie was wearing her school clothes—a simple-looking blouse and gray slacks. Her arms were folded, and she had a grim look on her face. He prepared for one more plea to forgo his plans.

Instead, she offered his pink-and-black jacket.

"You look nice, Todd. Even if you insist on spoiling a good dress with this ugly thing."

TEN

JULIE AND TODD had given their IDs to the brute squad outside The Attic. The lazy job at verifying their authenticity confirmed how last year's juniors got through the doors.

I wonder why a gay club, though. There are dozens of nightclubs in DC. Whose idea was it to come here? Who's in the closet? Julie slid her license into her purse.

"Bracelet?" The security officer held two green Tyvek wristbands.

"You bet your ass." Todd extended his wrist, and the man pressed the adhesive ends together.

My thoughts exactly. She took a bracelet and laced it around her arm unaided.

Julie could easily use alcohol to self-medicate. It didn't matter how many or what kind of anxiety drugs she took; alcohol was better at removing the edge.

If I drank enough, maybe I'd be able to be independent. Which is better? To be drunk or insane? Kill my liver, or end up in a padded room? She volleyed between those options when she was three beers, or two mixed drinks, into an evening. *That's when I start to feel like my old self.*

When the borders of her world became wooly, they also became safe. As of yet, nothing had happened to penetrate her alcohol bubble. Once she had a drink or two she'd stop looking for villains or packs of teenagers that threatened to destroy her fragile existence by exposing Todd's secret.

Despite being early, they were assaulted by the club's booming music and swilling crowd. At the bar across the room, where they'd camped last year, there were a couple empty spots. Rather than going forward to claim them, he'd cupped his hand to her ear.

"I hate to say it, but is this proof of getting older?" Todd leaned back with a smile and pointed to the ceiling.

She nodded and followed her brother toward the second floor's door. Even though it made her feel like a child, she pinched a corner of his jacket to ensure she didn't lose him. He gave no indication of minding, as he might ordinarily.

Small consolations are better than nothing I suppose.

Julie knew that in addition to tolerating her clinginess, the noise of the first floor didn't bother him. Relocating to the second floor was meant to put her more at ease. He was aware that packed rooms of strangers made her nervous. The lounge would also be safer in the event of a repeat infiltration. She'd been astounded that a group of Mormon teenagers made it across the dance floor without gouging each other's eyes to protect their purity. They wouldn't go upstairs.

Her anxiety dropped another level upon finding the lounge as deserted as she'd ever seen a bar or club. There were only a dozen people in the entire space, and she released his jacket.

Feeling the crisp frost on the outside of the beer bottle unwound her a bit more, and she drained half before they reached a table in the corner.

It'll be okay, Julie, she thought as she sank into a chair. She was already feeling the alcohol. She'd forgone breakfast and lunch so it hit her fast. She tipped her head and took several breaths.

"I know you don't want to be here, but I appreciate it," Todd said.

"It wouldn't have mattered what I'd done."

"But you could've been more difficult. You might've thrown yourself on the hotel room floor and started seizing."

"Would you still have gone?" She wasn't sure how to fake a seizure, but it might be a skill that could come in handy. Somewhere online there had to be instructions.

"After I dropped you off at the ER, yes."

Julie knew it was a lie. When she needed him, Todd was there and would put anything and everything aside for her. Her friend Suze had described how he'd dashed out of the bar to her rescue.

"Course he didn't know he was rescuing you. I told him to chill." Suze had her feet propped on the end of Julie's hospital bed and was twirling a long lo mein noodle around one chopstick. The noodle kept slipping off despite her best efforts. "I really had no idea. But he flew out of there. Fuzz clocked him going ninety-five in a thirty-five and said he almost flipped the car tear-assing around the corner of thirty-second. Hit the brakes outside your place and nearly skidded into the motherfucker's car—tires squealing like a mashed cat."

She thought she remembered the sound of those tires. Or maybe she imagined it. Before everything had gone black, she recalled wondering if hearing was the last thing that went when one died. And why else would she have considered it, if she hadn't heard a noise first? But she couldn't be sure what'd been real. Reality stopped when the cell phone fell from her hand onto the kitchen floor because a strange man had appeared in her house. It hadn't restarted until she opened her eyes in the hospital to see Todd's face.

"It's not like we were doing anything, but the way he dropped every thought in his mind except for you," her friend had continued talking. "I need to find me someone like that, you know?"

Suze looked at Julie and waited for an answer. Responses came seldom, if at all, for weeks. She'd been in Julie's room for hours without getting a reply to anything. This time was no exception.

"Not him specifically though. I couldn't be with someone prettier than me." Suze switched the chopstick into her left hand and held her right thumb and first finger a fraction apart. "If he were *this* much uglier, I'd swoop him up, cher. Hand to—God fucking damn it!"

She hurled the expletive as her lo mein noodle once again slithered into the white carton from the single chopstick.

"You're supposed to use two, you dumb bitch." Todd reentered the room after a short absence. Julie shared a smile with him. While she didn't mind if Suze visited, she'd already been focusing on the idea that she was only safe when her brother was there.

"I *am* using two! I use the one in this hand to drape it over the other one. I start to curl it around fine, and then it slips right the fuck off!" Suze demonstrated her technique, which had the same result. "See! This is why they're so thin in China! They can't get the food in their mouths!"

"Maybe I shouldn't give you this then." He dangled a fork in front of her.

"Are you saying I'm fat?"

"If the trough fits."

Julie knew he was trying to make her laugh. That's what Todd did. He rescued her, kept her safe, and attempted to raise her spirits.

"You're such a whore." Suze took the fork and shoved it into the nest of noodles.

"A pretty whore though. Too pretty apparently."

This also made her laugh, and it still made her smile to think of it. She drummed her fingertips on the table as she remembered her brother and friend bantering to make her feel better.

I should trust you more. Even if I could give you a bit more space, that'd be good. Let you make a grocery run or have lunch at school alone. I shouldn't have been against you coming here. Those kids aren't won't show after I scared the shit—

"Julie."

The swirling strobe lights behind her closed eyelids made her dizzy. When she opened her eyes and straightened her head, it took a couple of blinks to concentrate on him. Her vision bounced between the three empty bottles as if they were bumpers inside a pinball table. TILT flashed in her mind. Had she really had three already? But she met his eyes at last.

Julie knew he was lying when he said he'd drop her at the ER and then go. And she read him well enough to also recognize that he was conscious of her awareness to this deception.

I hope you also know that I'm lying when I tease you about how you look when you dress up. Genuinely, you look nice, Todd. You don't look like an awkward man in a dress.

His slight build and fine features made it easy for him to pull off. For some of the other men, their gender was clear straightaway. Since these were drag queens and not transgender men for the most part, it wasn't a huge deal. But she felt proud of him in a strange way. She'd never been embarrassed to go anywhere in public with him. You had to look closely to tell something was different.

His blue eyes were striking when he wore contacts instead of glasses, which he hardly ever did. And he accentuated them so well with the eye shadow and mascara that he could draw and keep a person's focus on his face rather than his body. This played to his favor, since he wasn't into padding himself. Sitting across the table from him, with his skillfully applied makeup and the wavy auburn-colored hair, he could be a normal twenty-eight-year-old woman.

I don't know why we play these mind games with each other. Those dipwads wouldn't recognize you. We could go out with you dressed at home. If I had a few beers first, and we drove to a bar a hundred miles away, I'd be okay. Maybe.

"Julie," he repeated, and she realized her mind had strayed. When they made eye contact, he was quick to finish his sentence before she could float away. "Thanks."

"For what? I make you miserable." She shrugged and set her fourth half-empty bottle on the table. Alcohol also tended to relax more than her tension. "Absolutely and completely miserable."

Through fuzzy vision, Julie watched him put his hand to his chin. He curled the tip of his pointer finger along his jaw and said nothing for several seconds.

"Not *completely*. I believe you have the capability to be a much worse bitch than you are." A slow smile spread across Todd's face. "Thanks for not fulfilling your potential."

He pushed his single, clear glass into one of her bottles. It clinked, and she smiled back before polishing off round four.

SOMEWHERE BETWEEN BEER six and seven, Julie became immediately sober.

Before this occurred, midway through six she foggily remembered Todd asking if she'd be okay if he left to talk with a couple of friends.

"Sure, but don't forget you're my ride," is what she tried to say, but it sounded more like "Sherbet donut floor git'ar my ride." Which made her laugh hysterically.

"You're okay?" He touched her shoulder.

"Sherbet donut? You can't put sherbet with a donut, Todd! Or a donut with sherbet!" Julie bent over the table with tears pouring down her cheeks.

"My study of the Constitution has led me to believe nothing specifically prohibits the intermingling of desserts, Julie."

This was even funnier. She could hardly breathe.

"Ice cream to fried dough we stand. No promises. No demands." She covered her mouth with her hand and tried to stop. "I forgot that's in there."

"That's Pat Benatar, cher. But true nonetheless. Dessert is a battlefield."

"Goooooo!" Julie waved him away between gasps.

She blinked and watched Todd leave his pink-and-black jacket draped on his chair to cross the room. For the first steps, he seemed to be walking sideways, so she tilted her head to avoid becoming dizzy. When he joined a small group, she squinted to lock the location and image of his back in her mind. Satisfied that he was no more than a few yards away, Julie then folded her arms and rested her chin on them, turning her stare to the abandoned jacket.

"You're not so ugly, are you? You just piss me off, you stupid thing." She chuckled at her inability to find a more derogatory term. What did one call a jacket to cause offense? She weighed a few options before narrowing her gaze. "You, sir...madam...polyesterish whatever. You are an asshat. A fucking asshat!"

Amid the laughter from a well-crafted insult she was sure had the garment bursting at its seams, she wondered why she picked at Todd for his jacket.

Instead of it reminding him of the hell he went through, he loves it. He wears it like a badge. I remember when I opened the first box to unpack my things in his apartment and saw that yellow dress.

Julie didn't spend time trying to make sense of what had happened to her. The events were too painful to sort and having a constant, buzzing anxiety was the lesser of two evils. But when the alcohol made her brave enough to think about the past and focus blame somewhere, there were many things she vacillated between.

Blaming the man was an obvious choice; however, it would've been easier if he hadn't killed himself. Not that being mentally ill absolved him, but she didn't feel he could be fully held accountable.

Julie could blame herself. For being too friendly and nice. For providing outstanding customer service. For not leaving the flowers on her desk at work until they died. For driving straight home instead of going to the bar and crashing on Suze's couch. For forgetting her cell phone the next morning.

And there were other things too. That rat bastard, God. Miniblinds in general. The bloodthirsty Doberman who hadn't been cute enough to sway her into purchasing him a few months prior to the incident. But what she continued to revisit was the yellow summer dress. The garment bore the most responsibility.

He said that's when he knew. He wasn't entirely sure when he sent the flowers; those were to see what I looked like. He said he knew I was "the one" because the other girls dressed like a "bunch of sloppy, stoned dykes." If I'd been like them, he would've driven away and never even called again.

Julie customarily dressed like the rest of the girls. There was no face-to-face interaction with clients, so what was the point of significant effort? Or any effort? Most days she threw on a T-shirt and jeans. She tied her messy hair back, and *maybe* if she was feeling "pretty," she'd put on lip gloss.

That day was special though. She was meeting the loan officer to review her business proposal. She couldn't stroll into an important appointment looking like a slob.

"Wear the yellow dress your brother made you buy," Suze had advised. "If you offer to go clothes shopping with him, he might even fix your hair."

"I can fix my own hair."

"With divine intervention."

Her hair had looked fine after she'd taken a flat iron to it and straightened the kinks. She'd done her makeup unaided by Todd as well. It took her an hour, and she'd stabbed herself in both eyes with the pencil and eye shadow. And unsurprisingly, when she'd used the mascara, the wicked brush had turned of its own accord and thrust itself directly into her cornea. But the redness went away, and she put on the yellow dress.

The meeting went smoothly. She knew she'd be approved and added the loan officer as a contact in her cell phone. He said he'd call in the next day or two with the confirmation. The morning at work was like any other, until the afternoon rolled around. Suze had slammed a ribbed vase of pink flowers on her desk.

"You fucking bitch."

"What?"

"You got flowers! What the hell? No one ever sends *me* anything."

Julie thought they were from the loan officer and smirked. She was sure it wasn't standard policy for him to call her *personally* with the confirmation. And to *insist* she call him by his first name. No, the pleasure of meeting her was *entirely* his, and he hoped to see her soon. It'd been such a good day.

"I hate you." Suze tapped her foot. "I like you just enough to let you buy me a drink tonight."

"I'm busy." She took the card from the floral pick. While she wasn't busy, having been awake early skewering herself with cosmetics, she was tired. To let Suze know the real reason would open herself to a new barrage of teasing though.

"With a new boy toy, apparently. *Some* friend!"

Julie opened the card and tipped her head. The flowers weren't from the handsome loan officer. They were from a man she didn't know and had never set eyes on.

"What?" Suze snipped the card out of her hand. Her mouth formed an O as she read the short note. "Ooo, well, la dee da. 'Thanks, Julia. Warm Regards, Sully.' I like that. 'Warm Regards.' Isn't he from some God-awful frozen wasteland?"

"I have no idea where he's from."

She had his name and account number on a sticky note by her computer. He was one of several clients who preferred to speak with her because she was good at schmoozing and shoveling shit up their asses. She'd spoken with him enough that he insisted she call him Sully, like his friends did. But she couldn't remember where he was from. Or any of the other inane things he might've said while she dashed in his orders and tracked shipments.

And he certainly doesn't know me. My name isn't Julia. Has he been calling me that the whole time? Shows how much I care or pay attention. I don't tell people anything personal. I don't even give my last name on the phone.

"I'm sure he's got an ice castle. 'Warm Regards'." Suze snickered and flipped the card onto her desk. "It's always warm in New Orleans, but it looks like it's getting even *hotter*."

"No, thanks." She pushed the flowers to the side of her desk.

"If you don't like them, I'll take them. Gladly. I'll make Darnell think I'm cheating on him."

If I'd only given them to you, Suze. Julie thought, staring across the table at the pink-and-black jacket. *You would've walked out with them, and he would've thought you were me. You dress like you're on your way to the gym. He would've driven away.*

Instead: "No thanks to the guy. Not the flowers." She grinned and pulled the vase closer to her keyboard. "I want you to look at them all day and be jealous."

"You fucking bitch."

Suze could only handle needling to a certain point though, so she made the decision to torture her just for the rest of the day. She'd then take the flowers home and put them on her kitchen table. When they rotted, she'd have a nice vase. And when the client called, she'd thank him for his kindness and try to remember he liked to be called Sully.

If he calls again before I quit. If not, fuck him. Thanks for the flowers, bucko. Come see me when you want a slot machine.

And as it had so far, things proceeded according to plan. Even better, since the weather report had called for rain. But the sun was shining when she exited the building at five o'clock. She left her long coat on her chair and walked to the car holding the vase of flowers.

It should've poured rain. The black coat would've hidden and protected me.

But the flowers identified her, and the yellow dress solidified the man's next actions as he followed her home in his white car.

Julie took her bleary gaze from the jacket and looked toward the last place she'd seen Todd. He wasn't there. But while "no-beer Julie" or even "one-beer Julie" may've gone into code red, "six-beer Julie" had a longer fuse. An internal timer began to count as she picked through the growing number of colorful patrons to find him. The time limit had nowhere near expired before she found him though. Or rather, before she heard his voice behind her.

"Julie, look who I found."

She released a breath she'd been holding when his hand touched her shoulder, and the relaxation of being intoxicated came back. She turned her head, expecting a strange character or mutual acquaintance.

But her smile disappeared as she registered the person standing next to him. The six-beer feeling vanished, and she felt immediately sober. And immediately furious.

ELEVEN

GOD-FUCKING-DAMN it, Todd! I knew this would happen! But you never listen to me! And now this cocaine-smoking— Do you even smoke cocaine? Fuck. Whatever. This cocaine imbibing-in-some-manner bitch will go to the Mormon school board and turn you in! Who knows what she's going to say! What she'll accuse—

"Take it down a notch," Todd said.

Julie realized she'd sprung from her chair too quickly. The dizziness swayed her brain from side to side, and Todd grabbed her arm to keep her steady. In what seemed like a single motion, Julie was placed in her seat and found herself glaring across the table at Amanda Porter.

"No need to get riled. The three of us will have a nice chat." And her brother sat casually as if the entire world weren't imploding.

"A nice chat? That's simple for you to say! How many pictures have you taken with your cell phone? Is it on the Internet already? Did you plaster him all over Twitter, you whore? Did—"

When Amanda's eyes grew wide and Todd touched her shoulder again, Julie realized she was saying aloud what she meant to be thinking.

Cry all you like. She narrowed her gaze as the girl's eyes filled with tears. *I will break every bone in your body. I'm afraid of many things, but not of you.*

"First, I assume Mrs. Farr doesn't know you're gone?" Todd asked. He looked at Amanda and nodded with encouragement, trying to coax her to not fall apart.

"No." Her voice shook.

Oh, you have reason to be afraid. I will break your fingers, you bitch.

"And are there others here, or just you?"

"Only me, sir...ma'am... Mr. K... Ms. K..." Amanda folded her arms on the table and buried her face in them. "Fuck. Just fuck."

Todd laughed, and Julie broke her scorching stare from the student to glance at him. Her anger leaked out, and when she turned to Amanda, she released the grind of her back teeth.

His amusement at her confusion and resignation to an unknown, horrible fate appeared to have also caught the girl by surprise. She raised her head and looked at him, her eyes red. But Julie noted something besides fear when Amanda looked at Todd. She didn't think her brother caught it, but that pinched face and its meaning were clear to her.

For years in school, Julie had defended her brother's behavior. Even though she was three years his junior, she pulled him from lockers and stepped into the ring with her own fists. Even after the stupid teenage shit had been left behind, she showed support in other ways. Whether by linking arms when they walked together, or proudly displaying a picture of them wearing the same dress on her shelf at work. It'd been a while since she'd had to voice her unwavering backing to anyone, but after years of recognizing when her aid was needed, she was hypersensitive to the look Amanda gave Todd. To that wince. That familiar fucking flinch.

He has nothing to be ashamed of. He's being himself and doing what he likes. It's more than can be said of most people. Especially dumbass teenage girls who only care about boys and cell phones. Even me. I'm not arrogant enough to not be able to admit that.

"In here, you can call me whatever you like," Todd said.

Again, the grimace crossed the girl's face before she lowered her stare to the table. It made Julie coil tighter inside.

"What are you?" Amanda asked.

If her brother hadn't put his hand to her arm, the seven beers might have served as enough fuel to launch Julie across the table. As it was, she remained boiling in her seat.

"That is a cheap white tablecloth, Ms. Porter." When Amanda looked at him, Todd continued. "If you're posing a question to me, I expect you to look at me. That's common courtesy."

"What are you?"

What the fuck, you stupid— His grip tightened on Julie's arm though he slid into an easy smile.

"You go first," he said.

They both watched her hesitate. She looked between the two of them and then back to the table while she chewed her lower lip.

"Go ahead," Todd added after a few more fleeting looks. He removed his hand from Julie's arm and leaned back in the chair. She recognized this move as well—opening and relaxing his body language to make himself more approachable. God, how he'd honed the skills of talking a crazy person down the past few years. "I think I know, but you should say it yourself."

Julie looked between them and wondered what she was missing. It was obvious, wasn't it? Amanda had cut her hair, ditched her makeup, and was wearing men's clothing. Combined with being in a gay nightclub? She was a lesbian. That also explained why she was being bullied. And if Todd had known this all along, it was additionally why he'd taken a special interest. While he wasn't homosexual, he knew what it was like to be persecuted for what one was.

It's a reassuring confirmation that you weren't lying when I questioned you about her. Tons of kids are bullied and you don't care. But identifying with this girl on that level as well? Now I'll buy it as the truth. You see yourself in her.

Amanda swallowed. "I'm transgendered." She took a breath, but before they could respond, she continued between the tears that ran down her face.

"I'm a boy. In here." She touched her chest. "And in here." She placed both hands to either side of her head and leaned her elbows on the table. "I always have been. My family doesn't know, but most of the other kids do. My old friends, who aren't my friends anymore because of it. They think it's a joke, and they spread it around like it's a dirty, disgusting secret. But I'm not dirty! And I'm not a joke! Nobody's laughing! It's awful! It's fucking awful to be trapped!"

The student coughed a couple of times and then sputtered on in a lower voice. "It's not like I want to be anything that great or special. I don't want to be a superhero or a rock star. I want to be a complete person. A normal person. I want to be myself, and I am a boy." Amanda looked at Julie. "I just want to be free."

The knowledge that Amanda was transgender was not in and of itself surprising. It might be to a conservative Idaho community, but not to a woman whose brother was a cross-dresser. Julie knew plenty of transgender people. More male-to-female, which was why "lesbian" had been her first guess; however, it was relatively old hat. What had caused a shiver to run through her core was what Amanda had said about it.

"It's fucking awful to be trapped. It's not like I want to be anything that great or special. I want to be a complete person. A normal person. I want to be myself." And then you look at me. At me, not at him. "I just want to be free."

Julie knew what it was like to be trapped. Yes, physically trapped with zip-ties cutting into her wrists and ankles—every window and door locked with no possibility of escape. But a material restraint was something a person could move past with time, even if by death. She also knew what it was like to feel trapped inside. To not aspire for prominence and to crave the mediocre. As long as it was normal. As long as it was her. To desperately want freedom.

None of her transgender acquaintances had expressed a desire for simple normalcy. Why? Maybe they were done. They had what they desired and wanted to leave a painful past where it belonged—behind them. Time had lacquered over prior experiences and made them something to be idly bitched about and nothing more. Julie had never sensed this relatable fervor from them.

Is it because you're stuck? You can't do a thing about it right now. And neither can I. The logical part of her knew the last statement wasn't true, but as usual, the emotional trauma won. *You're me.*

"I'd say I'm sorry for you, but I'm not." Todd's callousness caused them both to turn toward him. "In a few years when you've done everything you need to do, I don't think you'll be sorry either. I also can't apologize for the situation or the assholes who take pleasure in making you miserable. Both things—bad situations where you have no control and assholes—they aren't going anywhere. Their names and faces change, but they're reoccurring themes, and it's best to accept that."

Great time to be a hard-ass. You can't throw the kid any kind of bone?

Then he'd leaned forward.

"But tell me what I *can* do, that even in its smallest measure will help. Do you want to talk? Do you need to cry? Do—"

"Please," the student interrupted. "Please, never call me Amanda. Or Ms. I know you have to do what you have to do at school. But if you can, please don't call me either. It grates me. And not 'grate' as in irritating. It's physically painful. It's being scrubbed over the blades."

Scrubbed over the blades.

Julie understood how powerful a symbol could be. How any of the senses could evoke a visceral response. When there were so many tentacles and layers wrapped around it, a symbol ceased being what it originally had been. A name became more than a title. A picture was mired in emotional baggage. The feel of a yellow summer dress on her body. The smell of fresh lilies. The sound of a door opening and closing. These were no longer symbols. They were triggers.

How many times is the metaphorical gun fired at you a day? How do you possibly handle it? With having your palm forced to the grater and the instrument dragged across, shearing off the layers? I can order Todd to burn a dress or a picture. But I'm left alone for a few hours or I hear a door close, and I go to pieces.

Julie's filter was still partially dissolved in alcohol as she blurted another question that ordinarily would've remained unspoken: "How do you live when the thing that causes you that much pain is your name?"

"I have to. If I quit now, I'd be condemning myself. I'd be 'Amanda Porter' on a gray stone forever, and things would never change. And I want things to change. To get better."

If Julie Keegan died tomorrow, her name would be the same on a gray stone. But her obituary in Sunday's paper would be no more than a couple of sentences. Everything about her was a lie or tragedy verging on pathetic. And that's how people would remember her—as someone she never was, or a weak woman driven to psychosis after an unfortunate event. She was in the process of sealing her fate as a strange, wretched person she hated.

"What should we call you then?" Todd, as always, maintained composure and pushed forward.

That's why you've been clingy toward him. You're me. You need Todd like I do.

"Sam. My name is Sam Porter."

"Pleasure to meet you, Mr. Porter." Todd extended his hand. The young man timidly shook it as a smile crept across his face. "My name is Todd Keegan. Most people around your age call me Mr. Keegan, to my face anyway. But outside of class, you may call me Todd without suffering the slow and painful death that would befall your peers if they attempted the same."

He gestured to Julie, and she extended her hand across the table. "Julie Keegan."

Her brother's face didn't reveal if he'd expected her to divulge more—most relevant, the truth of their relationship.

No way. Especially since I'm not sure this one can be trusted. He can barely stand to look at you.

Julie needn't have wondered if Todd was aware of the awkward behavior though. He loved to call people out on their shit.

"In answer to your initial question, I'm a transvestite," Todd said with a blank tone after Sam released Julie's hand. "And you have a problem with that, which I find hypocritical."

"That's absolutely not true." Sam shook his head.

"We're all young here. None of us is near death's door. But life is too short. A large, rather tedious part of my occupation is listening to teenagers lie. Don't tell me your dog ate your homework. Tell me the truth. I'll still flunk you, but I'll be kinder if you haven't wasted my time by trying to lie. I'll use a black pen instead of a red one."

Julie could almost see Sam's mental action—one idea after another passing above the net.

Should I tell the truth, or shouldn't I? Am I clever enough to invent a reason and convince them I'm not lying? Is there even a rational excuse where I won't come off like a double-standard asshole?

Just admit it. Given your situation, there's no reason you should have an issue. No rationalization can possibly—

"It's not that I have a problem in general, sir. It's that it's you."

"Well, you're no less a hypocrite, but honesty isn't as prized as it once was. Bravo to you for that at least." Todd gave no indication of offense.

"It's just..." Sam went on. "I look up to you. So much, you have no idea. You have everything I want. I want to be like you. I want to be you. But now you're...this."

Julie wondered if the admission could soften her brother. She couldn't say for certain that it wouldn't have affected her to know she was held in such high esteem that the problem was only that she fell short of an admirer's expectation.

Who am I kidding? I know what it's like to not meet someone's unrealistic standards.

"Isn't the purpose of your journey to be yourself? Do you gain anything from trading one mask for another? I'd think, Mr. Porter, a particularly good role model for you would be an individual willing to be faithful to his identity despite it being unorthodox."

"Yes, but can you understand how difficult it is for me to see you like this?"

"And can *you* understand how I don't give a rat's ass how difficult it is for you?" Todd leaned back in his chair again.

Julie was sure only she could've interpreted the gleam in his eyes or the way his left cheek rose slightly.

It didn't take long before Sam met her brother's eyes without hesitation.

"Yes, I can. It's not about me. How you are and what you like to do doesn't affect me at all," he said.

"That's right." Todd shrugged. "So, fuck you."

"Well, fuck you too."

"Christ, that we *could* live in a world where everyone could fuck everyone else." He smirked. "I hope you're not wearing a wire, Sam. If you are, that sentiment flushes my entire career down the toilet."

"No, sir." Sam returned his smile.

Julie knew something had passed between them. It could've been the beer hanging on that made the concept confusing. Or perhaps she'd missed it, since she'd also failed to notice that her empty beer bottles had been removed, and a glass of water had been set in front of their new companion.

I shouldn't drink so much. I really need to show some restraint. For God's sake, I can't be this dense when I'm sober. She looked from the student to her brother. *If you think he won't turn you in, I guess I'm okay with that. Especially if he needs you. Even if it's to tell him to fuck off. You'd better never say that to me though.*

"So, tell me whatever you'd like," Todd said as he lifted his glass. "And then you can feel free to leave. I don't know why you came here tonight, but it wasn't for me."

"I'll tell you that then. Why I came."

And Julie listened to them talk until last call, and their Attic excitement ended for another year.

TWELVE

WHEN SAM CAME home, the first indication that something was wrong was the smell. It oozed from the brick rancher, rolling in thick, nauseating waves across the lawn. He didn't want the others to know where he lived, so Mr. Keegan had dropped him off a block away. Now he was even more relieved he'd made the request. His stomach churned as he wheeled his bag along the broken fence. God, why hadn't someone called the health department? People walked by the house every day, and the stench reached the curb.

Scarlet's house always smelled horrible. Even when it was free from the usual clutter, the floor cleaner added a fake pine varnish on the urine-soaked, decomposing rodent odor.

And there's no AC. It's a ninety-five-degree, piss-saturated dead rat.

Sam was accustomed to awful-smelling houses. Any home he'd been in for lengthy stretches had its own terrible aroma, and he'd find himself spending more time outside than in.

When Sam used to be welcome at his father's house, he remembered that it stank like a fish market. And with his stepmother preferring the heat and humidity of her country, it stank of heavy, rotting fish. Even clothes fresh from the laundry smelled like tuna wrapped in dryer sheets.

And his grandmother, God love her, everything in her house carried the scent of cold fried chicken and menthol cough drops. He imagined she had garlands strung with drumsticks and eucalyptus throat lozenges behind the drywall. It was better than the other places; however, it still made him sick.

His mother's house was the worst. In addition to promising himself that he'd never treat his children the way Scarlet treated him, Sam had also vowed that his house would never reek like hers.

But this time a different scent prompted him to pause, and he had to take several breaths through his mouth before entering. The old mouse hadn't congealed on the floor in a puddle of urine. The carcass had been swept away by a river of shit. Scarlet hadn't started using a new human-feces fragrance (though she would have if [insert boyfriend's name] had been into that). The house smelled like shit because there was shit. Ankle-deep raw sewage had backed up into the basement. Which, coincidentally, also happened to be the location of Sam's room.

He stood two steps above the bottom and couldn't peer around the corner into his room to see the damage. If one more gush came through, the sludge threatened to overtake the step he was on.

"Mom, what the fuck? What happened?" Sam held his hand over his mouth and nose, but it hardly cloaked the stench.

"Don't use that language in this house, Amanda."

This is literally a fucking shit pit, not a house.

"Can you tell me what happened?"

Scarlet turned from the television for the first time since Sam had walked in the door. She grimaced at him before going back to the screen.

"You look awful. That hair. Those clothes. Like a hermaphrodite. They had those on Springer the other day with a lobster-claw man and a woman who had three legs."

"Mom, the basement is filling with shit! What happened? And where's Stevie?"

"Language!"

Taking two steps forward, Sam pulled the television cord from the wall. The screen winked black, and Scarlet looked at him, her face red.

"What's the matter with you, Amanda?"

"What's the matter with *you*? There's half a foot of sewage in the basement! Have you called anyone?"

"Who am I supposed to call? Need I remind you that I, unlike your father, am completely alone in the world? I have nobody to call!"

"You have a phone book! You have the Internet! You could call a plumber, Mom!"

"Why would I do that? Even though you're *conveniently* absent when I need you, you can take care of it. Plug the TV in and go fix it."

"I have no clue how to fix it!"

"You fixed the kitchen sink and the upstairs toilet. Don't you have that coiled thing you can stick somewhere?"

Sam had fixed the kitchen sink. He got tired of emptying the orange bucket whenever he washed dishes, and Scarlet had refused to call anyone then. So, he'd gotten a book from the library and repaired it himself. He'd also fixed the upstairs toilet after it went on the fritz and ten-year-old Stevie was too scared to use the other bathroom in the basement. The boy had taken to urinating in a Clorox bottle upstairs.

"Do you know how dangerous that is, Mom? You can't mix ammonia and bleach." He'd shown Scarlet the revolting evidence. God knew where Stevie was doing his other business.

"Leave him alone, Amanda. You're always on his case. Let him do what he wants."

"That creates chloride gas. It's not even how disgusting it is. He could get a chemical burn."

"He's fine. Leave him alone. I don't have time for this." She'd stalked out of the room. She had a date.

Sam had tried to talk to Stevie, but Stevie was like Scarlet. He was never wrong. However, unlike their mother, who walked away in most circumstances, Stevie could be violent. And he had no respect for Sam, since while Scarlet had given him responsibility for his younger brother, she'd granted no authority. So, when Sam approached him, Stevie's collection of responses was typical of his volatile temper and idiocy.

Stevie would piss wherever the fuck he wanted. Under no circumstances was he going into that basement to use the bathroom. Yes, he'd always lived in the house, and Sam and Scarlet went to the basement without harm befalling them, but it didn't matter. No way. And he'd keep using the Clorox bottle. He liked that bottle. The handle placement was convenient.

And as often punctuated the end of Stevie's tirades, the boy had picked up the nearest object—a mug from the coffee table—and lobbed it into the wall.

As a result of Scarlet and Stevie's reactions, Sam had learned how to fix the upstairs toilet. His brother was a stupid asshole, but he deserved better than a Clorox bottle. Besides that, as he tinkered with the trip lever in the toilet tank, the possibility of a certain scenario kept Sam motivated until he'd prevailed. Even when his parents had been together and they had two incomes, Scarlet had made it clear there was no money to spare if he or Stevie became sick or got hurt.

"That's why you can't go roller-skating, Amanda. And stay out of those damn trees. If you fall and break your arm, it's staying that way."

Whenever he became frustrated with the toilet, Sam pictured Stevie burning himself and suffering. In the back of his mind, he knew that Scarlet couldn't allow either of them to languish in pain, but part of him believed her.

"Plug the TV in. I've probably missed who the father is." Scarlet pointed the remote at the television and repeatedly pressed the buttons, as if one of them would reconnect the power.

"Do you at least know where it's coming from?" Sam swallowed. "Is it the toilet?"

"It's everywhere. The toilet, the shower, the washing machine."

"I have no idea how to fix any of that. I guess I can try to snake everything."

"I don't care what you do. Plug the TV in and take care of it," she said.

"But how am I supposed to get...everything out of there?"

"Don't you have a wet vac?"

"You expect me to wade around in raw sewage? In ankle-deep human waste and hose it out a window in—"

Sam had to stop. The stench, in combination with imagining his shoes squishing through the brown slush, was too much. He had to lean over the kitchen sink, coughing and gagging.

"You're such a boob, Amanda." Scarlet got up and reconnected the television. "Do you know how many of yours and Stevie's diapers I changed? I ask for so little, but you fight me on everything. Everything—"

The show had resumed. Sam spit into the sink and held the edge of the counter with his eyes closed. There was no way. To even try to fix it, let alone clean up. Not only was it disgusting and *nothing* like changing diapers, but it wasn't safe. Could E. coli be spread through the air? That's what was down there. A swamp of E. coli and other bacteria and germs. What the hell had happened? Had the toilet stopped working so they'd taken to dropping their pants at the top step? Were they a couple of elephants? How the fuck had they filled a basement full of shit in a week? And how dare she expect *him* to clean it? Absolutely not.

The shit-filled basement was his breaking point. The second breaking point and what had to be the final. The first had happened last year. It was what prompted him to stop playing the "Amanda game" for Scarlet and what'd broken the flimsy belief he'd clung to for years—that deep down, his mother loved him as much as she loved Stevie, or her boyfriends, or herself.

He thought back to his conversation with Mr. K days ago at The Attic.

"Here's a question. You had the teenage 'all,' Sam." His teacher had curled his fingers into air quotations. "What everyone wants—the looks, popularity, and friends. What made you throw it away?"

"I couldn't take it anymore."

"Doesn't answer the question. You could've continued the act for the rest of your life. Something had to have happened that pushed you over the edge. If you feel like sharing, I'd be interested to know what that was."

Sam had been careful about keeping eye contact with him. As he'd admitted, looking at Mr. K when he was dressed like a woman was difficult. It became easier the longer he did, but God it'd been a shock.

There he was. In a stretch-knit, black dress with Alençon lace cap sleeves. Wearing a shoulder-length, wavy auburn wig. His face made up with such expertise that he would've been unrecognizable if Sam hadn't spent the last two years studying and idolizing him.

Couldn't you have any other secret? I'd rather you be anything *but a transvestite. You could be a closet skinhead, a drug addict, a necrophile. I'd rather have you be transgendered.* Sam had stumbled along behind him to the corner table where Mrs. Keegan looked like she was falling out of her chair. *But you* want *to look like this... I didn't choose to be how I am. How could you ruin yourself?*

It was a repeated punch in the stomach every time he looked at Mr. K. He reverted to staring at the tablecloth.

Where are your slacks? Your shirt and tie? For God's sake, where are your glasses? You wear glasses! I can't believe this is happening. And despite Mr. Keegan's kindness, including that fabulous moment when he'd called him by his name, Sam couldn't help it. *How could you be this?*

"In answer to your initial question, I'm a transvestite. And you have a problem with that, which I find hypocritical."

Further proof that Mr. K knew everything. Everything worth knowing anyway. Even when Sam tried to explain, hoping that Mr. Keegan would take it as a compliment that the reason for his disappointment—

Despair. Crushing despair.

Was only because of how much he admired and wanted to be like him. Absorb and imitate everything he did. His clothes, his mannerisms, how he spoke, how he walked, how he sat...

You've got your right knee crossed over your left. You don't sit like that, Mr. K! You bring your right leg up and rest your ankle on your left knee! You can't do that in a dress! Why are you wearing a dress? How could you do this to yourself? How could you do this to me?

"And can *you* understand how I don't give a rat's ass how difficult it is for you?"

Mr. K's statement resonated with him. Almost as strongly as the sight of his idol wearing a woman's wig and makeup.

I'm grieving for you as if I lost something. But I haven't lost anything. I can admire you all I want, but you're not mine. If you want to dress like a woman or a giant panda bear, it has no bearing on me.

He'd swallowed as the next thought was the most chilling of all.

I'm treating you like Mom treated me after I told her I was gay. I'm treating you how she'll treat me when she discovers I'm transgendered. Like it's a personal affront and there's something wrong with you because you aren't what I want you to be. Like it's all about me. You're right. I am a hypocrite. You shouldn't give a rat's ass how I feel. And I shouldn't give one how you or anyone else feels about me either.

Sam had met his eyes. His blue eyes that weren't covered by stately rectangular frames and were instead accentuated by a dark eye pencil and silver shadow.

I refuse to be my mother. We are what we are. You're important enough to me that I'll move past what I expected you to be.

"Yes, I can. It's not about me. It doesn't affect me at all."

"That's right. So, fuck you."

"Well, fuck you too." Sam had smiled.

"Christ, that we *could* live in a world where everyone could fuck everyone else."

If only people weren't fixated on pushing everyone into cartons. Classifying and reclassifying based on their own agendas. Setting expectations about what or who someone should be, and not being willing to let go when they were wrong. And also, if the individuals who were being pressured and squeezed had the courage to tell their would-be ring masters to fuck off. If everyone accepted that the only person they could control was themselves, and they had no right to try and manipulate anyone else. Everyone could fuck everyone else. Brilliant.

It was hard, but Sam tried. And it was made easier not only by the time spent, but by Mr. Keegan's interest in him. No one had been interested in Sam since his grandmother passed. And he'd never anticipated that anyone would care about his gender identity struggle. But Mr. K asked question after question. Some he had to puzzle over before he could answer. Like the question placed before him on what his breaking point had been.

"Something had to have happened that pushed you over the edge."

He broke eye contact with Mr. Keegan to think about it. What had made him decide to tell everyone else to fuck off? He rewound several events until it came to him.

Sam looked from Mrs. K, who'd stayed silent but seemed attentive, and then to Mr. K.

"Last year, I got really sick."

It'd been during Christmas. His teacher might remember, as Sam's extended absence began before the break, and he hadn't come back to school or returned to work until the end of January.

"I don't get sick a lot. Couple of days, over-the-counter meds, and I'm fine. But this was different. I couldn't move."

It was near to literal. Days prior to Christmas Eve, Sam had barely left the couch. He had a bowl on the floor that he was responsible for emptying, which was the only reason he got up. He couldn't keep anything down to need to use the bathroom, and he couldn't stand long enough to shower. Both toilets were working at the time and were within yards from the couch, yet it took upwards of forty-five minutes to make it there and back.

Scarlet and Stevie kept operating their lives around him, as if he were part of the furniture. After waking one afternoon when Stevie was sitting on his legs to get a better view of the television, Sam considered moving to his bedroom in the basement.

"I know it makes me sound like I'm a hypochondriac and I'm paranoid, but it'd crossed my mind that I could die. And I didn't want to die in the basement and not be found for four days. If I died on the couch, they'd have to do something." He forced a shy smile. "They liked that couch, you know?"

Sam had continued to get worse. He hadn't eaten anything in days, which at least made it unnecessary to empty the bowl. No matter how many painkillers he took, he couldn't break his fever. And there were periods of time where he was losing consciousness. Not sleeping, but blacking out. He felt as if he were seeing the world through a 3-D viewer.

He closed his eyes, the lever was pulled, and the reel frame changed. What hour was it? What day was it?

On December 23, he started coughing blood. He knew the date because of Stevie's regimented television schedule.

The boy was "up" at five in the morning every day to claim the box. He'd flip to his cartoon channel and go back to sleep on the couch until seven, when Scarlet got half an hour before heading to work. Then to the cartoon station with Stevie snoring away until eight. Awake again to change the channel at nine. His alarm clock was the theme music of a show he didn't like, even though until one in the afternoon, he wasn't awake for any of it. Stevie bounced the channels around two dozen times in a strict timetable. When he wasn't feeling like he was losing touch with reality, Sam found it comical. It reminded him of a person obsessed with workouts at the gym. Only instead of dashing from treadmill to elliptical to bicycle, building muscles until he could lift a car, Stevie moved from *Pokémon* to *Flintstones* to *Married with Children*.

"Liquefying his brain until he can only speak in vowels."

"I can't *wait* to get this kid."

"You won't, Mr. K." Sam said. "There's nothing *wrong* with him besides laziness, but he's kept in special classes because he can't get along with people."

Stevie could barely coexist peacefully with inanimate objects. When the television programming changed, and they moved his shows around, Sam sometimes checked if the four horsemen were outside. The boy had an absolute meltdown.

"The day before Christmas Eve they were airing old holiday movies on TV Land, which is his 'cardio.' I woke to him howling and screaming."

And the sound of the coffee table being flipped, dishes crashing to the floor. And the closet door being slammed as Stevie hung on the knob and smashed it repeatedly in his rage.

"What the fuck! It's December fucking twenty-third! I don't care about *White Christmas! It's a Wonderful Life!* Fuck Jimmy Stewart! *Miracle on 34th Street!* Who cares? I want my shows! What am I supposed to watch now? God-fucking-damn it!"

The toaster had flown across the room.

"Are you sure he's not on the autism spectrum?" Mrs. Keegan asked.

"Yes, he's been tested. He's just an asshole."

A lamp met its untimely end being thrown down the staircase. And Sam had pushed himself up from the couch gasping. His chest felt tight and painful, but he leaned over his bowl to cough. He'd been hacking for a couple of days, which had only served to incur Stevie's yelling. He'd cough until his throat was raw, but there'd never been anything in the bowl. Until there was one big cough where something moved in his chest, like an air bubble rising to the surface. And when he opened his eyes, there was blood in the bowl.

"Mom, are you there?" Sam had woken hours later. The frame had changed. It was dark outside. He was devoid of the energy required to roll over and peer around the couch to see if Scarlet was in her rocker, but since he heard Betty White's voice, he was sure she'd stolen the television from Stevie's clutches temporarily.

"Quiet, I haven't seen this one."

"I don't want to watch this," Stevie whined from the other couch. "Mom, Amanda has been watching stuff all day. I hardly got to see anything and—"

"Shut up, both of you. I said I haven't seen this one."

While Betty White played the fool with the three other women, Sam took his temperature. Still a fever. And he could feel more of those bloody air bubbles in his chest. If he moved too quickly, they'd come up. They would eventually but—

A cereal commercial interrupted the show and his thoughts.

"Mom, I need—"

"Turn it to twenty-six during commercial, Mom. Come on, please."

"No, Stevie. I've had a long day, and it's my turn."

"But I want..." His brother trailed off in a whimper.

"Go to your room and play your Xbox."

"The screen's too small," he blubbered, and Sam heard him kicking the coffee table. "It's not fair. All they had on today was Bing-fucking-Crosby tap dancing on fake snow! It's not fair!"

"Get upstairs, Stevie!" Scarlet ordered. She never reprimanded Stevie's language or corrected his behavior. Exile in his room with his Xbox, PlayStation, and all his other stupid toys was as close to punishment as he received.

But Sam didn't focus on another of his mother's double standards. He was glad to hear Stevie trudge upstairs. He was also glad a toilet paper commercial was on.

"Mom, I need you to take me to the doctor."

"Why? You have a cold."

"I haven't moved from the couch in a week. I've had a fever for five days that I can't seem to—"

"Take more meds. I'll even get them from the kitchen on the next commercial."

"No, I need to see a doctor." Sam had paused. Thankfully, a microwave sandwich commercial began to play. "I've been coughing up blood all afternoon."

"I don't have money to take you to a doctor, Amanda. You know that."

"I have it. You don't have to spend anything."

Sam had been employed for more than a year. He worked part-time doing legal transcription for a law firm his mother used to work with. From three o'clock until ten on weekdays, and usually a few hours on the weekend, he sat at a computer and typed what an attorney dictated via tape recording. It was simple, paid better than many other jobs, and he could get close to forty hours a week.

The job also enabled him to have a degree of independence. He bought his own clothes and paid for his cell phone and bus pass. He had a savings account, so he could afford to go to the doctor. Of course, Scarlet could as well. When Stevie had an ingrown toenail a few months previously, she'd rushed him to after-hours urgent care.

For me, it's always been different.

"And when am I supposed to take you? I have a full-time job, Amanda."

"You could take an hour tomorrow. Half an hour."

"No."

Scarlet preferred being paid for unused vacation and sick time at the end of the year.

"Can you drop me off on your way to work then?"

"Take the bus."

"I'm really sick, Mom. I don't know that I could make it to the bus stop, and even if I could, I shouldn't be around people."

"If you're coughing anything up, I don't want it in my car. Suck on some ice cubes or something, you'll be—God, can you stop that damn coughing? The show's on, and I can't hear a thing."

Somehow Sam made it to the bus stop the next morning. The doctor's office was booked solid, and he sat in the waiting room on Christmas

Eve with a white mask over his face and his bowl between his knees for six hours.

"I had pneumonia. They weren't sure whether I could be allowed to go home with antibiotics, or if I needed to be admitted to the hospital. But I didn't have insurance, so I asked to go home. I don't remember how I got home exactly, but I got there. And I lived. Obviously." Sam had smiled as his story ended. Both teachers stared at him in disbelief.

"When I woke a few days later, and my head was starting to clear, that's when I decided. My mom would've rather let me die on that couch than take fifty dollars from her checkbook or half an hour from her day." He heard his voice shaking. He'd never told anyone about Scarlet's behavior, and saying it aloud wasn't easy. "But I'm worth more than that. Amanda might not be, but Sam is. I'm tired of investing time in something that isn't just a lie, but that's of no value. That was the breaking point, Mr. K."

And here Sam was, at another crossroads with his mother as he leaned over the kitchen sink and tried to control his nausea. Because while, after his illness, he'd veered toward taking the steps to eliminate Amanda on the outside, he persisted in toughing it out at home. The reality of the situation was that he had no place else to go. His grandmother was dead. His father didn't want him. He didn't even have friends that he could use to couch surf.

He was also a minor, and therefore at the mercy of any adult. Every school principal, every government official, every psychiatrist. Anything he said, wrote, did, or was even *accused* of doing could, and would, be held against him. He was powerless. Or as Scarlet had put it numerous times: "That's why you have kids. Slaves."

But I won't wade through sewage for you. This is the end. I'll force you to do the right thing.

Back in the house, Sam pushed away from the sink and cleared his throat.

"Are you through with your hissy fit, Amanda? I've been waiting a week for this stuff to get done while you've been playing around."

He ignored her and walked outside before the stench could either overcome him, or like her, he could be desensitized by it. Several feet into the backyard, the smell of shit faded enough that he could breathe. He retrieved his cell phone and skimmed the contacts. As he passed Mr. Keegan's number, he hesitated.

"If you ever need anything, call me."

Mr. Keegan had said this as they waited for their bags to cycle around the luggage carousel in the Boise airport. It was the last time they'd be alone. Or as alone as they ever were since Mrs. Keegan was always there too, though Sam didn't mind. The more he was around her, the stranger she seemed, but not necessarily in a bad way.

"I will, sir. Thank you for everything."

"Sam, I mean it. I'll be there, whatever it is." Mr. K had put a hand on his shoulder.

At the time, and now remembering it, Sam wanted to cry. Not only due to the compassion or similarity to what his grandmother had said when she rescued him. But feeling Mr. Keegan's hand on his shoulder was special. No one squeezed Amanda's shoulder. They lightly brushed her arm, or her hand, or her wrist. But you only touched the shoulder of a young man, pressing it firmly because behind the touch was belief in him. Was pride. Was the solidarity of strength between men.

He coughed back the tears and continued down the contact list. He really *was* a man. And he'd prove it. No matter how much he wanted to be saved.

I'm the rescuer. Not the rescued.

Sam selected the contact for directory assistance and held the phone to his ear.

"I'm looking for a twenty-four-hour plumber, please."

THIRTEEN

THREE WEEKS LATER, things seemed to be improving for Sam. He'd started to consider that Scarlet's basement flooding with sewage may have been a good thing. His new set of problems was more surmountable. Both his eighteenth birthday and graduation were a month away.

At the time though, it'd seemed like he was at the end of his rope and might not survive a week.

"The pipes in this neighborhood are old, sir," the plumber had said to him.

Sam had decided to risk introducing himself as Sam Porter to the plumber. Coming off the Washington, DC, trip, he felt confident enough that he could pull it off. It wasn't like the man would ask for identification. And Scarlet wasn't going to interfere. When she found out he called a plumber, she'd stormed upstairs and locked herself in her room, which was fine.

"I've had calls to six other houses within three blocks from you in the past couple of years. Same problem. Tree root grows into the pipe up the street, forces all the waste down your lines and into your house."

He didn't know if it could be considered a relief that Scarlet and Stevie hadn't been using the basement as a toilet when the sludge was really the neighborhood's combined sewage.

"But usually people call me in before now." The man raised an eyebrow.

"I've been away all week, and my mother can't do things by herself," Sam explained. "She relies on me to take care of her."

Relies. Expects. Commands. It's only semantics.

"Well, you've got yourself a big problem, Mr. Porter." It was hard to not smile, exceedingly difficult. It wasn't the time for smiles. "I can clear your lines, but it's bad. You need a cleaning crew. A disaster team."

"My mother was thinking I could use a wet vac." Sam wanted to see the professional reaction, as he'd been feeling guilty after Scarlet shut herself away to throw a tantrum.

"You've got to be kidding me!" The plumber laughed. "That's sewage! Almost a foot of it covering the lower half of the house! Tell your mom that any time a toilet has been flushed within a two-block radius, the contents have landed in her basement. A wet vac? That's hazardous human waste down there."

"Hazardous human waste?"

"You bet! I'm wearing a full suit before I go in there to fix it. Head to toe. And you need a disaster crew to clean it." His smile fell. "If you plan on trying to wet vac that mess, I'll call the health department."

"No, I realize it's bizarre. Just an illustration of why I'm the one handling things."

I made the right choice, good.

"Point taken! A wet vac? Good Lord!" The grin returned. "They're going to have to gut that basement. Cut the drywall halfway up. They'll have to chuck everything that's been contaminated."

Everything?

There was no chance of the title making him smile again. His bedroom was down there. Would everything he owned aside from the clothes he'd taken to Washington, DC, be considered contaminated? Or was it just things the sewage had come into contact with? Sam had never thought about what touched the floor of his room. He prepared for all the possessions he could consider gone. His bed. A nightstand. A chair. His dresser and some of the clothes inside. A few rows of books. For years, he'd played the violin, and the case with the instrument was on his closet floor.

I can live without all of it. It's replaceable.

Irreplaceable items he kept on shelves. And the more he considered it, something couldn't be contaminated if it hadn't been touched. If that wasn't the case, they might as well raze the entire house.

But there's Stevie. One of his brother's favorite activities was to rifle through Sam's things. Sam would come home from work or school and it would look like a tornado hit his room. His clothes ripped from hangers and drawers. Books torn off shelves and sentimental objects cast to the floor. Stevie wouldn't have left his room untouched an entire week. He could be down to a single suitcase of clothes.

Unless he's tossed that into the slime while I've been out here. Sam ran a hand through his hair. *But even if he has destroyed everything, I can replace it.*

"Here, Mr. Porter." The plumber handed him a business card. "You can go with any crew you want, but I can vouch for these guys. They're top-notch and do their best to save what they can. They can also be on site within a couple of hours, which is how long it'll take me to fix the line."

"Thanks, buddy. In your experience, how long does it take to clean it all?" Sam took the card and fished out his cell phone.

"There is *quite* the mess," he said as he pulled a protective suit from his truck and slipped it on. "You may want to get your mom used to the idea that she might have to spend a few days in a hotel. I doubt she'll be able to stay in the house." He flipped the hood over his head and his voice became muffled. "It's not fit for human habitation."

She won't have that. Neither of them will.

But he called the disaster crew recommended by the plumber. If it was left to Scarlet and he refused to use the wet vac, she'd wait for the mire to solidify into a solid layer and treat it like a ground cellar.

You might've been okay with letting me die on a couch, choking on my own blood. But I'm better than that.

The cleanup team had been shocked.

"How has your mom lived in there for a week? We could smell it from the driveway!"

"She can't smell anything. She thought it was mud." Sam did wonder if years of living in squalor had burned off Scarlet's olfactory nerves. "How long will it take you to clear it?"

"Two or three days. First, we'll get out as much of the liquid portion as we can. We'll move the bigger stuff tomorrow morning. I'll put a dumpster in your yard, if that's okay." Sam nodded, and the man named off the large items. Everything that had been on Sam's mental list from his room was on it. "And you're going to lose the washer, dryer, water heater, and furnace. I'll need to rip out that shower, toilet, and sink as well."

"What can you save?"

"There are a few things on shelves that we'll put on a tarp. I can't let any of you down there to retrieve anything."

"Is the house livable?"

"The drywall has to come up four feet, and then we'll check the beams behind. Hopefully they're salvageable."

While not an answer to Sam's question, now he had something new to worry over. If the supporting beams couldn't be saved, how would he tell Scarlet the house was condemned? Stevie wouldn't mind as long as the television moved with them.

"But is it habitable while you're cleaning?"

The man laughed, and the two others behind him smirked.

"I mean no disrespect, kid, I'm sorry. If you *want* to stay, if you *can* tolerate it, I don't have a problem as long as you keep out of the basement. The first and second floors seem okay as far as I've seen, unless you've been tromping around in the waste and spreading it elsewhere."

Sam made a note to check for footprints.

"We can put a wrapper over the staircase to isolate most of the fumes, but I would strongly recommend you spend the week somewhere else. Even though they've been able to stand it a few days, if you'll pardon the language, there is literally a week's worth of shit from fifty different people in that house. You're risking all kinds of disease and infection by breathing that air, let alone eating and drinking in there. I can't evict you, but it would be in your best interest if you left."

Sam tried to explain the need to leave to his mother in a logical, calm way even though he knew what her answer would be.

Scarlet sat on the edge of her bed with her arms folded. Her lips were pressed in a thin line, and she stared at the wall. Along with the sound of vacuums, the theme music of *Sanford and Son* permeated to the second level of the house, because neither the noise nor smell of sucking up sewage could keep Stevie from TV Land. He cranked the volume and held the chip bag closer to his mouth.

"The man from the disaster crew thinks we should leave for a few days while he cleans the basement. I'll take care of everything, Mom. I've already called the insurance agent and—"

"You go to a big city for a week, come back, and think you own the place." Scarlet didn't take her eyes from the wall. "This is *my* house, not yours."

"I know that. But like I said, it's hazardous waste. I couldn't have fixed the problem or used the wet vac to clean it."

"It's all about you, Amanda. It's always all about you."

After spending the last few hours talking with the plumber, disaster crew, and insurance agent, and having them call him Sam and refer to him as a male, it was striking to hear that awful name again. He'd tried to present the information as gently as possible, but now he felt less inclined. And he was also irritated with her refusal to look at him. He considered correcting her as Mr. Keegan had corrected him, but they had bigger things to fight about than respecting his elders.

"This has nothing to do with me. There's six inches of sewage in the basement and I'm trying—"

"You *had* to go on your stupid vacation to be with your nasty *girlfriends* and sin." Scarlet clenched her arms until her knuckles were white.

"I didn't make a tree root grow into the pipes! I didn't ignore gallons of raw sewage pouring into the basement for a week!" Sam stood. He considered shooting a nice stream of lighter fluid into the fire. Oh, what the hell? "What would Gary think about that, Mom? About how your basement is half a foot deep in the entire neighborhood's shit, and all you did was watch TV? And then asked me to wet vac it? What would he think?"

She met his eyes with the deepest look of anger she'd given him to that point, and each word from her lips cloaked an underlying threat.

"Did you call Gary?"

"Why would I call Gary? He's no good in a situation like this! Can he clear blocked pipelines or shovel shit from a—"

"I told you to not use that language in this house, Amanda! Even if you want to think it's your house, it's not! It's mine! And Gary loves me!"

"Then where is he? Where has he been all week to tell you it's unsanitary to let your basement fill with sewage?"

"You know he doesn't come to the house because of you and Stevie! Yet *another* way in which you're trying to ruin my chances of ever finding anyone!"

None of her men came to the house. And it wasn't out of respect for her children. It was because Scarlet could cloak her body and clothes with Calvin Klein perfume, but there wasn't enough Eternity on the entire fucking planet to keep that house from smelling like dead rodents and urine.

But there was no purpose to arguing that her house was disgusting even when it wasn't filled with human waste.

"I could be loved! I've been loved before!" Scarlet shouted. "But every time I am, you destroy it!"

"If they all love you, why is it me cleaning up after you?" The toilet. The sink. Stevie constantly. Scarlet's sanity itself. Countless other things.

"*You* owe *me* more than I've ever asked from you. I gave birth to you. I changed your diapers I—"

"Exactly! I am *your* child, not the other way around!" They were at the point when the fuse was hitting the powder keg, but Sam didn't care. "And neither of us is old enough for me to be changing your diapers! Yet here we are! There are gallons of shit in your fucking basement!"

"Amanda Michelle! I won't tolerate that mouth of yours a second longer! Get out!"

"Or what? You'll hit me? Repeat performance sixteen years later. Go ahead!"

If there was one positive thing to be said of his mother, it was that she avoided violence. While her own mother had often resorted to physical punishment, Scarlet had never put a hand on Stevie. And she'd only hit Sam once, which was how she learned her lesson.

"Amanda was maybe one. Barely walking. I can't remember what she did, but I hit her so hard that she flew across the room. That's when I decided to keep my temper in check. I just send them away when I'm angry now."

Scarlet told this story often when child discipline surfaced in adult conversation. She was proud of herself. Proud that it only took one incident of hitting a toddler with enough force to knock her across the room to realize that violence wasn't a good idea. She never understood why she received strange looks when she finished this charming anecdote of her parental prowess.

Because you should be ashamed that you struck an innocent baby. That you hurt your child, Sam would think when Scarlet retold it and people gave him the confused looks he often received when his mother opened her mouth. *You should want to bury that secret instead of continuing to get off on it more than a decade later. The last thing you should feel is pride.*

But sometimes he'd rather have a slap to the face than the emotional abuse Scarlet dealt. Bruises healed. The damage from seventeen years of being blamed for every negative circumstance? The constant feeling of rejection? The thousands of times when something or someone else was of more importance than him? His father. Stevie. The boyfriends. Work. The fucking *Golden Girls*.

I'll never get over it. Even when I'm free of you. Even when I'm free of Amanda. Sam stared Scarlet down and waited for her to respond. *You're a cancer to me. I'll cut you out. But I'll always have the scar.*

"Get out, Amanda! Get out!"

"Oh, I'm going." He lowered his voice and took a step into the hall. "But so should you. That's all I came to tell you. You should check into a hotel for a few days. It's not sanitary. And that's not even my opinion— it's the disaster crew's recommendation. You could get sick."

"This is *my* house, young lady. I won't be told what to do by you or anyone else."

It was the most below-the-belt thing he could be called, and his skin was smoldering. Sam didn't believe he was capable of laying a hand to anyone, especially a woman. But he needed to leave now before he said something he'd regret. Like yelling in her face at the top of his lungs. Like using every profane word he could think of until her ears bled. Like divulging his secret when she had some power over him.

"Well, I'm not staying here."

"As long as it's out of my sight, I don't care where you go." She'd turned away from him again. "But Stevie and I are staying here. I'm not paying for a hotel room because the basement is dirty."

"You know what else lives in their own shit? Pigs. It's too bad Gary's condo doesn't allow farm animals, or you could stay with him."

Scarlet spun around and slammed the door in his face without another word.

FOURTEEN

THE DINGY, CARPETED steps had been marred with brown sludge a few times, so Sam picked his footsteps carefully as he descended. He chose to not tell the cleaning crew that the first and second floors had been contaminated. His bag thankfully hadn't been moved from the location he'd left it in hours before. He picked it up and entered the living room, where Stevie sat mesmerized by the television, licking cheese crunchy powder from his fingers.

The same fingers that put on and took off the shoes that squashed through the bowel movements of the entire neighborhood. You don't bathe. You don't brush your teeth. Why would you wash your hands? He watched his brother dig another handful of crunchies from the bag squeezed between his legs. *But it's not your fault. You're a kid.*

Sam pulled the television cord from the wall. He didn't have time to wait for a commercial.

"Hey! What the hell do you think you're doing?" His brother screamed as if he'd been disemboweled. He unfolded his legs and the bag of crunchies fell, its contents spilling on the carpet.

"I assure you, there are no new episodes of *Sanford and Son*."

"I don't care! It's my show! Plug it in!"

"Keep your voice down." Sam wondered if the cleaning crew could hear the yelling, if they'd heard the fight with Scarlet.

It doesn't matter. This is not my fault or my problem anymore.

"You can't tell me what to do! Plug the damn thing back in!"

"I will, but I need to tell you something first. I've been talking with the men who are working in the basement, and—"

"They aren't half as annoying as you! Plug my TV in, Amanda, or I'll go get Mom!"

"Stevie, listen. They said it's not safe for you to stay here until the basement is clean. Call Dad and go with him for a few days."

"Forget it. Dad doesn't have cable."

"You could get really sick."

"Good. I like being sick. I hate school." Stevie howled around a finger in his mouth. His fingernails were as long as a woman's, and Sam could see a stratum of black grime underneath the layer of orange cheese his brother was getting out by sliding the nail along one of his lower teeth. With his other hand, Stevie picked the cordless handset from its cradle and brought back his arm. "Now plug the TV in before I beam you, you fucking bitch!"

There was a pair of scissors sitting on the entertainment center.

"Well? Are you gonna do it?" Stevie shouted. He made a sharp motion as if he was launching the phone and grinned when Sam flinched.

Yes.

Sam swiped the scissors from the table and cut the plug off. He ducked as the phone smashed into the wall and was outside before he could witness more of Stevie's explosion. From the wails of grief and shrieks of rage that came through the door, he imagined his brother was dissolving into the floor.

"Oh, what a world! What a world!" You'll get over it. In an hour you'll be slurping the cheese doodles that've been marinating on the floor in the shit from your shoes. You're both going to die. And I'm not sadistic enough to watch it.

After Sam had wheeled his bag a confident seven or eight blocks, it occurred to him that he didn't have a plan. Or anywhere to go. And it'd be dark soon. The triumphant march slowed to a contemplative pace.

Okay, options.

Stevie might be welcome in their father's house, but Sam wasn't. Even if Scarlet had radioactive waste in her basement instead of human waste. It'd been made as a clear statement of fact that his father wanted nothing to do with him. Because before Sam had announced he was gay, before the incident at Target, even before his parents' divorce... Before his father looked for a mail-order bride, Sam's future stepmother had a baby girl. A girl who didn't remind his father of Scarlet, and therefore made his existence unnecessary.

"She doesn't have her look or her cocky mouth. Min has none of the many attributes that make your mother the bitch she is. She's training you to be like her, Amanda. And I won't have it. I don't need you anymore."

Fortunately for Stevie, their stepmother hadn't had a boy and didn't appear capable of producing one. There was room for Stevie.

I wish I had friends. Just one. He sighed and parked his bag at the bus stop. *Well, I do have two friends.*

Sam removed his cell phone but hesitated to call Mr. Keegan. The man had promised he'd be available if Sam needed him, and there was no reason to doubt his support was true.

But you didn't make that guarantee thinking I'd call on you so quickly. That I'd beg you for a place to stay. No, I can't. I'm going to try to solve this myself.

Few ideas came to him as he waited for the bus. He wasn't sure at which stop he should exit in order to find a good park bench to spend the night. But when the large gray vehicle pulled to the stop he got on anyway. Instantly, he was glad he had.

Sam opened his wallet to flash the driver his bus pass, and the answer was staring him in the face. The fake ID. Of course! He didn't need anyone. The ID might have been for Amanda Porter, but it was for a nineteen-year-old Amanda Porter. And a nineteen-year-old individual who had a job, his own bank account, and debit card could get a cheap motel room for a week or so.

Perfect. Fuck you, Mom. Fuck you, Stevie.

That sequence of events was how Sam ended up staying for three weeks at a motel. It wasn't a great place, but it had reasonable weekly rates and everything he needed—an onsite washer and dryer, a microwave and mini fridge in his room. It was also along the bus route, so he could get to both work and school.

And there were other "amenities" the motel *didn't* have which made it even more pleasant and convenient. There was no Stevie or Scarlet.

A week went by before Scarlet contacted him. Sam would've liked to think she'd called the school or his job to confirm he was attending, and therefore had known he was safe. But he was tired of making excuses for his mother and imagining that she was a better person than she truly was. Not that checking on him and then ignoring him would make her a good person. In a way, it was the kind of mind game Scarlet liked to play and fantasy she loved to create. She'd probably relished all week not only in thinking she was "teaching Amanda a lesson," but also that she'd have a new "mother of the year" story to tell.

"I called that school pronto to make sure my baby was okay. I sure as shootin' wasn't playing into her tantrum though. I let her squirm and think I didn't care for a few days to show that she can't treat her mother with such disrespect, and that she has it good here!"

But I'm not squirming. And I don't *think you don't care. I* know *you* don't.

Then the text message came in at two in the morning. He didn't bother mulling over that *maybe* the hour it came in was indicative of a seventh sleepless night worried about him.

You just got home from Gary's, who invited you to Pokey for the weekend, and you want a babysitter. Or Gary learned something about the situation—your side, which includes a quarter of what really happened—and convinced you to "be the bigger person." And you agreed because Gary *said so, and you'd do* anything *for Gary.*

But then he thought of his brother. Asshole Stevie eating cheese crunchies dipped in diarrhea and disintegrating into the carpet. Once upon a time he was a sweet innocent boy. Before their parents had done things to him. Sam imagined that he'd also been a sweet innocent boy. Only by luck had he become a strong person, instead of the fat slob his brother was. Stevie couldn't bear the entire blame for his situation. He was a weak-minded dumbass. As a result, the boy might not have possessed the self-control to *not* eat cheese doodles from a carpet saturated in human feces and could now be in the hospital.

So, instead of deleting the message, Sam opened it to ensure that his brother was okay.

—*Are you staying with your dad?*

He'd already decided he wasn't returning to Scarlet's house. After his birthday, he'd rent an apartment and until then, he was staying put. Yet he was sensitive to the fact that he was technically a minor. If Scarlet learned his location, she could tromp down to the motel and drag him back. Why risk it? An affirmative response was best. His parents weren't on speaking terms, and his whereabouts wouldn't be discovered.

Maybe I should teach you *a lesson and wait a few days to answer. Make you think* I *don't care about* you. Sam hesitated on sending the message. *But no, I'm not like you. I don't like to mindfuck people.*

He sent it and waited. He wasn't sure why. Scarlet was as likely to not respond as she was to respond. Chances of a reply were better if she was with Gary.

The phone buzzed.

—Tel him I'm not paying child support for you. Not a dime.

Sam turned the phone off and was glad he hadn't hoped for more.

Scarlet, realizing who you really are isn't like finding out that Mr. K is a transvestite. There's no shock in you not fulfilling the expectations I used to have. He pulled the clean comforter around his shoulders. *And you're not important enough for me to waste time getting over. Fuck you.*

SCHOOL SEEMED TO improve as well. The week spent in the swimming pool for gym class had arrived, forcing Sam to use the girls' locker room, but otherwise things were going smoothly. Following DC, no one had hurt him or threatened him. All he received were strange, disgusted looks, and he was left alone, which was better than persecution. And he believed his reprieve was due to Mr. and Mrs. Keegan.

Sam doubted they'd *actually* done anything. They hadn't pulled his bullies into the office and given them a "talking to." But for the remainder of the trip, it'd been made clear in nonverbal communication that Sam was under their protection. Where Mr. K had been subtle about watching him, he now allowed more of the concern to show. There hadn't been *much* time, but it'd been enough. He openly made sure Sam was in his group and sat at his table for meals. And he spoke and treated Sam as if he were on the same level. Like when they'd been alone before, but now for everyone to witness.

"Can you pass me the *obituary* section?" asked a girl at the six-seater table with Sam, Mr. Farr, and the Keegans on the morning they were flying home. Sam had glanced from his scrambled eggs. She held out her hand for the newspaper, but was looking hopefully around to see how much attention she was receiving for her "dark" request.

Does it take a case of pneumonia to make you realize life isn't about impressing people?

"I *love* to read the obituaries. I *love* death. Nobody *understands*. It's so *deep*. So *obtuse* and *pterodactyl*."

One of the many things he admired about Mr. K was the amount of control he had over himself. Sam had choked on his eggs, and even Mrs. K brought her hand to her mouth and coughed. But Mr. Keegan sat there with the same serious look on his face. Sam could only tell from the glint in his eyes that he was amused.

"Give me that." Mr. Farr swiped the section being handed across the table.

"See, no one *understands* me," she whined.

Well, when the words coming from your mouth make no fucking sense.

"Outrageous, you know?" Mr. Farr said to no one specifically as he perused the obituary columns.

"Are you in there, dear?" Mrs. Farr sat at the next table, where this was apparently a funny joke to everyone but Sam, the Keegans, and Mr. Farr. And the girl pouting over the paper. Because death wasn't funny. It was abstruse and esoteric—triangles and flying dinosaurs.

"It looks like everyone is dying of the cancer here too," the old man grumbled behind the newspaper.

"Must have leaked. Crossed the border sewn into a car seat or in the stomach of a drug mole."

"You mean 'mule,' Mr. Keegan. Drug *mule*," corrected Death Girl.

"Mole, mule." He shrugged with a straight face. "It's all the same. Cinnamons of each other."

She didn't get it.

My generation is going to bring about the end of the world. Some imbecile will confuse the "detonate" button for the "decorate" button. The planet will explode because Beavis thought balloons would drop from the ceiling.

"It astounds me; the liberties writers take nowadays. The lies that are allowed to be made in print." Mr. Farr folded the paper in half. "This 'fought bravely, valiantly, courageously' hogwash. I don't know how they get away with putting that stuff in. It's not true. In the end, they're all screaming and writhing in agony. Nothing brave about that."

Sam wondered how individuals with this level of brash dickishness lived as long as they did. Without someone beating *their* heads into a brick wall, or someone—

"What about making it that far?"

The words left Sam before he could think. And since a stream of teenage diarrhea didn't spray constantly from his mouth even in the prime "Amanda" years, people paid notice to him. But he couldn't help it. He'd thought of his grandmother picking him up in the rain at a

Target when she needed a seat belt extender because her tumor was so large.

"When you could opt out," Sam continued. "When you could deliver yourself, enduring is brave. Carrying on is meaningful, even if it takes you in the end. Holding on *is* brave."

Somewhat to his shock, his newfound ally had given the rebuttal.

"Both roads lead to the same place. 'To suffer unnecessarily is masochistic rather than heroic.'"

Sam took the wrapped bundle of silverware next to him. He broke the paper ring, unfolded the napkin, and removed the knife. Then he slid it across the table, where it clinked into Mr. Keegan's untouched water glass.

"Do it now then."

If it'd been any other teacher, and Sam had been any other student, he might have been suspended. But when Mr. Keegan hadn't hidden his smirk, Sam realized he'd been baited.

Or batted. Whatever. They're just cinnamons.

But it'd helped. Allowing Sam to make the final bold move in a battle of wits between two classically opposed foes garnered a degree of respect from his peers. It was a small sword taken, but a sword nonetheless.

There'd also been that gesture of unity in the airport. What Mr. Keegan said couldn't have been heard, but his hand on Sam's shoulder had surely been seen.

Which is partly why you did it. I'm sure you wanted me to feel acknowledged as a friend and as a man. But you also wanted them to recognize I'm under your protection. That I'm not alone anymore.

Not feeling as assailable had instilled a distinct confidence in Sam. Combined with the daring and successful break from Scarlet, he walked taller through the school hallways. He was independent, but he had people who believed in him. In the *real* him and not the Amanda mask. So, he wasn't as afraid anymore.

Was he untouchable? No. But even the boys in gym were less interested in harassing him. Sam was now supported by a teacher who commanded the high respect given to one of baller status, but there were also only a few weeks left of school. Their opportunities had also become limited. For two weeks Sam was forced to use the girl's locker room by the swimming pool. He wasn't as convenient to pick off when in a group. And even though the gym teacher only called roll and then retreated to her office to smoke crack or look at porn, the class wasn't left alone. There was a swim instructor and a lifeguard. And they hadn't left the group unattended yet.

SAM TOOK HIS place in the horseshoe shape to the side of the swimming pool. He waited to give his number as the woman ticked attendance off her clipboard without looking at them.

"Five."

"Six."

"Seven."

The first day of class, the gym teacher had used their names. She only used the names to tell them their numbers in alphabetical order. This was their identity in her class. It was easier to split them into teams. It made roll call faster. It was "sporty." But mostly, they didn't pay her enough to learn how to pronounce whatever jumble of letters their parents had decided to throw together for a name. So, they were numbers.

"Fourteen."

"Fifteen."

"Seventeen."

Sixteen was absent. Whoever he or she was. Or he or she had forgotten his or her number, which was equivalent to an absence. You had to be quick too. The gym teacher didn't like to wait to get back to doing cheap tequila shots off her desk. The next student's number had to be given sharp.

"Twenty-one."

"Twenty-two."

"Twenty-three," Sam said. He smiled though. Despite the parallels between jails and concentration camps, the number was nicer than "Amanda."

He'd had high hopes for gym class at the beginning of the trimester because of the number method. It could be a fifty-five-minute break from that name. Of course, the violent bullying had erased this tiny pleasure.

But things are different now. They feel that way. I have less than a month left. Less than a month of being Amanda, or twenty-three, or anyone I don't want to be! I'm almost done! The finish line is in sight!

"Mr. Donovan and Wayne will be in soon."

"Can we get in the pool until they're here?" asked thirty-five.

"I don't care." The sound of her athletic sliders slapping against the tiles echoed away.

If Sam thought about it, it wasn't a single finish line. It had been a series, and he'd streaked through several in the last few weeks alone. From cutting his hair, being brave enough to go to The Attic, telling Mr. and Mrs. Keegan his secret, and cutting ties with Scarlet.

Next step, birthday. Graduation. Apartment. Hormones. Name—

"Play in the pool, girly!"

The wind was knocked out of him as one of the boys bulldozed him into the swimming pool.

Sam hit the water hard, and the side of his face stung from the impact. But the pain was immediately replaced by streaks of panic and adrenaline as he thrashed to get to the surface.

He reached it only once.

His head broke above the water, and he gasped for a single breath of air. He heard laughter before they grabbed his shoulders and thrust him under.

This time, they held him there.

And Sam's world became a 3-D viewer again. Each struggle was a click of the lever. The frames kept cycling and cycling, splintering one individual moment into the next as he fought desperately for freedom. Until his lungs filled with the warm chlorinated water, and the reel completely ripped out.

FIFTEEN

JULIE HAD BEEN on her way to Todd's classroom to see if he was ready to leave when she heard the racing footsteps.

"Ma'am!"

Her heart hammered and the muscles in her legs tensed to start running. She knew the voice of every male staff member. This one was strange. It was deep. It was loud. And it was accompanied by a quick pace that bounced off the lockers and reverberated into her eardrums.

"Ma'am! Wait!"

Todd's room was a few doors away, and she could make it. If she didn't waste another second, she had a chance. No matter how fast or big he was, or what kind of weapons he might have, or—

No. Julie stopped in the hallway. She pushed the "what-could-be" horrors from her mind and forced herself to think of something else. Of someone else. *If a seventeen-year-old can go through the gauntlet every day, I can face a stranger. I can refuse to run. If he can do it,* I can do it.

Her chest ached as she compelled herself to turn around.

The man's voice may have been unfamiliar, but his face wasn't. He was the athletic middle-aged man the school employed as a lifeguard.

Trusting him with kids doesn't make him safe. Maybe teenagers aren't his thing. Maybe he likes twenty-five-year-old women with brown hair and blue eyes and—

The lifeguard planted his sandals to avoid plowing into her and skidded with a piercing screech into a row of lockers.

"Jiminy Christmas!" He stumbled to the side and regained his footing.

I have no reason to worry. If Jiminy tried to assault her, she'd not only be able to outrun him in his silly flip-flops, but she could stop him in his tracks by screaming every obscenity she knew. Like a good Mormon, when confronted with the F-word he'd fall to the ground and clutch his bleeding ears.

"You're a teacher, right? I need help at the pool."

"I don't get paid to clean pools, or polish buoys, or whatever it is you do," Julie snapped.

"It's a student." Jiminy's forehead furrowed, since like any respectable Mormon, he was also thrown off by snarky remarks. "I need you to come with me right now. I can't find anyone else, and I don't know what to do."

If it was a student, Julie really was responsible. But facing a stranger in a hallway was different than following someone she barely knew to a swimming pool unconnected to the main building. She could outrun and outswear him right then, but the tables could turn in another environment.

Someone could be waiting outside the door. A dozen someones. They could push me into the trunk of a car and drive off— She put two fingertips to her right temple. *Stop. Stop. Stop!*

"Come on!" The lifeguard waited for her to follow, but there was a sense of urgency in his tone.

Julie considered telling him to hold on while she got her brother. If Jiminy was willing to receive help from a man instead, that would prove his harmlessness. And even if he *still* wasn't innocent, once the band of goons saw him exit the building with Todd instead of her—

Julie. There is no band of goons. There's an idiot who falls out of his sandals. And a student who probably just shit his pants in the pool. And furthermore, I'm tired of running. She took a breath. *I'm worth not hiding anymore.*

Julie followed the lifeguard. It was at a slower speed than the man wanted to move, but with two-thirds of her mind screaming and trying to convince her that she was insane for *willingly* entering a den of bloodthirsty wolves—

Jaguars. Tiger sharks. Silverback wolverines. Velociraptors. Man-eating—

She could only move so fast.

BEING "WORTH NOT hiding anymore" was a remark Sam had made. Not on the first night at The Attic, though he'd said something similar. But in one of their many subsequent conversations.

"Their" was a stretch. Sam didn't seem to mind her constant presence, but it was clear he was there to be around Todd. It was no longer unexpected to find him in the classroom after school. He did busy work if there was stapling, correcting, or arranging; however, when she walked in two weeks following the trip she'd found him doing nothing.

Todd sat on his desktop, and Sam was across from him, talking excitedly. And her brother listened instead of lecturing. Without derision on his face or tuning out to think of what *he* was going to say next and developing cynical commentary. It'd been a long time since Julie had seen the smile and lightness in his eyes which confirmed the cogs weren't turning and the inner dialogue was silent. He was happy.

You like having him around. Todd was so focused on Sam that her presence hadn't even been noticed. *You used to feel that way about me. You used to feel that way about a lot of people and things. But then* I *happened to you.*

Julie had thought before that she might be holding Todd back, but it'd only been fleeting. What was he *really* held from? He had everything he needed. He didn't want relationships or more than what he had. When that changed, she'd leave. Until then she felt a little guilty being dependent, though not overly. But then there was that look on his face while he listened to Sam.

I'm preventing you from pursuing happiness. You're almost thirty, Todd. You could be really married. You could have kids and friends. People you enjoy being with. But because of me, you're stuck.

The second epiphany hit her. Julie had spent the last couple of weeks around Sam identifying with him. When he told Todd about his family and the emotional abuse, it was a closed-circuit connection in her mind— *You're me. Everything you say, that's how I feel. We're so alike. Beaten down. We're both screwed.* Being around Sam was like looking into a mirror.

But how could the damaged help the damaged? The only thing that helped was Todd, and she was willing to share him with Sam. So, she sat in near shock and rarely spoke when the young man was there. Watching herself. Stuck.

But the day she'd noticed her brother just taking pleasure in listening to Sam, it'd hit her. *You're not me. You easily could be. You could shut off. Curl into the fetal position and never unfold. But you choose to not be defeated.*

When Sam talked about being transgender and his toxic family, it wasn't a bitch session or a pity party. It just *was*. It *existed*. He was trapped, but in a vastly different way from her. Sam was trapped the way her brother was.

He's not me. He's you. And his god-awful mother? That's who I am. I do to Todd what she does to Sam.

She felt bowled over with shame, and there wasn't a hint of the sweetness that accompanied a painful realization. Because she had no idea how to fix it. She'd tried and failed. Multiple times.

How do you do it? Julie looked at Sam's back and tears stung her eyes. *How do you avoid being me? And why? When I'm not thinking what a drain I am, it's easier. Especially when I have Todd to depend on. Bury the past under a cross-country move, a fake marriage, snipes, and cynicism. There are more reasons to quit than fight. Plenty of—*

"Why?" She walked toward him. When the young man turned his head, she stopped and wiped a hand across her eyes. "Tell me why."

"It was nine o'clock and nowhere else was open," Sam answered slowly and looked at her as if her hair was turning fuchsia. Todd had his eyes on her also, with the same confusion.

"Why do you do it? Why do you struggle?"

He understood. Not the reason she was having an emotional outburst, but he knew what she was referencing.

"I told you at the club, Mrs. K. I have to."

"You don't *have* to do anything. You *want* to make things difficult and suffer. You *hope* they'll turn out all right, though they won't. And you'll find yourself at the beginning and scared waiting for it to happen again." Julie knew she was talking too fast and not making sense. "And it would be *easy* to not do a damn thing. Build a good wall and cover it up! Cover it! Why—"

"Because I'm worth it," Sam had cut her off. "I tried all that. It didn't do any good and brought me nothing. It made me feel I was empty and insignificant. But I'm *not* worthless. I am worth not hiding anymore."

Julie had mentally repeated the words a few times. She thought of the strong, independent woman she used to be. Who did only what *she* wanted to do. Who let nothing stop her. Who had plans and aspirations. Who could exist without another person checking under her bed for monsters. What was Julie now? A pathetic shell. Safe, but afraid of her own shadow. Miserable. And Todd may care about her, but he had to.

She'd seen it in his eyes when he spoke with Sam. He didn't *like* to be around her. No one did. She didn't like to be around herself.

But I spent eighteen years being happy and liking who I was. Being excited about who I was. Being in love with me! And if I can spend my time being her or this thing I am now, then she's worth it too. You're right. Who I want to be isn't worth hiding anymore.

Her path wouldn't be easy or overnight, but she was determined to start taking steps to recover. And she'd make the journey not only for herself, but also for Todd. So he could get *himself* back too. He could return to New Orleans and embrace a part of his identity that he loved but had hidden for her benefit. She'd separate from him. Give him space so someday he could enjoy being around her again.

He's been my constant companion for years, but I really have lost him. For her, Todd had become who he was never meant to be. He wasn't her husband, father, or guardian. As much as she missed herself, she missed her brother. And Julie wanted him back.

This time maybe she had enough strength to propel her forward. Something beaten into the ground with shame and violence, made to feel weak and inferior—it could rise. Fragment by fragment, a person could be pulled together no matter how shattered they'd been. A seventeen-year-old transgender young man was proof of it. And that's what she'd keep in the forefront of her mind: *If he can do it, I can do it. I'm worth not hiding anymore.*

Those statements ticked in Julie's head as she followed the lifeguard from the building. No thugs attacked her. She wasn't pushed into the trunk of a black car that didn't come spinning across the grass. And when she walked through the door the lifeguard impatiently held for her, no exotic or extinct wildlife emerged.

The smell of chlorine engulfed her. From the humid concrete lobby, she saw the pool area through two large panes of glass that comprised the upper half of a counter. The walls of the other room were lined with rows of plastic bleachers. A diving board was near the deep end and corded red-and-white buoys separated the shallow portion from defined swim lanes. It was nice enough—clean in a sticky way.

Unlike what she expected, there was no student in the pool. Or in the lobby where she stood *alone* with a strange man. Isolated, with the door closed and no one able to hear her scream. But wait. She'd made it this far without falling to pieces. Julie gathered her courage before it could be dismantled by her anxiety.

"What's the problem, Jiminy?"

"My name is Wayne."

"Does it matter? Where's the fire?"

"You don't get paid to polish buoys or clean the pool, and *I* don't get paid to deal with this stuff. Or to stay past two thirty." Wayne folded his arms. "I have an appointment at three, and I can't lock up while a kid is in the locker room. The last two girls said one of them is in there. I've been hollering at the door, but there's been no answer. I need you to check if there's anyone, and if there is, get her to leave. I'm going to be late!"

"You dragged me out here to be your bouncer? Where's the gym teacher?"

"She leaves the class with me and Mr. Donovan. And they get to go on time every day." He walked down a corridor on the right. "I'm not sure if those girls were pulling my leg. Like I said, I've been calling, but there hasn't been a peep."

"Why would there be anyone left? They run for their lives as soon as the bell rings." Julie stopped at a wooden door painted with a crude dress-wearing stick figure.

"Girls said there was some horseplay before Mr. Donovan and I came in. One of them got pushed in the pool. Probably in there crying. But like I said, I didn't hear anything." Wayne looked at his watch. "Can you please hurry?"

Julie pushed open the door.

The humidity was worse in the locker room—every time she inhaled there was a weight on her chest. She had to stop herself from wheezing as she looked around. It seemed deserted, and there was no sound beyond water droplets from the shower heads on the left side. She circled an island of square lockers in the middle of the room. There were no legs in any of the seven bathroom stalls lining the back or in the half-dozen changing rooms on the right wall.

"Hello?" Julie turned. There was no answer. "Anyone in here?"

The only noise was her heavy breathing, and she began to walk along the locker island beside the changing rooms.

Dumbass kids. But this was good for me. I should be proud that—

A slight movement from the crack in a changing room door caught Julie's eye as she passed. She retreated a few steps. Nothing looked unusual.

"If someone's in here, you need to leave! Pool boy has an appointment!" Julie dropped her voice as she went by the rooms. "It's with his hand, but—"

The movement again. Or maybe it wasn't movement, just color. The walls of the room were gray, but when she walked past the fifth changing room there was a blue flash. She looked in the small door crack.

Oh, my God.

There was a figure huddled on the wooden bench. Her legs were folded, her arms loosely hugging her knees. Julie couldn't see a face as her head was turned to the wall. And the color of the blue shirt was indeed what had caught her eye. Because there was no movement.

"Kid! Wake up!" Julie pulled the aluminum door handle.

It didn't open.

"Kid!" She hammered on the door with her fist.

The figure didn't stir.

"Kid! Wake up!"

She got to her knees and ducked her head, crawling under the stall door into the room. She stood and clapped a hand on the small blue shoulder. It was cold, but she shook it anyway.

"Kid!"

Julie released a breath when she felt the muscle in the shoulder tense, confirming the cold was due to damp clothing. But absolute relief was short-lived. When Sam turned his head, he had the same expression she must've had when she woke in the hospital bed.

Sam looked like he wasn't sure he was alive. She remembered how it was to feel so lost inside her own body that she couldn't move. The entire world had faded away and nothing was real. Each sense came slowly, if at all—everything on a delay. Her thoughts paralyzed to the extent that she couldn't speak. Even recognition was impossible. It'd taken minutes to piece together that the face in front of her was her brother, Todd, and he wouldn't hurt her. She remembered not knowing his name or even her own. And this was the look Sam had—a slate wiped of everything except terror.

Julie had drawn back her hand at Sam's movement. When she raised it and placed it to the side of his face, he flinched. But she kept his eye contact and smoothed her thumb along his cheek.

"Sam, it's Julie Keegan," she said slowly. "You're safe. I won't let anyone hurt you anymore."

SIXTEEN

"THAT'S QUITE THE story, Todd," Charlie Smith said.

Throughout Todd's explanation of the bullying and assault of Sam Porter, Charlie kept a placid countenance. Sam had advised them of the principal's indifference when he'd sought help before, but Todd was convinced that it couldn't have been that bad. Sam had likely misread him. Many educators hid their real emotions under a cover of gravity. It was a necessary skill honed from being surrounded by immature stupidity.

Sam might be able to read Todd after making a two-year study of his mannerisms. But the young man's ability to interpret others? Todd had no reason to question it per se; however, Charlie had a lot of kids being "picked on" whining in his office. He probably gave pushback to feel out if Sam's report had been real or tattling. Knowing Sam, once he sensed the abrasion, he folded a little, which would've confirmed the principal's assumption that he was exaggerating something minor. Once the entire situation was brought to his attention by a fellow instructor, the reception would be different.

After Julie had coaxed Sam out of the locker room and into his classroom, he'd eventually calmed down enough for Todd to try to clarify the logic.

"Think of it this way, Sam. The last thing Charlie wants is a lawsuit. Reducing liability is a huge part of his job. If he knows the severity of what's going on, it wouldn't matter why they're doing it. He'll *have* to do something," Todd had explained.

"What more could I have said?" Sam protested. "I'm not a troublemaker. He had no reason to believe I was lying."

"Usually when a student has these issues, the parent is involved as well. That could be why he may've thought—"

"I told you. My mom doesn't give a shit what happens to me. She'd do *less* than nothing if she could."

Todd also wasn't sure what to believe about the mother. He'd met Scarlet once at a parent-teacher conference, and she seemed normal. Sam had advised this was part of the "mother-of-the-year" persona she put on for small increments of time. She hated attending those meetings for Sam. Unlike Stevie, she told him there wasn't a point. All his teachers only ever said good things. Why waste her time?

"It's *not* a waste of time to me," Sam had told him. "It's nice to hear myself praised in front of her. To hear people tell her I'm worthwhile. I thought that maybe one of you might say enough. If other people like and appreciate me, she should too. She likes fads."

This was one of the sadder things Todd had heard. Most of the time, the pathetic, attention-whore little Snoochies wanted accolades for themselves. To slake their own pride and boost already inflated egos. Here, the boy wanted his mother to listen to the commendations. And he held the hope that someday the right tribute or honor would convince Scarlet she should love him.

Like with Sam's account of Charlie, Todd wasn't certain that Sam understood these people correctly. But though his mother seemed more outlandish, she was more believable than the principal. With Charlie it was business and business had to rule the bottom line.

"If the bottom line is business, he should've checked into it then." Sam had folded his arms. "You say he's supposed to reduce liability? If I could prove he wouldn't even investigate, how much legal responsibility does that put the school under? The district under?"

"Exactly. Which is why I'm telling you, let me talk to him. I'll explain what's going on and verify that what you're saying is true. I'll give it validity."

"I don't need you to give it validity, Mr. K," he snapped. "It is valid. Your retelling doesn't make it credible."

"To a man who puts up with jerkoffs crying over paper balls, it does," Todd said.

"I'm not a jerkoff. I didn't go to his office with spitballs in my hair. I had a fractured wrist! And you saw the back of my head! You both did!" Sam glanced at Julie. "And they tried to drown me! Those are physical things! They don't need the word of an adult to make them real!"

Todd ran a hand through his hair. All he wanted to do was help, but it was impossible to explain these concepts to a person outside the education field. Especially when they were this close to the issue.

"I'm not meaning to come off like a dick. But let's face it—you said yourself, your mother doesn't give a shit about you." He received a tentative nod and continued. "Consider which problem is given the higher degree of attention: one accompanied by a screaming mother, or one with only a student where the mother *should* be screaming but is markedly absent?"

"That's right, Todd. Talk to Charlie in a dress. Wear your pink jacket. He'll *really* take you seriously." Julie had apparently begun to feel the third beer.

Todd chose to ignore his sister. "Sam, if he needs to know you have support to take action, that's all I want to do. If in order to believe you, Mr. Smith needs to see you have an adult who won't back down..."

He trailed off when Sam shook his head. The young man's grim face had moved into a cynical smile.

"You're missing it, Mr. K. Lack of belief isn't the issue. He said, 'Kids get hurt in gym.' He knew it happened. He knows it's happening. I don't want you to go. It'll make things worse for me and maybe for you."

"You can't *possibly* be considering going back, Sam." Julie placed her bottle on the counter.

"Of course, I am. I was shaken, but I'm going tomorrow."

"That's absurd!" She laughed, and Todd pictured the thoughts running through her head. Not being able to go to her house or to even allow him to drive down the street it was on. "Going back is suicide!"

"No." The smile was gone. "Letting myself be beaten is suicide."

Todd had kept his expression unmoved as he looked from Sam to his sister when he really felt like beaming. He was proud of Sam. Of his strength and determination, even if it was partly stupid and risky.

I do see it, Julie. The past week you've been different. You've stopped quadruple checking the locks on every door. I came downstairs last night to play that damn machine, and you didn't follow. And you waited for me to come to your classroom after school the other day. You're trying.

"Well, we can't let you. You'll stay right here." Julie nodded. "Believe me, you'll be safe here."

Julie hadn't told Sam what had happened to her, but Todd wondered if she might. He'd also noticed by her comments, the way she looked at Sam, and how she acted around him that she identified with him. As of yet though, her past remained a secret. Neither of them had even disclosed the reality of their relationship.

"Being safe isn't my primary objective. And you can't make me do anything, Mrs. K. Neither of you can."

His sister looked at him, but Todd shrugged in response. Even if they could force him, it wasn't something he'd be a party to.

"You can only keep him if he wants to be kept, Julie. And if you promise to feed him, brush him, and pick up any presents he leaves in the yard." Todd turned to Sam. "Let's be clear though: I'm not giving you license to shit in my yard."

Sam smiled. "And I appreciate what you both want to do, but I don't need any help. There are only a few weeks of school left, and I don't want to make them any more difficult than they will be if you interfere. Your willingness to listen is enough."

And at first, Todd acceded to Sam's request. He promised not talk to the principal, and he stopped Julie from building an electric fence and tagging the young man's ear. Instead, once Sam was feeling better, Todd had driven him home. Not to his mother's house, but to a motel. Apparently the house was being fumigated, so they were staying there a few days.

"You didn't mention that," Todd said when Sam asked him to head in the opposite direction.

"Do I need to tell you everything, Mr. K?"

"I'd probably prefer you didn't."

"That's a correct assumption."

But the situation had still bothered him, and he knew it was troubling Julie. These kids hadn't put Sam's head in a toilet. They'd held it under water until he had blacked out. They'd hurt him because they wanted to and saw purpose in it. It was too dangerous to let it go, even if that's what Sam wanted.

He's not little Snoochie, but there's a reason for the age of majority. Kids are entitled to the same constitutional rights and protection as everyone else, but they aren't mature enough to make some decisions. Whatever he's been through and however adult he may seem, everyone makes stupid-ass choices sometimes.

Todd knew Charlie would listen to him. Sure, he'd sat through Todd's report without concern on his face, but the man was very accomplished at the appearance of apathy. It wasn't until Charlie smiled after his comment of it being "some story" that Todd realized Sam had been right.

"Story?"

"Yes, story."

"That word has a strong implication of something fictional, Charlie."

"Well, did you see it happen?" The principal folded his hands behind his head. "Did anyone over the age of seventeen see it happen? If not, it could be just a story."

"No, I didn't personally see anything and Sam advised—"

"Amanda?"

"*Sam* advised that no teacher was—"

"Amanda Porter is her legal name, Todd. If she asked you to call her Bubbles the Elephant, would you? No," Charlie said.

"*The student* advised no teacher was present at the time, which is also—"

"This right here is part of the problem. It's our responsibility to reinforce the correct things. That's our job. We support what's accurate. We *correct*, Todd. And you're letting those boys do your job when it comes to helping a confused girl accept her role as a daughter of God."

It'd taken a great deal of effort for Todd to not boil over when he'd been interrupted three times, and when the principal adopted the lecturing tone. But Charlie's last statement knocked everything, including the rage, out of him.

"You cannot be condoning the behavior of these students."

"You don't need to slow your speech for me." Charlie laughed. "I don't condone the behavior of one student. But Heavenly Father gives us free agency to make gross errors in judgment. However much it may grieve my soul that—"

"Leave your dogma out of it. Whatever you personally believe, one of your students has been assaulted. Repeatedly. It's your responsibility to do something!"

"Something about *what*, exactly? You saw nothing."

"I saw a bleeding head wound!"

"Which could've happened due to anything since you didn't witness it. Right, Todd?"

"A child came to my classroom nearly catatonic at having been almost drowned by—"

"That's silly, if you think about it." Charlie looked at the ceiling and swiveled his chair. "'Almost drowned'? 'Drown' is a finite word without degrees. You can't 'almost drown' like you can't 'almost suffocate' or 'almost starve.' You either do or you don't. You drown or you don't." He turned his stare to Todd. "We're not responsible if she held her breath too long under water. Kids get hurt in gym class."

Todd was determined this encounter would be different. He may have a lot in common with Sam, but unlike him, Todd didn't care who he was talking to—he wouldn't back down.

"You're saying it's *okay* for a group of boys to torture another student?"

"No, but it's *commendable* for young men to try to lead a sister onto the path of righteousness and into her divinely ordained role. I *know* the students you're referring to. I went to school with their parents. Several of those boys serve the sacrament."

"If some dink hadn't wanted to watch a person die and intervened, those boys would've been murderers!"

"And do you know what sin is next to that of murder? Sexual impurity. Homosexuality and bestiality. Women who dress like men, men who dress like women. And you can't defuse the toxicity of it. The Lord can't look on sin with the slightest allowance."

Todd's face was burning. Desperately he wanted to tell Charlie that he was talking to such a "sexual deviant." That he'd had lunch with a man who dressed like a woman. That he'd invited this man to his home for summer barbecues and to spend time with his perfect Mormon family for a taste of the "other side."

You know what I loved about being around your wife, Charlie? Her clothes. I'd love to have five fucking minutes in your wife's closet.

"I know it's difficult for you to understand, Todd." Charlie sighed. "It's not a church; it's a culture and a way of life. But you know inside that what we have in this community is true. And you know you need it. Both you and your wife. Trust in Jesus to heal what troubles her."

Todd paused as the unexpected involvement of Julie pushed his anger to a lower level. The red he was seeing faded, and it was like being thousands of miles under the ocean. There'd never been any light to illuminate color. It was blackness.

"We all see it." The principal smiled. "We're acclimated to seeing weakness in many young women. But you've done a good job. You've taken her as far as you can without us. She follows you meekly and obediently as a helpmate should. You're in the right place and—"

"And if I told you that she was my sister?"

On the Mormon totem pole of sins, incest had to be worse than being a transvestite. But Charlie didn't bat an eye.

"Then I'd say you're even more in the right place. Two of our prophets have endorsed a brother marrying his sister. Brigham Young cited Adam and Eve's children marrying." He placed his hands on the desk and leaned across with a grin. "I *knew* you were hiding something. That *something* was weighing heavily on your heart. But, good news! Our prophets have said that children from a sibling union will be as healthy and pure—"

"You're a sick motherfucker." Todd was astounded. Did the depravity of this institution have no limit? Women were weak subordinates. Children could kill each other. A brother could fuck his sister. No problem. But be attracted to someone of the same sex? Dress outside the gender norm? Have the misfortune of being born with the wrong reproductive organs? Well, fuck you. Straight to hell.

"It's these latter days we're living in, Todd." Charlie shook his head. "The lures of Satan are strong. We're a very accepting church, and you'll come to understand that the more—"

He forgot Julie and Sam. He only remembered himself.

Thank your God for that. Because the time I forget myself is the time I'll be coming across the desk at you.

"I won't come to understand anything more about this place. Consider this my resignation. I'm done." Todd pushed back his chair and stood.

Charlie's smile melted and his lean across the desk snapped into a straight posture. "You can't be serious."

"I'm as serious about walking out as you are about not doing a damn thing to help a student being physically abused in your school."

"Are you saying that if I put an end to it, you'll stay?"

"No. I'm sick of your Mormon shit. I'm going home."

"I wish you'd open your mind to develop a testimony. You'd realize there's a bigger picture. What sexually impure individuals like Amanda do is an abomination to the Lord, but they can act how they want, dress how they want, and do disgusting things to disfigure their physical bodies. It won't make a difference," Charlie said. "In the preexistence, Amanda was a woman. That's why she was born a female. In the hereafter, she'll realize the truth along with all the other derelicts. They'll receive the opportunity to be instructed in the ways of the church and repent. Even Gentiles like you."

"Your religion is garbage. It's pollution on the minds of good people." Todd skimmed the framed academic certificates on his wall. "And I feel sorry for you, Charlie. That you, a seemingly educated person, are such a fucking moron."

In response, the principal folded his arms. "If you intend to stand by your threat of leaving, I expect you to fulfill your contract by staying until the end of the school year."

It was only a few weeks away. Todd wanted to bitch-slap him across the face and then go home to his slot machine, but during Charlie's discourse, he'd regained some consciousness of who else was hanging on the line. Sam was determined to graduate. If Todd agreed to stay, he'd be in the building if Sam needed him. He could continue to offer any protection he was able to provide.

So help me God, if it happens again, I'll skip your fat fucking ass and go to the police. If they'll do anything. They probably "know" the boys too.

"I'll stay until the end of the school year. Then I'm done." He walked toward the door.

"Will your sister-wife be staying? Or do I need to interview for two positions?"

Julie would also bear the consequences of both his resignation and the awkwardness with Charlie for the remainder of the year.

But I'll figure that out later.

"I don't own her. She'll do what she wants."

"I stand by what I said. You've done a good job with her, and she could have a place among us," Charlie said.

The *Freaks* chant played in Todd's head. How had he allowed Julie to convince him to move to this horrible state? Christ...New Orleans. Where he could dress how, when, and where he wanted. So could Sam. And if *anyone* gave him trouble, the principal would nail the responsible parties instead of defending them with noxious religious doctrine.

"Go fuck yourself. I know she'd rather let you bastards beat *her* head into a brick wall rather than be one of you."

"Before you go, that reminds me of a final point to tell you, Mr. Keegan."

Todd's hand paused on the doorknob. The only thing that stopped him from leaving was that he'd prefer a ceasefire with this man for the next few weeks.

"Something to crystallize my take on Amanda's issue. A simple concept from one of our Quorum of the Twelve: 'Better dead clean, than live unclean. Many is the faithful Latter-day Saint parent who has sent a son or daughter on a mission or otherwise out into the world with the direction, "I would rather have you come back home in a pine box with your virtue than return alive without it.""

The man returned Todd's stare with a smile. "As I said, it doesn't matter what happens in this life. Sometimes a 'pine box' and blood atonement are the only ways to absolution and salvation. In the days of Israel, they gave the death penalty for—"

Regretful that none of the principal's appendages were in the doorjamb, Todd walked out and slammed the door.

SEVENTEEN

JULIE DIDN'T IMMEDIATELY panic when Todd made it clear he intended to return to New Orleans with or without her. Maybe it was time to go back. Another step toward facing her fears and regaining her independence. She'd planned to move out on her own in safe Idaho before New Orleans, but Idaho suddenly wasn't safe anymore. She could handle this. Especially if she didn't think about it much.

In refusing to give consideration to what would happen in the next few weeks, she was able to postpone a panic attack. She emailed her own resignation, but otherwise went about her daily life, choosing to focus on making those small improvements she could wrap her head around. She ignored Todd sending off packets of teaching credentials to Louisiana school districts, filling boxes with his books and nonessentials, and taking house pictures with a realtor.

Finally, a couple of things forced Julie's head from the sand when only a week of school remained. One morning the realtor slid a white "SALE PENDING" panel on top of the "FOR SALE" sign in the yard. Its presence only nibbled at the edges of her brain, but what pushed her into disintegration was Charlie Smith noticing the sign and stopping by her classroom.

"Hi, Julie."

She looked away from the book she'd been reading behind her desk during prep period. He hadn't spoken to her even to acknowledge her resignation.

And then Charlie closed the door.

"I'd like the door open, please." It was one of the things she was working toward. She never closed her door, even while teaching. There was always an open space for screams to echo in the hall.

He moved away from the closed door. "I need to speak with you privately."

Julie stood, her pulse thudding in her ears. "Anything you have to say, I want Todd present for."

"You know he's in the middle of class."

So do you. Only not even in the middle. It's the beginning. The bell just rang. Did you wait outside my room until the last student emptied from the hallway? She tried to hide a deep breath. *Calm down, Julie.*

"Besides, you know what 'privately' means. I've wanted to talk to you for a while. I apologize it's taken me so long to find the spare time."

Julie forced the muscles in her face to stay relaxed as he walked up the aisle of desks toward her. He stopped at a front desk and hopped up on the desktop.

It was similar to how Todd liked to sit, but there was something different in Charlie's manner. Todd was casual and loose, leaning back with his frame open and confident. Charlie had a brash slant forward that, combined with his narrow stare, gave the impression of him looming above. The terrified prey animal feeling came over her. She'd only been looked at this way by one other man.

This isn't that man or that place. This is a school, and even if the door is closed, I'm safe here. She cleared her throat. *At most, he could hold me here for fifty minutes.*

"I don't have anything to say to you, Mr. Smith."

"Oh, you do. And please, call me Charlie," he said, and her mind froze. "Let's talk about that resignation letter."

He is not *that man, Julie.* Yet she eyed the stapler on her desk. She could hurl it at him and run. Or would he catch it and then lose trust in her? *Yes, it's better to keep their trust as long as possible. Todd will rescue you, if you play your cards right and draw this out before it escalates.* She tried to not think how the same strategy hadn't worked last time.

"What about it?"

"I didn't think you were serious until I saw the 'SALE PENDING' sign on your house this morning."

"You saw the sign?"

"'And it opened up my eyes; I saw the sign.'" Charlie chuckled. "Of course, I saw it. I've been driving by your house for some time."

Julie knew where Charlie lived. In order to drive by the house, he was going out of his way. And her safe haven suddenly felt violated. As if he hadn't only been driving by but had been inside. The watertight security within its walls had failed. She didn't want to go home. It wasn't home anymore. It was another prison. And who knew? Maybe he *had* been inside. The thought made her legs weak, and she had to sit.

"I don't think you want to leave, Julie." He left a slight pause for a response, but her head wasn't clear enough to formulate a complete sentence. "I know you might feel obligated to stay in that hovel of sin with your brother. You depend on him, as you should. One of our wisest leaders advised that women are given to us 'to be their head, their patriarch, and their savior; to teach, instruct, counsel, and perfect them in all things.'"

Had Sullivan been a Mormon? Her head spun.

"So, I *completely* get how you're feeling." Charlie put his hand to his chest to convey how emphatically he understood. "I admire it. Following with a submissive and gentle heart is the right thing to do. But you needn't feel compelled to stand by someone insistent on leading you in the wrong direction. Your rewards come in the next life. Did you know that?"

It seemed he was no longer willing to give her an opportunity to reply as he rambled.

Stay cool. He seems prone to lecturing. Let him vomit his garbage. The dismissal bell will ring, and Todd will come looking for you.

"With the right preparation and leadership, Julie, when your worthy husband receives you into the celestial kingdom, you won't just be reborn. You'll be a goddess! Reigning with him for time and all eternity! Don't you want that?"

This is where the lofty and inflated self-worth comes from. You don't worship God. You live with the anticipation of becoming gods and being worshipped yourselves.

Not that either she or Todd were religious. Of all the lies told about their private life, they'd never professed to be spiritual. Charlie had been informed immediately that they weren't Christian and weren't on the market. They believed in God, but not some micromanaging general who "had a hand" in *everything.*

The world was a clockwork motor which God wound and let go. There wasn't a divine being steering the rudder of your boat, sometimes crashing your vessel into the rocks for shits and giggles. An inventor of unknown origin and motivation had tightened a mainspring and stepped back to let the gears turn of their own accord. Did He even survey His handiwork? Regret it? Enjoy it? Irrelevant. There was nothing to be done, so why waste eighty-some-odd years worrying. And death?

"Heh, I'd like to *hope* we're not worm food," Todd had said to Charlie. It'd been during one of the last times he'd invited them to his home in attempts to exchange gelatin salad and rice cereal treats for two more "Christian" souls.

"You're not, Todd. You're much more than that," Charlie insisted. "You—"

"Of course, the whole 'poof you're gone' theory does counter the first law of thermodynamics, being that energy can't be created or destroyed."

"Sure, I guess."

"But energy not being able to be created also throws a hitch in the LDS grand master plan, doesn't it? Damn that bitch, science. Physics specifically." Todd tossed his plate into the garbage can like a Frisbee. "Stellar cornflake casserole though."

Remembering Todd's ability to put the kibosh on religious idiocy gave Julie the strength to break into Charlie's harangue.

"No. I'm going home."

"You are home, Julie. You haven't even heard my real offer yet."

"Offer?"

"As I said, I'm cognizant of your womanly need for a protector." Charlie drummed his fingers on the desktop, an action that made her cringe as much as what followed. "Remember when we met? I asked you out, and you declined. Well, I'm asking again. Let me take you to dinner."

It was repulsive for more reasons than she could list in her head before replying. He was under the impression that she was married. And Charlie was now married himself. With small children. He was also an absurd, pedantic cretin. Furthermore—

"You're married, and I'm married." Julie figured it couldn't do any harm to maintain this lie.

"What Todd thinks doesn't matter to me. And my wife is fully aware of my intentions. I like you, Julie. I liked you the first time I saw you. You're lost now, but with counsel from priesthood-holding brethren, you can be turned around. You're malleable and obedient. And there's time for you to fulfill your purpose." Charlie nodded, giving a big smile that caused her chills. "It's your duty to 'bring forth in the name of Israel's God—'"

"No! Get out!" Julie stood.

She regretted upsetting the house of cards as the principal sprang off the desk and took the two steps toward her. She shrank against the wall as he slammed his hands onto the desktop, making her stapler and pencils jump.

"I'm not accustomed to being refused by a weaker vassal! I won't tolerate defiance of any—"

Charlie dropped his voice and turned around as the classroom door opened.

"Well, if it isn't the girl responsible for all this recent unpleasantness." The principal adjusted his tie with one hand, leaving the other on Julie's desk as a sign that he wasn't finished. "Shouldn't you be in class, Amanda?"

Sam looked between the two of them and deciphered Julie's distress. But unlike what she expected, and what she would've done, he didn't leave to get Todd.

"Are you okay, Mrs. Keegan?"

"Young lady, I asked you a question." Charlie snapped his fingers. "Why aren't you in class?"

"This is my free period, Mr. Smith." Sam lied. He was supposed to be in gym. But while he'd returned to school, he hadn't been able to go back to gym class. Another student had happily accepted a monetary bribe to throw her voice and announce number twenty-three in the horseshoe roll call.

"Then should you be on school grounds? Why don't you go home?"

"Mrs. Keegan asked me to help her sort through papers."

"I'm helping Mrs. Keegan. Go home, Amanda."

Julie's heart sank when Sam broke the eye contact with her and shrugged. He turned to exit the room and leave her with the volatile lunatic.

"Okay, I'll pop over to Mr. Keegan's room to see if he needs any help then. I'll let him know you've got everything under control, Mr. Smith."

Charlie's flat hand curled into a fist.

"Well, since you're here..." The principal's hand relaxed, and he removed it from the desk, the plaster smile on his face. "There are other things I could be doing if you want to finish helping Mrs. Keegan."

"Important things, I'm sure," Sam said as the man walked up the aisle. "Keeping the school and *all* its students safe and whatnot."

I wish I had the balls to bait people like you and Todd.

"It takes a strong leader to keep the ship afloat." Charlie stopped in front of him. "To keep everyone's head above water, you might say. It'd be a shame if anyone were to *drown*, wouldn't it, Amanda?"

"It sure would. For many people. My mother, who works for the largest law firm in the county, she's seen cases where due to the gross negligence of an institution's leader, someone gets hurt. Sometimes it takes a single incident to capsize everything. One diminutive lawsuit. And the captain goes down with the ship."

"Depends on the proof though, doesn't it?" The snide smirk was a parry of its own accord.

"There are many factors beyond physical evidence. Petitions, affidavits... At any time, anyone could be court ordered to give a deposition. Even minors. You never know who might've seen something. Or what could be uncovered in a negligence investigation. My mother and I have discussed it. Recently. And at length."

"Have you now?" Charlie's voice didn't seem to reveal anxiety, but he advanced to the door.

"Yes, but these types of decisions are weighed carefully since they can have catastrophic consequences." Sam took a step in the principal's direction. "I'd hate to see you locked in the pilothouse when the ship goes down, Mr. Smith. The windows cracking from the water pressure. Thousands of gallons filling the room inch by inch until there's no space left. Not that water is respectful of spatial capacity. That's what drowning is, after all. An invasion by an element. I'd hate for that to happen to you. To anyone."

"So would I." Charlie stopped in the doorway. "But I'd rather go down like a real man, than finish in a pine box."

"I'll take a pine box over clinging to the steering wheel of a ship going nowhere any day."

"And that is fully able to be realized, Amanda. *Fully*."

"We'll see. In court, or otherwise."

This time, Sam allowed the principal to leave and closed the door behind him. When he turned around, Julie stared at him. Her eyes were wide with panic, and her hands shook. But though the door was shut, her claustrophobia ebbed and receded.

The young man held her gaze with the same care in which she'd held his upon finding him terrified in the locker room a few weeks prior. It was like he was on top of a cliff, and Julie was dangling above a sheer drop. What kept her from plummeting into the abyss was the look they shared. Without saying a word, he transmitted that she wasn't alone and to hold on, as he winched her onto the plateau.

After several long seconds of silence, Sam must've felt she'd found a foothold in the crag somewhere. "Are you all right, Mrs. K?"

Unfortunately, he was wrong. There were no footholds. No handholds. Julie turned her face and plunged into the chasm.

EIGHTEEN

"YOU KNOW WHAT I love about your house, Mrs. K?" Sam pressed a throw pillow to his face. "How it smells!"

Julie sat in her rocking chair across from him and gave a small smile. The confidence and progress she'd built had crumbled, but she was starting to feel better. Being free of the school building helped. And so did being around Sam, who she'd decided was almost as good as Todd. And the rocking motion was soothing too.

"It smells like lavender and—" He inhaled deeply. "—lemons."

"Thanks."

"My mom's house smells like dead mice." Sam paused. "It was my birthday a couple of days ago."

"I'm upset. I don't have memory loss," Julie replied. She and Todd had invited him over for dinner on his birthday.

"I haven't been living with my mom since we came home from DC. There was no fumigation. I left, and I've been staying alone at that motel. I can tell you now, since you can't make me go back."

"You think we would have?" Julie wasn't surprised. If Sam wasn't happy with something, he showed no fear in breaking away.

Meanwhile, I build and build. I think for sure I'm gaining ground. Then one thing happens, and I relapse. Well, I guess it's not a total relapse. I'm here.

Somewhere between the gasps for air she'd taken while crying into her hands, Sam had suggested they go to her home. It was polluted now with Charlie Smith having driven by that morning; she wasn't supposed to leave until half an hour past dismissal, and there was no Todd, but after a few minutes of gentle persuasion, she relented.

Walking home with anyone was a huge accomplishment. What could be less safe than strolling in the open with only a boy for protection? And to any creepazoid driving by, she didn't even have a male safeguard. She was walking with an androgynous young person who didn't look like a threat. Yet she'd done it. She'd had to get out of that building, and by the time Charlie could be on the prowl, Todd would be home.

Sam had seen Julie safely to her rocking chair. As he had the night she almost had the panic attack in Gettysburg, he fetched a cool washcloth and glass of water. He left a message on Todd's cell phone to not worry; she was safe at home.

Now you're revealing secrets that don't matter. We wouldn't have made you go back.

"I knew you wouldn't want to," Sam shrugged. "But as my teacher, it would've put you in a difficult position. I figured I'd save you an ethical dilemma."

"I'm not your teacher. And Todd let you have a screwdriver on your birthday. He could go to jail for that. We wouldn't have forced you to do what you didn't want." Julie stopped the rocking motion of her chair. "Being upset doesn't cause memory loss and having anxiety doesn't make me an idiot, Sam. A secret for a secret, right?"

Either he didn't care about being found out, or he really was embarrassed but had mastered the ambiguous expression. Both possibilities reminded her of Todd, and she settled more comfortably.

"I wouldn't presume that you'd trust me, Mrs. K, but if you feel you can, I'm glad to listen." He put aside the pillow and leaned into the couch, looking like he was anxious to hear, but wouldn't be hurt if she declined.

"I'm surprised Todd didn't tell you." Julie wasn't, but she was considering if she could.

"I didn't ask. It's none of my business. That's why I won't be upset if you don't feel you can. But in my experience, and I realize I only have eighteen years of it"—Sam smirked—"it helps to talk. It's hard to get over something without facing it. And sometimes, you need to face it multiple times before it becomes concrete enough to be what you even *can* get over. Until it's solid, you can try all you want, but it's like jumping an invisible fence. If that makes sense."

Once she'd emerged from that stupor in the hospital, things hadn't seemed real. And even though years had gone by, it felt more like being haunted by a dream than scarred by an event that had actually occurred. She hadn't told anyone everything that had happened. The police pieced together what they needed. And while Todd had cajoled a few additional details out of her, what she'd revealed was only so he could make sense of her various anxieties. Like the yellow dress. Or quadruple locking the doors. Or the picture of the two of them where she was wearing the yellow dress—the explanation she'd given behind that had been somewhat a lie.

Was that why she was still paralyzed? It wasn't "concrete enough to get over"? Because she'd been battling with the anxiety rather than confronting what'd transpired? Talking gave it form. Reality. Existence. A place in time and space. Keeping it locked in her head made it a mental illness. Which it wasn't. The anxiety *from* it was. It'd happened. But if no one knew, it might as well not have, and she was just some crazy woman.

You're right. How can I land something without an anchor? I've been sailing around and around for years. Julie pulled her legs into the chair. *If I want to get better, I have to land. And you're a good place to start, Sam. Better than Todd even, since there are some things I can never tell him.*

"I wore the yellow summer dress the day before it happened. And of everything that could've made the difference, everything that was at fault, the yellow dress is the most responsible."

Julie skipped the backstory of the dress, including why she'd worn it that day. And she skimmed through the receipt of the flowers and the business relationship between her and Sullivan. In telling what needed to be told, these things were important to make sense of it, but weren't worth delving into. She started in detail where it became difficult to talk about. Her nightmares began in the car, when she realized she'd forgotten her cell phone.

Goddamn it. Now I'll be late, Julie had thought as she made an illegal U-turn. *Fucking electronics. Two years ago, I didn't even have a phone. But now I have to be* constantly *connected. If I don't have my phone, it's like I forgot my shoes or to do my hair.*

She actually had forgotten to do her hair that morning. It hadn't been one of those days of feeling like being pretty. With how dolled up she'd made herself the day before, she doubted there'd be another pretty day for a long time. It was a day to wear blue jeans and sneakers with a band T-shirt in such worn shape that it barely passed the dress code. And her hair that she'd painstakingly straightened the day before? She'd scooped it into a messy ponytail and hadn't even brushed it. Most days she left the house like this, not thinking a thing of it.

"But everything became relevant." She hugged her knees to her chest in the rocking chair.

A white car had been outside her house. Unfortunately, she couldn't control curbside parking. As long as it wasn't blocking her driveway or a hydrant, any errant vehicle could make its home outside hers.

It could be a disgusting RV. Julie pulled into her driveway. *And it'll be gone when I come home.*

She jogged to the door and put her key in the lock. On turning it, the tumblers hadn't slid out of the way. The motion met clean air. The door was already unlocked.

Must've forgotten to lock it. She shrugged and pushed the door open. *Guess it's good I came home. Okay, phone, I forgive you. Now where are you?*

The house had been quiet. Nothing unordinary. Julie stood in the entryway and mentally retraced her steps. Where did she last use it? Every morning, it began the day at her side. Shower. Getting dressed. Breakfast.

That's it. Todd sent that text at three in the morning to deliberately wake me up. So, I texted him at six to return the courtesy. Even if it doesn't get him up, the first thing he'll see is a message telling him what a mother—

Julie had just walked through the doorway into the kitchen and found her cell phone. It was next to an empty bowl of cereal with a thin layer of milk crusting at the bottom, and across from the ribbed vase of pink stargazer lilies. She turned around when she heard a door open behind her.

All she could see was the empty hallway connecting the living room and kitchen. The front door wasn't visible.

She waited.

No further sound. So, she laughed.

I didn't lock it behind me. Blew open.

The phone was on the counter, the screen glowing blue. With a smile, she retrieved it and unlocked the keypad. It was a reply from Todd.

—Love you too, Cher.

Ha! She had woken him up! If he'd been awake at three in the morning, he wasn't planning on being conscious before noon. Which was why she hadn't sent him one text message. She'd sent at least twenty. Her entire message split one word at a time. His phone would fire one annoying tone after another, forcing him awake. She'd sent so many it'd filled her outbox, and she'd had to empty everything after sending the mega-message.

Serves you right. I have no idea how you teach when you party all night. I mean you—

The sound of the door closing behind her. The lock sliding. The footsteps. And when she turned to the doorway of her kitchen, there he was. She dropped the phone.

A sudden coldness hit Julie's core. Like someone had punched a syringe into her chest and pushed units of liquid nitrogen into her heart. She imagined the organ freezing, swathes of smoky frost curling from the solid rock.

He had the intimidating build of a linebacker. He was older than her, but not old enough to have lost the massive amount of muscle tone. Unlike how she'd pictured a home invader, his face had been uncovered. And there was no indication on it that he was anything other than a normal man. A normal man who stumbled into the wrong house? Sure. That was it. The houses looked similar.

Yeah, buddy. You're in the wrong house. Just go. It's all good. She struggled to lift the corners of her mouth.

But upon realizing one had accidently entered the wrong house, one wouldn't set down one's large duffel bag as if preparing to stay. One wouldn't step closer. One wouldn't smile.

"Julia." The stranger said. "I didn't think you'd be home for hours. Did you know I'd be here?"

She hadn't known what to say. Her mind was as calcified as the rest of her. He recognized her. He was there for *her*.

"You *felt* that I was waiting for you, and you rushed home." He stooped to unzip the duffel bag. "Silly girl. You've ruined your surprise by being anxious to see me. I was planning to have everything ready when you came home."

Run. Run right now. He's blocking the doorway, but turn around. Throw open the French door and run.

Before the command made its way down a half-frozen neuron to the muscles of her legs, the stranger had retrieved his object. He took a few more steps toward her and offered a golden-brown teddy bear.

"I know you like bears."

Julie hated bears. Hated stuffed animals. She'd never been that type of girl. The men she dated took her to dinner. Bought her drinks. And although it was cliché, she'd accept traditional gifts of—

Flowers. Oh, my God.

"Sullivan."

"We're way past that. Call me Sully." He pressed the bear forward. "I picked him for you. You see how he has the light-blue bow? Are you impressed that I remembered it's your favorite color?"

Julie didn't like light blue. Her favorite color was green. Even if it'd been blue, she wouldn't have told a client that. She didn't talk about herself.

You have to be smoking something. She tried to calm herself enough to think logically and devise a way to escape. She had time. *You're a nut job. But you seem like a well-meaning nut job. You're sticking a stuffed animal in my face and not a gun.*

"Don't you like him, Julia? Take the bear." Sullivan shook the bear's paw, and his smile fell.

I won't be one of those victims who fights and gets killed. I'll go with it. Gain his trust. And when the opportunity presents itself, I'll make a run for it or call for help.

Julie took the bear.

"I do like him. Thank you."

"You're excited to see me, that's it?"

"Yes."

"Hug the bear."

Julie hugged the bear, and she stroked the soft fur between its ears for good measure. But the intruder frowned.

"What are you wearing, Julia?"

"What I always wear."

"That's not true. You look awful." Sullivan examined her. "You wear things like what you wore yesterday. The yellow dress. That's how I knew it was you. Well, I knew it was *you* from the flowers; that's why I sent them. But even without you carrying them..." He reached forward as if to touch her hair, but didn't. Instead, he brought his hand back, rubbing the fingertips together, and looked to the floor. "I would've known you were the one."

When he glanced back at her, Julie saw the first unstable flash in his eyes. Though he didn't raise his voice, the cold tone shocked her.

"If you'd been dressed like that bunch of sloppy, stoned dykes, I would've wanted nothing to do with you. I would've driven away." The warmth of only being disappointed returned. "And now look at you. You're dressed like one of them. Why?"

"I wore the yellow dress yesterday, Sully. It's dirty."

"You have other dresses."

"I really don't."

"Yes. You do. You don't like wearing pants. It's not ladylike. Since you're home early, I want to take you out. But I won't be seen with you looking like that." Sullivan rubbed his eyebrows. "Go change your clothes."

Now Julie had two plans. Plan A: "Okay, I'll call work to tell them I won't be there."

Keeping her eyes on him, she bent slowly to retrieve her phone. Any sudden movements could cause him to pounce. Or shift into what she'd seen lurking behind his eyes.

"Not necessary."

"They'll worry. I can't no-call, no-show."

"Doesn't matter. You won't be returning."

A chill ran down her spine, and her hands trembled. She couldn't have grabbed the phone even if she dared.

He's going to kill me. He really is planning to do it.

"Sweetheart, don't be sad. You don't need to work anymore. I'm taking care of you and will bring you home with me." Sullivan was smiling, and he reached out his hand, but as with the last time, he withdrew it before making contact, and she noticed his left eye twitch. "But not like that. Go change your clothes."

Leave the phone. Keep cool. Plan B: "So, where are we going? There's a diner in the French quarter that has a great breakfast," Julie said. The diner was a shitty boxcar, and the food was terrible. But Todd's apartment was next door. She'd go to use the restroom, crawl out the window, and—

"No. I want to take you ice-skating."

"Ice-skating?" She lifted an eyebrow.

"I want to see you do the double-axel jump you told me about."

I'm fucked.

Julie didn't know how to *roller* skate, let alone what the hell an axel jump was. She fell over blades of grass. And she had no idea where an ice-skating rink even was in New Orleans.

"But, Julia, for the third and *final* time—" The mini-explosion happened. "I cannot take you anywhere when you look like a dirty, grungy whore! Go change your fucking clothes right now!"

She moved so quickly that she dropped the bear, although she saw him retrieve it, along with her cell phone. She would've rushed to the door had she not heard his footsteps on her heels as if he were herding her into the bedroom.

He's going to rape me and then kill me. This is where it ends, Julie, she told herself as she opened her bedroom door. *In your ugly beige bedroom. Nineteen and having done nothing with your life. They'll find you years later, hacked into pieces behind the drywall.*

But Sullivan didn't follow her into the bedroom. He stopped at the threshold. Like a light switch had gone off, he held the bear with the blue bow.

"You dropped your bear."

"Toss him on the bed," Julie drew her hand under her nose. She looked at the clothes in her closet. There really weren't other dresses.

"I can't. I don't want to hurt him. You take him."

Play along. Play the game. She cleared her throat before crossing the room and taking the bear.

"I don't want to hurt you either, Julia," Sullivan said. "If I have to correct you, I will. I brought things to do that, but I don't want to use them."

So, the black duffel bag wasn't full of stuffed animals.

Guns. Knives. Drugs. I'm going to die. Unless I can get out of here. Julie combed through her closet for something to satisfy him. Even if they went ice-skating, they wouldn't make it far enough for him to realize she could barely handle flat sneakers. *Let me out of the car. There will be people. I'll scream. I'll run. I'll—*

"Why aren't you finding anything?"

"Um…" She fumbled. Goddamn it! Why had she insisted Todd needed to stop using her house as a second junk pile? She didn't give a shit how little closet space he claimed to have. Need more room for the double wardrobe? Buy a storage unit. Or better yet, get rid of that ancient eighties shit—

"Where is everything?"

"The dry cleaner. My dresses are dry clean only, Sully. And I take them all in at once to get a volume discount." Julie prayed to the hands-off deity to please for once intervene. She heard the intruder sigh.

"You did have an awful job that paid you peanuts. I understand."

Thank God for understanding psychopaths.

"I have this denim skirt. Will it work?" Julie hoped it fit. It had to. Her only chance was leaving the house.

"I suppose, but we can stop at your dry cleaner for your normal clothes. I prefer those. I *strongly* prefer those."

"Well, I just want to make you happy."

This was a good move—it made Sullivan smile. In turn, she was infused with more confidence.

I can do this. Focus. He's easy to manipulate. She walked to the bathroom adjoining her bedroom. She cursed the architect for not putting in a window when the man didn't follow or prevent her from shutting and locking the door.

"Julia, I did a walk-through of your house to see what we'll need to bring with us." Julie heard his voice through the door as she slipped on the ill-fitting skirt. She imagined his fingers touching her things and his slimy stare rolling over each room.

Pervert.

"Why do you have those gambling machines in your garage? And there's some in your spare room. Every time I opened a door, some of those *things* were there."

"They aren't mine." She ripped a brush through her hair, anticipating that complaint. "They belong to a friend. She had to move to a smaller space due to flooding damage. I'm storing them until she moves home."

A genius lie.

"That's nice of you, but we need to have your friend get them today. I know you don't play them, but even having them in the house isn't conducive to how you should be living."

And an unexpected ray of sunshine.

"You're right. I'll send her a text message as soon as I'm finished getting ready."

"It's okay, sweetheart. I have your phone. I'll do it. You shouldn't be having friends interested in that stuff. Talking to people with such filthy habits. Now, what's your friend's name?"

Not ideal, but okay. Julie clipped a barrette in her hair. *He can text Suze. It's her day off. She'll think I'm insane, but she'll come save me.*

"Suze. Text her to bring Darnell to carry them, okay?"

There'd been no response. She heard a couple beeps as the phone keys were hit, but not enough to have sent a message. She waited, but there was only silence, which made her more nervous.

"Sully?"

No reply again.

Maybe he'd had an aneurysm. I swear to God, if he did I'll convert. To whatever deity caused the blood clot to stick in his brain and end this madness. Christianity. Judaism. Buddhism. Islam. I'll worship Ronald McDonald for fuck's sake if—

When she opened the bathroom door, hoping to see her captor sprawled lifeless on the floor, she felt his hands at her shoulders. He used so much momentum to force her into the bathroom she couldn't stumble. Her lower back hit against the sharp edge of the marble counter and her head slammed into the mirror, cracking the glass.

At this point in her story, Sam became the only person who knew what really happened. This was where she divulged only tiny details to satisfy her brother. Where she became too upset to continue and purposefully changed events. But this time, instead of relaying that her captor was in a rage demanding to know who "Darnell" was, she told the truth.

"Who the fuck is Todd? Who in the motherfucking world is Todd, Julia? Who is he?" The man was screaming and mashing the cell phone to her face. "Tell me now!"

"He's my brother. He's just my brother!"

"You lying bitch!"

He'd balled his fist and slammed his knuckles into her cheek. Once. Twice. A third time below her eye, before he regained self-control. Julie opened her eyes, the skin around the left beginning to swell. Something in the side of her jaw moved, and she coughed. But she didn't dare spit the tooth out. She held it and the blood in her mouth as he glared at her.

"Do *not* lie to me." He'd stopped yelling, but looked ready to explode. "Tell me the truth."

Julie swallowed the blood and tooth. She looked from him to the phone he held. The screen was speckled with her blood, but she could read the message:

—*Love you too, Cher.*

"I promise I'm telling the truth. He's my brother." Her voice came painful and clouded with tears. "That's how we talk to each other. I swear."

"You *never* mentioned you had a brother. In all our conversations!"

"Why would I? He's not my entire life." Julie brought her hand to her cheek, squeezing her eyes closed. She'd never been in so much pain.

"You told me your favorite color! You told me you like brown teddy bears, pink lilies, and ice-skating! And you don't like pill bugs or the smell of roses! Are you saying you *would* tell me all that fucking nonsense, but you wouldn't throw in that you have a brother who sends you text messages that say 'I love you'?" Sullivan snapped the phone shut. "Who calls you by a pet name? Your name is Julia! To everyone but me, it's Julia!"

"It's New Orleans dialect. He calls everyone cher. I call *him* cher."

"Show him to me. I want to see your lover!" The man pulled her from the counter and pushed her from the bathroom. "Go! A picture! Now!"

Julie staggered forward, clutching her head as her mind split in two directions. Where was a picture of Todd? And was there any way to recover from this? To regain his good side in the hope of an opportunity to bolt.

The only one I can think of is the one we took last week. I don't do pictures! We don't do pictures! But God, he's dressed in drag in that picture. Wait. She paused from shuffling through her side table drawer. His eyes were on her, and she heard his angry breaths.

Maybe that's it. He's used slurs. He's offended by homosexuals. And he said if I hadn't been wearing that yellow dress yesterday, he would've "driven away." Is it too late to drive him away?

Julie found the picture and handed it to him. She picked a tissue from the table to press under her eye as she watched him study the photograph.

"This is you and a woman."

"That's my brother, Todd. Can you see the resemblance?"

"Your brother is a woman? Your lover is a woman?"

"No, he's a man. He's a transvestite. He—"

"He's a faggot?" Sullivan dropped the picture to the ground, and she sensed the light switch being in the middle. Was he deciding if he should continue bothering with her? If he should bail?

Yes. You want nothing to do with me. I dress like a dyke, and Todd is whatever you imagine him to be. Just leave.

"You let *that* touch you, Julia? You let that freak touch you? Even your perfect hand?"

"We grew up together. Of course, he did."

Julie could've wept. She was ready to fall to her knees and become a nun. Sullivan stomped off down the hallway.

Thank you, sweet Jesus. And thank you, Todd. For being who you are. Your offensive, yet loveable, handsome, yet beautiful fucking bitch self. Thank—

The footsteps returned. She opened her eyes as a bottle of bleach and box of wire scouring pads fell at her feet.

"I will boil water. And you'll get in that bathtub and start scrubbing yourself from head to toe with this bleach and that water until every. Last. Motherfucking faggot germ is off you! Until you're clean!" He kicked the bleach bottle into the wall. "I want the water pink, Julia! Fucking pink!"

Nineteen

MOST OF THE information Julie said wasn't new to Todd, but hearing it from beginning to end in one horrific story was. When she'd spoken before, she hadn't *said* as much as he'd *inferred* by her behaviors and then asked closed-ended questions to confirm. It was daunting to hear not only the psychotic words of that devil, but his sister's strategies for escape and ultimate defeat.

"Every time Todd sent a text message, he'd beat me." He heard Julie's voice from the hallway outside the living room. He'd been sitting against the wall since he came home. On overhearing the conversation and her *finally* opening up, he couldn't interrupt. Or resist eavesdropping.

"And when he'd call—" Julie's words caught in her throat, but she forced them free. "Another pink bath. Afterward, he'd check my skin to ensure it was raw and hold a pink sample card from the blinds we manufactured to the water. The water had to be the right shade." Todd could hear her crying. "If there wasn't enough blood, he'd force me back in."

How many times did I call?

"He called every day. Multiple text messages, and at least one call a day."

She might've said more, but he couldn't understand her. Before she stopped speaking, her voice had sounded nearer and louder than it had an hour ago. He hoped this change indicated her moving from the rocking chair he'd first heard to wherever Sam was. If Todd had been in the room, if his presence was known, he would've sat next to Julie and held her while she cried. He was confident that if she'd relocated, Sam would fill the place he normally would, which made him feel better.

You should feel nothing but guilt though. If you hadn't sent that text message, the fucking freak would've taken her out, and she could've gotten away. If you didn't cross-dress, or if you chose to hide it. He would've been upset, but he wouldn't have tortured her. And if you hadn't called— A decent human being would feel responsible.

Yet he didn't. An ache surrounded his chest, but it was because of what happened to Julie and had nothing to do with him. He couldn't perform the mental gymnastics to make himself feel in control by taking blame. And it was a waste of time playing the "what if-if only" game. There was no rewind. No redo. The events were archived, fixed, and permanently sealed in the pockets of time. A mentally ill man had physically and sexually assaulted his sister for a week. It wasn't productive to wonder if anything could've prevented or changed it.

I did the best I could with all the awareness I had at the time. That's all I can ask of myself, or that anyone has the right to ask of me.

So, it was only for a second that he considered giving into irrational guilt. He continued to sit in the hallway and listen to his sister describe her hellish week in graphic detail until she arrived at its close. At the part that, in a way, Todd knew more than she did.

"He became too frustrated with 'correcting' me. It was taking too much time and effort." Julie's voice was stronger now. Flatter. She was near the end, or at the time she'd been past hope.

When you've given up and there isn't a purpose to further investing, how emotional can you be in losing what you don't care about anymore?

"He said, 'It's too late for you. You're too polluted for me to set you right.' And I knew he was going to do it. I was ready to die."

Todd had never been "ready to die," even when being bullied in school. He hadn't imagined his own funeral and his persecutors remorseful for their actions. It didn't matter even if they would've felt bad. He wanted vengeance in the form of frustrating their attempts to defeat him. No other option had been considered—seriously or half-heartedly.

The closest I've come to death has been that bullying. I've had it mild in comparison to both of them. Death has stayed on the other side of the street from me. I don't know what it's like to be close enough to the brink that there ceases to be meaning in trying to regain stability. Your shoelaces are already dangling over the edge. Might as well jump.

Julie had jumped a while ago. Todd thought of her sitting as he'd found her—in a kitchen chair with zip-ties securing her ankles and wrists. Her face had been swollen, but with the frequent beatings, it hadn't bruised much yet. It was a mass of puffed pillows.

"That's where he preferred to hit me," Julie had mentioned before. "He said that in his experience, it 'exacted the best results' because looking beautiful was important to a woman."

Apparently Sullivan hadn't received an acceptable outcome from beating her face beyond recognition, scrubbing her skin with boiling water, bleach, and a wire brush, and raping her repeatedly. Julie still wasn't performing to his expectations.

"He told me it was time to 'start over.' I didn't know what he meant. I just sat there. Not answering him was unacceptable though, which is why he hadn't gagged me. He said, 'You will not speak unless spoken to, but when I speak to you, you will respond.' When I made no reply to the 'start over' comment, he whipped the butt of his gun into my jaw. I barely felt it. By then, I felt nothing."

But her silence made Sullivan more certain that his efforts had been futile.

"He was so angry, he struck the other side as well. When I didn't cry out, he said, 'This is what I'm talking about. You're too far gone and can't learn. We'd be here forever. We need to go back to square one.'"

"He was convinced I was 'the one.' I have no idea why. Or where any of it came from—what I was supposed to like and dislike, the things he was adamant I'd told him. Why he latched onto this fantasy I don't know."

"There's value in trying to make sense of what happened to you. But worrying and speculating why a severely mentally ill person thinks or does what they do isn't productive." Sam spoke for the first time in more than an hour. "You'll never solve it, Ms. K. You're not at that level. You're not insane. He is."

I know she feels like she's crazy. Have I ever specifically told her she's not? Assured her that being scared, even if it's sometimes irrational, doesn't make her like him? I didn't think to. But maybe that's what she needs to hear. Good.

"He was," Julie corrected.

"Square one" wasn't just restarting *her*.

"He left the kitchen and went outside. I heard the garage door open and my car start in the driveway. Then I heard the garage door close. He kept the engine running." Julie's voice was matter-of-fact, as if she were reading stage directions from a script. "He grabbed the chair I was tied to and took me to the garage. I was glad this was how I would die. No pain."

Sullivan didn't have "the heart" to kill her with his own hands.

"He brought another chair and sat opposite me. And he said, 'Julia, I've tried to fix you, but you're unfixable. And I'd let you fall asleep out here and wait forty or fifty years until my time, but I can't live knowing you're waiting for me. So, I'll go first, and then you'll follow me, as you should. When we meet again, you'll be fresh and new. You won't need me to correct you. It's best that way.'"

Julie described how Sullivan retrieved his gun from the kitchen. He'd entered the garage and shut the door behind himself to seal the room.

"He sat in the chair, put the gun to his head, and pulled the trigger." She took a ragged breath. "Do you know what it's like to see someone shot in the head?"

"No," Sam said.

"It gets everywhere. The top of his head came off. His blood splattered across my face, and there were pieces of skull and chunks of brain in my lap. When his chin fell forward onto his chest, I could see the inside of his head; it was a ravaged meat cavern. And the blood pooled toward his forehead and dripped onto his pants. Like a tiny waterfall."

Julie had expected to die quickly, but it crept up on her.

"Dying from exhaust filling your garage isn't what it used to be. I'd recently replaced my catalytic converter, and he hadn't made the garage airtight. The gas was diluted by the space under the kitchen door and one window that had been cracked open a couple inches. I waited for what seemed like hours. My head felt like it was coming apart, and the room began to rotate and tilt. Have you ever seen a roulette wheel?"

"Not in person."

"The ball whizzing around the track is life. Cruising at top speed in a continuous length of time and moving so fast you barely notice the middle wheel. All the numbers meld together. And then the ball starts and the wheel slows. Where you'd focused on the ball before, attention is now on the individual pockets. And you just wait for it to drop into one of them. That's how dying was. The ball slowed, and time broke from a long stream into separate sections. I might've heard the squealing brakes outside, or hallucinated them because the ball dropped. The next thing I remember is waking in the hospital."

Todd knew he couldn't have been much later.

Finding you doesn't consume me like your anxieties do, but it does haunt me. And I've had my fair share of nightmares about it.

After pushing open the door, not only could he see the blood, he smelled it. That heavy, metallic stink made him nauseous. But he went in and followed the sound of the running car engine.

The police officer who'd shouted for him to stop came through the living room as Todd opened the door to the garage.

In the dim light, there were two seated figures. But barreling into a garage full of carbon monoxide might result in him also crashing. He reached around to the switch on the inside wall and yelled her name. The garage door climbed, letting in the fresh air and sunlight. When he saw Julie's head was forward and there was no movement, he threw caution aside and ran into the garage.

Todd paid no attention to the body opposite his sister. He tried to lift Julie's body, but found she was attached to the chair. He tilted it on two legs and dragged it from the garage like a dolly cart.

"Julie! Wake up!"

He'd pressed his fingertips to her neck, but hadn't felt a pulse. He barely recognized her— Her face was so swollen she could've had her eyes open, and he wouldn't have been able to tell. He smoothed her hair as he spoke to her. It didn't seem like there was anywhere else she could be touched that wouldn't cause pain if she was alive. Even the backs of her hands were red and crusted.

"Ma'am, an ambulance is on the way." The officer beside him spoke in a hurried voice. "The man is dead. Looks like a gunshot—"

"I don't care! This is my sister!"

When the man gave him a second evaluation, Todd remembered he'd gone to the bar in drag, and the officer had just realized he wasn't a woman. He would've taken this as a high compliment had he not been panicked that Julie was dead.

The other man's hands were steadier in taking her pulse. "She's alive." He brought a pocketknife from his belt and cut the zip-ties binding Julie to the chair as sirens howled in the distance. "God almighty, what happened to this poor girl?"

Todd leaned his head against the wall. *Sam is the first person to know everything. What exactly happened and how her anxiety drove her into this intense dependency on me. How we moved here, and she created this false relationship so she wouldn't feel as susceptible.*

"But I'm stationary, no matter what I do. It's not that I can't do the things I did before," Julie was saying in the opposite room. "I can't walk into my own house by myself. I can't be more than a few yards away from Todd without having a panic attack. I can't be independent and alone. I can't do anything."

She trailed off and there was silence for several seconds. He wondered if she was crying or too shattered to say more. And even an unusually mature eighteen-year-old faced with such a weighty, awkward situation didn't know how to respond.

"Today you can't. But what you can do today has no bearing on what you're capable of doing tomorrow. What you *will* do tomorrow."

Todd was struck that he wouldn't have said anything like this. When Julie lamented of her limitations, his replies were a mix of "I'm sorry" and "It will be okay." To throw out that she was broken seemed counterintuitive. No one wanted it flung in their face that they were damaged. People disparaged their circumstances and lamented to hear the other person protest and give encouragement.

That's part of the problem. We've pretended for years that you're normal. Neither of us has acknowledged how bad the situation is. We cover with lie atop lie and accommodation after accommodation. It's the elephant in the middle of the room, and we've thrown a tablecloth over it. I get pissed that my coffee mug slides off its ass, yet I keep putting the mug back on.

And the second half was more concrete than "It will be okay." Although it was the same sort of sentiment, what exactly would be okay? What Sam had said conceded the current struggle, but recognized that it was temporary; not only *could* she regain her independence, she *would*. Yes, this was more valuable than "I'm sorry" and "It will be okay." He was glad Julie had found someone who understood her and she could trust.

The next thought entered his mind aided by the silence from the room. Julie hadn't given a verbal response to Sam. Why? Was she crying again? Or was something else happening?

Could you take my place? Would I be okay with that?

Todd admitted that as much as he wanted his own life, the last few years had left an indelible impression on him. Her dependence on someone else might not be as much of a relief as it may have seemed. He would have to trust that she'd be taken care of.

I'm going down this path for nothing. We're leaving in a couple of weeks. I'm not—

"You want to get out of here, Sam," Julie said. "I want you to come with us to New Orleans."

Sam had taken the news of his only two friends leaving with resignation. He hadn't asked to go along, and Todd hadn't thought to invite him. He knew what the answer would be.

"I want to leave, but I found a doctor here. I need to get that taken care of first."

Yep.

He knew the young man would make the move without assistance. But Sam was taking a disciplined approach in resolving his identity conflict, which included getting his name change before leaving the state and seeing the sex therapist until he received the approval letter for hormone therapy.

Sam had filed the name change petition on his eighteenth birthday and was waiting for the background check in order to schedule a court date. And he was certain that he was close to being granted the letter from his therapist. He wasn't going to restart that process, though if he did, he'd be less anxious since he was now really eighteen.

"Sam, you don't technically have to wait. If you can afford to start, go now," Todd had said. Sam advised a couple weeks ago that he'd located a therapist willing to work with a transgender person.

"She won't see me without parental permission, and there's no way I'll even try to get that."

"You weren't stupid enough to give your age with the email inquiry were you? Not that she'll ask, but what's the harm in some additional use of your fake ID? You may as well get your money's worth."

"You don't think she'll ask for it?"

"Don't give her a reason to not trust you and she won't."

The therapist hadn't asked and was already talking about providing his golden ticket. Todd knew with being so close, Sam wouldn't restart.

"You'll find a better doctor in New Orleans," Julie protested.

"But I have one here, and she'll give me my letter soon. I don't want to explain from the beginning. Give the same spiel and answer the same questions."

"We're not leaving tomorrow though. The house won't close for a few more weeks. You'll have your letter by then, and you can fly back for the court date."

"I don't think Mr. K would approve."

"I don't care what he thinks." Todd imagined Julie crossing her arms. "Now you know the truth. He's my brother, and he doesn't tell me what to do." She paused. "And after you're handed your diploma, will you stop calling him that? It's strange."

Todd smirked. She'd said more than a few times how odd it was to hear him addressed in that way. Even their father hadn't gone by "Mr. Keegan."

"Hardly anyone puts stock in names even though it's *vitally* important. Not only in how a person views themselves. How you address someone is a reflection of how you feel about them and what kind of relationship you have," Sam said.

That's why I refer to my students by their last names. I care enough to tell them apart; however, we have a strictly business relationship. But I haven't called you by anything but your first name since the trip. And I invited you weeks ago to drop my title.

"I understand that you have a great deal of respect for him. It's not that I don't want you to have respect for me, but I'd prefer you not call me Mrs. or Ms. anymore. Please call me Julie, and please come with us."

"I'll consider it, Julie."

When seconds passed in silence, Todd's curiosity got the best of him. He scooted to his right and snuck a peep into the room.

As he'd predicted, they were sitting together. But while they sat closer than two friends might, they just shared a look of rapt attention. His sister's hand was resting on the couch with Sam's hand atop, his fingers curved around it. Todd smiled, and despite having overheard the majority of the conversation, for the first time he felt like an intruder.

Before he could withdraw and slide down the hall, Julie abruptly took away her hand and broke the intense gaze. Todd barely caught Sam's look of confusion as he dodged around the corner.

The couch cushion creaked as someone stood. *God damn it. I'll know you're one hundred percent when you cut this hypersensitive shit.*

"We shouldn't sit here any longer. I'll forget what you are."

"And what's that exactly?" Sam's voice was sharp and bristled.

"A student."

"Not your student, as you said yourself."

"Still currently a student."

"A student you shared deeply personal things with, that you trusted to become emotional around, that you invited to move cross-country with you, that you—"

"Yes, all of the above." Julie cut him off. "And I can't express how much it means to me." Her voice cracked. "But even if you aren't a minor, you're a student. And that's too much fire for me right now."

"Right now?"

"Yes, right now. Just..." Todd knew she was struggling with what to say because she was now aware he was listening.

Weren't you saying that you don't care what I think? False bravado at its finest. But you are making an effort to satisfy both of us.

"Just right now. Okay? Remember not wanting to put us in a difficult position? Ethical dilemmas? You understand that, Sam."

"As far as ethical dilemmas go, I'd rather be reported for the fake ID, and I'd forgo the screwdriver if I could sit with you a few more minutes."

"It wasn't a good screwdriver then. He puts in too much juice." Julie raised her voice slightly. "Speaking of my brother, I wonder where he is. He's late coming home."

Todd crawled to the front door and waited a second or two before opening, then closing it. He took his briefcase and walked with heavy footsteps back down the hallway into the living room.

He met Julie's glare easily, especially since it was coupled with flushed cheeks. "Not that it matters since we won't be staff much longer, but you missed the staff meeting. It was a wild party. They had those Danish butter cookies in the blue tin and fruit punch. I was waiting for the wet T-shirt contest to start and—"

"You're vile. We have a guest." She flipped her hand to Sam.

"I'm a guy. And our guest would enjoy a good wet T-shirt contest if certain staff members had been present."

Todd retreated to the kitchen before her head exploded.

"IT'S NOT POLITE to listen in on other people's conversations. Did you know that? Or have you inhaled so much Juicy Couture perfume that you've burned all your etiquette brain cells?"

Todd was awake at one in the morning battling the New World Order. His sister's voice in the doorway of his library startled him, and he dropped the animal cracker bucket. Thankfully, it was only half-full of quarters.

"I recall growing up with a younger and less attractive sister who'd often eavesdrop on my conversations. I'd call that overdue payback," he said as he scooped the quarters into the container. "Also, I wear Viva La Juicy perfume. There's a difference."

"A *huge* difference."

He put the bucket on the barstool beside him. Julie stood with a tight posture and her arms folded. He returned to the slot machine and hit Max Bet without responding.

She'd been seething all evening, but Todd made it impossible for her to corner him and demand to know how long he'd been listening. Sam had been there all night and was still there. After admitting to Todd that he'd been living in the motel for the past few weeks, he'd eventually been persuaded to stay with them until they moved. It was safer and more cost-effective.

They drove over to collect his bag, but when Julie made an attempt to confront him after Sam left the car, Todd exited as she began. She tried again after dinner when he was alone in his library, reading. But as soon as she opened her mouth, he called Sam's name. The young man responded and was in the room almost immediately.

"Did you need me?"

"Oh, I *apologize*." Todd had looked over the book at his red-faced sister and grinned. "I thought you'd called for *me*. But as long as you're here..."

I want you to think about what you'll do if I disapprove, Julie. Think that the reason I don't want to talk to you is that I'll criticize. If you'll fold like you did when you caught me, you need to cut the shit now.

And he loved to get under her skin. Which ignoring her was doing. Until, as he hadn't expected, she mimicked what he'd done weeks ago. She walked to the wall and pulled the slot machine plug from the outlet. The screen zapped black.

"I'm tired of games, Todd. You had no right to spy on me."

"I had no right through my ubiquitous, pervasive presence to put a crimp in your style?" He rotated the chair to face her. "No right to invade your life with an omnipresent obsession and—"

"How long were you there, how much did you hear, and what did you see?"

"There's normally a car battery involved when I'm interrogated to this extent. Don't shortchange me."

Julie sank onto a barstool and propped her elbow on the counter. She closed her eyes.

"Please give me a straight answer."

"Enough. On all three questions. Long enough, heard enough, saw enough."

"For what?"

"To find myself highly amused that you sat in that same place not more than two months ago and accused me of having a thing for the same person. That's not tables turning. It's tables on the ceiling."

All her anxiety didn't leave, but she turned her head to him. He took this to be a sign of relief that he hadn't heard the part he'd unknowingly played in her week of hell. It didn't overly matter to him that the reality be exposed. It'd neither enhance nor depreciate their relationship. And there were more important things.

"What do you think?" Julie asked.

"Does it matter what I think?"

"There's nothing wrong with your opinion meaning something to me." She swallowed. "But I'm going to make my own decisions. I haven't done that for a long time, but I'm starting with this one."

Taking ownership had been what he wanted to hear, but he kept his face blank.

"You're in a position of power, and it's unethical to have more than a platonic relationship with a student." Todd crossed the room to pull a couple of beers from the fridge. "However, you weren't his teacher. You never wanted to teach; you probably won't continue doing it, and he'll graduate in a few days. All that neutralizes the situation.

"It also helps that you're not a gross old hag who's twenty years older than him. You're only twenty-five. But—" He kept his hand on the bottle he held out to her. "He's been through enough, and he's my friend, Julie. You need to make it a high priority to not hurt him. And *you* also need to get better. In both of your best interests, I won't just transfer you to someone else."

"I'm not a fucking car you can sign over." Julie snatched the bottle and twisted off the cap.

"I'm glad to hear you say that. I'm tired of your broken-down ass sitting in my driveway. All dented and rusted. At least your tires aren't shot to hell."

"In the near future, I'm going to leave, and you'll have no one to take potshots at but yourself."

"It's good I find myself so hilarious then. Here's to you restarting your engine." Todd held up his bottle. "I do think it's wise if you lay low until we move. Then you can spend all day writing sleazy love letters to each other."

Julie averted her eyes—confirmation that despite plenty of opportunities, she was too afraid to mention the idea of Sam moving with them. Todd would have to—

"I want him to come with us." She surprised him again. "Is that all right with you?"

"Why would I care? I don't own the entire city, Julie."

"Really?"

"No, I bought it all. Lock, stock, and barrel. On my multibillion-dollar teacher salary. Of course, I don't give a shit. It'll be better for him there. It'll be better for—"

Todd stopped when she hopped off her barstool, took the three steps closer, and hugged him.

"Thank you. You're a good brother."

"My magnanimity knows no bounds." He folded his arms around her, giving a brief squeeze. "If I'd known there was someone who could give you the courage to set out on your own, and all I'd have to do to identify him is dress like a woman. Well, I would've spent a lot less time wearing pants the last few years."

"The goal of every misogynist, transvestite, or morbidly obese slob—as little time spent in pants as possible." Julie shook her head and set her empty bottle on the counter. He'd stood to retrieve another for her. "No, thank you."

Todd had expected their conversation would extend a couple of hours; however, she placed the bottle in the garbage can on her way to the door.

"I don't drink and drive." Julie winked at him. "Have a good night, cher. Don't stay up too late. Everything will be okay and the New World Order will never triumph. The power of Steven Tyler cannot be defeated. He is stronger than any mere mortal."

"Truer words have yet to be spoken." For the first time in several years, he had confidence everything would be okay. Julie was on a good path to recovery, and he'd restart where his life had broken off. He was going home.

Though it was only two in the morning, and his medicine cabinet was full of DayQuil, he didn't need to stay up any longer. Everything would be okay. Aerosmith, Julie, Sam, and himself.

Todd left the electrical plug on the carpet, set the animal cracker bucket aside, and went to bed.

TWENTY

IT WAS DIFFICULT for Julie to remember that Sam was a student. She wanted to forget. She hadn't been excited to move back to New Orleans, but now she wanted the entire stressful nightmare to just end.

Her initial inclination had been to not return to school; however, Todd and Sam had convinced her that she was more secure there than alone in the house. If she was cornered in the school building, there were people nearby to hear calls for help.

The week was slow, but it finished without further incident. On Friday afternoon she and Todd left two empty classrooms, and that night Julie put on the first dress she'd worn in years. She wanted to look nice for Sam's graduation.

"I swear to God, if you get anything on that, I'll take a crowbar to every fucking machine in that garage." Todd's dress was light green and similar to the style of the yellow summer dress.

I'm going to confront this thing and not be afraid of a piece of clothing anymore.

"There'll be such electronic carnage that nerds worldwide will wail in the streets for days. If you spill one damn thing on it. One spot of grease. You need to wear a drop cloth. I'll cut a hole in the middle, and you can wear it like a goddamn poncho."

"You're just jealous it looks better on me than you."

Todd gave her his middle finger and left without another word. She knew he was bitching because it would've been odd otherwise. He could hide his feelings from most people, but not her. When she'd asked for the dress, he hadn't shuffled away the pleased surprise fast enough.

Julie didn't feel as exposed or anxious wearing the dress as she'd anticipated. She looked in the mirror and smiled—satisfied that she could transform from a grunge ball in jeans or teacher in dress slacks to something she hadn't been in a long time: a young woman wearing a nice dress to look beautiful for someone special.

"Lovely." Todd returned, carrying his circus wagon makeup case and a few accessories.

"I said I only wanted the dress."

"You *wanted* the dress. You're *getting* the whole look. Do you think I'd allow you to pair such a gorgeous garment with sneakers or combat boots or whatever else you were thinking? Or let you tie your hair in a rat's nest? It's sacrilegious. Besides, you're going to ruin it by pouring tomato sauce down the front. It should go out in style. A twenty-one-gun salute."

Any apprehension about pushing herself with Todd's assistance vanished when she saw Sam.

Sam had been distracted all day and that he broke cleanly away from his thoughts was significant. Walking into the room was like placing a fingertip to a plasma globe—all his energy centered on Julie.

"Wow." Sam turned from the mirror he was using to straighten his tie.

"Creature from the black lagoon, wow?"

"Stunning, wow. I'm glad I have to sit on stage instead of with you since I can look at you the entire time." He smiled. "You must have a hot date afterward."

"I might."

Sam resumed adjusting his tie, but he studied her for a few more seconds as she entered his room and sat on the edge of the bed before he was again in his own head. She didn't mind though; he'd tell her what was bothering him when he was ready. Until he was prepared to talk, they were content to be in each other's company and share the silence.

I've never known someone I could sit in a room and be quiet with. Todd is always yakking, and so were my friends. And every man I dated was too busy showing off. But amusing or impressing me isn't a priority to you. You're sure of yourself, and you don't care if I like you or not. I do like you though.

Julie should've seen it coming. Since that first conversation in The Attic, there'd been many things about Sam that reminded her of Todd, which made her relax with him.

But there were also qualities that weren't like Todd and were equally appreciated. Sam didn't have her brother's cocky swagger or brash irreverence. He made her feel safe, but retained a vulnerability she could relate to. Todd was impenetrable. Sam knew what it was like to feel targeted and weak. He knew how it was to think you were going to die. However, unlike her, he had the persistence to bounce back. He inspired her, something Todd had never done. And Julie was constantly forgetting that not only was Sam a student, he was also seven years her junior and transgender.

The first time she'd forgotten those three things had been the afternoon she revealed what had happened to her.

I was so upset, and you were kind and sweet. You were letting me talk and not trying to break in and draw a parallel. And when I was crying, you held me and let me do what I needed without rushing me.

That'd been what pushed Julie past rational thought. It occurred to her that when she'd told fragments of her story before, the reaction of the other person was to promote their own agenda or try to console her. Either way was an attempt to shut her up. Being distraught, crying, sobbing made people uncomfortable. The things they'd say *sounded* nice and like they cared. But they were in a tight spot and wanted the awkwardness to stop. Maybe that's why it took so long to get over anything anymore—the world kept saying: "That's enough, calm down."

You pour out a glass of your soul, the bastards swig it right away and then expect you to put a cork in it.

But Sam had let her breathe.

When she could breathe, while the things and feelings she relayed were horrible, they took on a mellowness they never had before. Softness like a piece of paper folded and refolded until it became a swatch of worn cloth. A distance was created that made the events easier to deal with, and they even seemed possible to leave behind someday. She'd felt *almost* calm.

Time is the most valuable thing in the world, she'd thought. *You can't press pause, save it, or recover it. There's only a certain, unknown amount, and it keeps winding down. Everyone is in a rush. But you're willing to give me as much of your time as necessary. To sit here and hold me in absolute silence while your watch runs.*

She'd looked at him and expected to see a sense of urgency in his eyes. Something that said, "We good now? I've got things to do and places to be."

But there wasn't even the uneasiness, like other people. With others, you can tell they feel caught and don't know what to do or say. There's a tempest inside them. Julie pushed a piece of hair behind his ear. *You're stable, but you're also not adrift. You're anchored and invested in me and whatever I have to say. No matter how terrible it is, or how much time it takes to get it out.*

She'd been thinking this during the silence following her disclosure of being "stationary" and that she couldn't "do anything."

"Today you can't. But what you can do today has no bearing on what you're capable of doing tomorrow. What you *will* do tomorrow," Sam had said.

The atmosphere became a buzzing baseline, its tone so low that it drove away every other thought. She forgot he was a student. And how, at best, he looked like a young man barely old enough to get behind the wheel. She felt too much of a connection toward him. She didn't know what to say, so she hadn't said anything. She'd lost her mind, folded her arms around his neck, and kissed him.

Before her experience, when she'd been at her pinnacle of independence and was regularly socializing, it was still unusual for her to initiate anything. Julie was like her brother—aloof. Very "electric bug zapper," as Todd put it.

"As in, I'm the ultraviolet light, cher. *You* are coming to *me*. I'm not going anywhere."

When she reluctantly revealed to Todd that she'd been the one to kiss Sam, he'd laughed his ass off.

"Zap!" he said. She picked a book off his shelf and flung it at him.

But her brother only teased her as much as he did about anything else. He liked Sam and thought he was good for her. But he was appreciative of how she was willing to refrain until the school year ended so no unethical line could be drawn that would damage his career. He'd been right; Julie didn't want to teach anymore, so it didn't matter if anyone found a school connection between her and Sam—she was just older than him, and that happened all the time.

"But it's hard enough for me to get a job in my area since I don't give a fuck for coaching sports. I don't need a legitimate reason they can cite to not hire me."

It'll be much better once we leave. If you come with us. You have to. You can't stay and—

"My mom sent me a text this morning," Sam said and Julie met his eyes in the mirror. "First time in a couple of weeks. Since my birthday. When she didn't wish me 'Happy Birthday' as much as my birthday happened to be on a Friday night, and she was hoping I could babysit."

"What did she say?"

"That if she had time before meeting Gary she might drop by to see me."

"Where?"

From Todd's ten-minute impression of Sam's mother, he told Julie that while he didn't think Sam prone to exaggeration, she seemed harmless. But with what Sam had told her, Julie got the feeling that if there was an easy way Scarlet could make trouble, she would. Bringing to the school district's attention that Sam was living with an unmarried male teacher would be simple, and it could capsize everything.

"At graduation. I told you, she thinks I've been living with my dad. You're safe. So is Mr. K."

You'll know him twenty years and call him that. But she smiled.

"Do you think she'll come?" Sam asked.

"Do you want her to?"

"I don't know."

Sam's feelings and relationship with his mother were some of the stranger things Julie didn't understand. While he'd had the courage to leave an extremely toxic environment, he still cared for Scarlet and was bonded to the notion of her as his mother. He wanted and hoped to someday have that parental gap filled.

"That may be why I've had this attachment to teachers, even before Mr. K. He's been different, but in middle and elementary school I was desperate for their attention," he had said. "When I was in sixth grade, for Easter I wrote my teachers sappy notes and put them inside plastic eggs. In one, I said that I thought of this woman like a mother. She probably chucked it in the trash."

A disconcerting thought struck her. "Do you think of *me* like that?"

"God, no!" Sam took her hand. "That woman was old enough to be my grandmother."

Julie believed him, but it was sad that he would always be searching for something he'd never find. People didn't change, and nothing could make Scarlet love him. But Sam felt a need to protect her and to see her happy. As he'd further explained when he began giving them the whole story, she didn't have anyone to take care of her when adult things needed to be handled, like when the house flooded with sewage. She was incapable of more than hiding in her room. And Gary? Like most of her boyfriends, he was MIA when there was any inconvenience, let alone a crisis.

And maybe that's part of why you haven't agreed to move with us. Doctor and name change aside, if you leave your mother behind, you sever the possibility of a turnaround from her. She may drive ten minutes to your graduation, but she won't come see you in Louisiana. And if you're not here to do her favors, there'll be no reason for her to call you. It may not be much of a relationship, but you're afraid to abandon what little you have.

Julie thought of repeating a version of his own words—he was worth it. Even adding that *she* was worth it too. He'd be happier once Scarlet was completely flushed from his life. It was hard to advise someone they should tell their own mother to fuck off though.

"I don't know if I want you to meet her. And she might bring my brother. What will you think of me?" Sam tried to smile, but she saw the worry in his face.

"That every unmutated scrap of DNA somehow found its way to you," she answered.

"For years I've been waiting for her to tell me I was adopted. She's saving that knowledge for a special occasion. And I'm likely worrying for nothing. She won't come."

"If she does, how will you introduce me?"

"I won't introduce you. I'll give you the signal to run for your life."

"Are you prepared to let the ball drop on your situation tonight if she's there when you receive your diploma?" Julie asked.

"Why else do you think I'd signal you to run away?"

Sam's name change wasn't final yet, but the background check had come through, and he was now waiting for a court date. He'd decided that the official filing of the court document combined with more veiled threats of a lawsuit should be enough to prompt Principal Smith to announce his name correctly when he was handed his diploma. What did he have to lose?

To Julie's amazement, he'd faced the man alone. And along with his notarized petition, he brought a secret weapon that no one had been aware of—pictures of his head injury.

"You should've seen his face when I whipped those out, Julie." Sam reported. "He was in the palm of my hand and would have given me anything I wanted."

His actions helped defuse the Charlie Smith threat further. If the man could be controlled by an eighteen-year-old threatening a lawsuit, this man couldn't sneak in and abduct her. And if she needed help, Sam may not look intimidating, but he'd proven himself capable of stepping on someone's neck.

Under duress of having his career torched by a transgender student who'd have his name changed in a matter of weeks anyway, Charlie had agreed. The transcripts would stay in the birth name until the order was signed by the judge. But the name that would be read at graduation, in front of his class and his mother (if she deigned to show herself), would be "Sam Porter."

"Unless he wants his balls in a vice."

Sam really had no means or support to bring legal action against the school, although Scarlet worked for a large law firm. However, perception was reality, and Sam had made it seem like a mangled lawsuit was a genuine possibility that could only be minimized by the principal's cooperation.

But if Scarlet came, Sam would have no choice but to reveal his secret. Not that there was anything she could do now, but he'd said he wanted to tell her in his own way.

"How?" Julie had asked.

"Arriving on her doorstep with a beard would be nice."

She hadn't pressed him to describe an ideal scenario, but she knew taking his mother by surprise wasn't how he wanted it.

You want to tell her in the gentlest way possible. That'll give you the best shot of a favorable outcome.

Sam turned from the mirror. Julie was thrilled to see his face light up as she replaced his worries about Scarlet.

"I have a deal for you," he said. "I'll ask you a question, and if you give me the answer I want to hear, I'll tell you something you want to hear."

"Something I want to hear?"

"Well, I hope so."

"Okay."

Sam sat beside her and took her hands. He smoothed his thumbs over her knuckles, which gave her a cool feeling in her stomach.

"After this crazy ordeal is done, will you go out to dinner with me?"

"I didn't dress to the nines to sit through a graduation with my brother. I would've worn the usual for that."

"I don't mind the usual. As long as it's you."

"That's sweet, but if all you have to say is a cheesy line, that wasn't a fair deal." Julie failed to push past a grin.

"No, it's not." Sam raised a hand to touch her hair.

She saw an image of Sullivan putting his hand forward and then bringing it back to rub his fingers together as if he'd changed his mind.

But Sam wasn't like that man, and he possibly even understood why she flinched. Despite the slight recoil, he didn't shy from running the ends of his fingertips through a loose section of her hair.

"If you still want me to go with you to New Orleans, I will."

Julie stopped fighting the smile. She knocked the hand from her hair to hug him. She didn't think she was ready to be on her own, and she'd desperately not wanted to leave him. She was so relieved that she could hardly think of anything else for the rest of the event. She even pushed Sam's mother from her mind.

SCARLET WASN'T AT the stadium before the ceremony, or in the audience during it. She appeared as the three of them were walking through the parking lot.

Sam dropped Julie's hand as a pale, gaunt woman stepped from behind a car. Her presence overshadowed all the good feelings and relief that graduation and school were over.

"Mom, are you okay?"

The glance Todd traded with Julie confirmed that no, Scarlet hadn't looked this way at their parent-teacher conference.

Maybe she's been missing you, and she's made herself sick with worry, but was too proud—

"I'm fine. But look at *you*! What on God's green earth are you wearing? You look like a boy, Amanda!"

Sam winced, and Julie remembered his description of how it caused literal, visceral pain to be called that name. She thought of reclaiming his hand, but didn't when Todd shook his head and put his own hand on Sam's shoulder instead.

The movement caught Scarlet's eye. It was like she was seeing that Sam was accompanied for the first time, and she had to manually adjust her vision to concentrate on three people, instead of one.

"Who're your friends?"

"You've met Mr. Keegan. Don't you remember?"

"The married one you have a crush on?"

Sam's confused expression verified that the behavior was unusual.

"I never had a crush on him. I don't like men, Mom."

"Is that what she is?" Scarlet made a side gesture to Julie, and the effort threw her off balance. She leaned against the trunk of the car to stabilize herself. "One of your lesbian girlfriends?"

"Are you drunk?" Sam asked.

"I'm a good LDS woman. I don't drink. I've been feeling under the weather the past few days. But I've dragged myself from my sickbed to see you graduate. And you're parading around dressed like a boy with one of your lesbian girlfriends!"

She turned a watery glare to Sam. "How could you do this to me? In public! Can't you keep your filthy sin behind closed doors instead of prancing with your bimbo for the world to see? What if I'd brought Gary? What would Gary have said?"

"Does Gary know you're sick?" Sam started to approach her, but Todd held him in place.

"I'm not sick!" Scarlet yelled. "And for your information, Gary *doesn't* know I'm sick because—"

"How can Gary *not* know you're sick if you're *not* sick?"

"Because this explains it! Gary saw you gallivanting with your lesbian girlfriend, and he blames me! Like it's my fault you're this *thing*! That's why he hasn't returned my calls! He came by once after you left, and I haven't heard from him since. Now I know why! Good job, Amanda! You can move out, and you *still* sabotage my happiness! Are you proud of yourself? Are you—"

"Gary didn't call after he took one whiff of your sewage-filled dump and decided to not date someone who wallows in the neighborhood filth!" Sam finally came out of the daze to see past his mother's weak state. And as he mentioned it, Julie noticed that since Scarlet had appeared, a fecal musk had hung in the air.

"That's *my home* you're talking about!"

"Whatever fancy words you want to use to dress up an oversized public toilet, Mom."

"It was good enough for Gary! I was good enough for him! But then there was *you*! And there was *this*!" Scarlet glared at Julie and began to cough.

"Don't talk about her! Don't even look at her that way!" Sam's face was as red with anger as his mother's was from coughing. Again Todd squeezed his shoulder to restrain him.

Julie wasn't able to control the warm feeling in her chest at his willingness to defend her. *Thank you.*

Scarlet stopped coughing and put the back of her hand to the underside of her nose. It'd begun to bleed, but she didn't seem alarmed. "See! I'd be able to get through a cold if you were around to help me! But I have no one! And you've chased away another prospect! You're intent on—"

"Ruining your life! I know!"

"Stevie! Stevie!" she hollered into the sky as if Sam's brother were floating on a cloud.

A hobbit-looking creature rolled out of the car and approached them, his eyes glued to a handheld video game.

Stevie wore black jeans that'd previously come apart in the zipper area. A shoddy job with a glue gun had mended them together but also created rivets of rolling goo from the heated plastic. A woman's tie-dyed shirt was pulled over his massive stomach and tucked into the pants. He sported six-inch-long brown leather cuff bracelets on both arms, and a large pentagram dangled halfway at his chest. His greasy black hair was partially covered by a gray Confederate cap with two gold muskets crossed on the front. What appeared to be an attempt at growing mutton chops looked like two mice had died clinging to his face, and half their fur had rotted off.

"What is it? I'm busy." Stevie's open mouth revealed an incomplete set of yellow teeth.

"Get Momma a tissue from the car, honey face."

"I have to do everything!"

Stevie shoved the game in his pocket and punched his fist into the car frame as he waddled to the front seat. When he returned, he dropped the tissue on the trunk without handing it to her.

"Thank you, sweetie pie."

The boy retrieved the game from his pocket and leaned against the car. Julie exchanged a look of equal surprise and disgust with Todd.

"You're the sick one, Amanda!" Scarlet held the tissue to her bleeding nose. "I cannot believe a child like you came out of me! I don't know what sin I committed in the preexistence to be saddled with such a selfish daughter intent on driving me into the grave! All I have is my poor, sweet Stevie to rely on."

"That's right. Poor—" Stevie had been chewing a wad of gum. He blew a bubble and popped it with his hand. "Sweet." He blew another bubble and popped it. "Stevie." When he popped the last bubble, part of the gum stuck to his palm. Without taking his eyes from the game, he rolled his hand down his pants to curl the gum off. "All she's got. That's me."

"And someday he'll start his own life without me. I'll be left old, ugly, and alone. And it's all your fault!" she shouted at Sam. "Because you can't stand to see me happy!"

"That's not true! All I've wanted is for you to be happy!"

"You're a vindictive snake in the grass! You told me to start dating after your piece of shit father left us! You encouraged me! You helped me select profiles and get dressed up to go out! And then you blame me for doing what you told me to do and you sabotage all my relationships by being a whiny bitch and turning lesbian!"

Sam inhaled slowly to lower his temper, and again Julie thought of Sullivan. How his rage had been a light switch he seemed incapable of controlling. Part of why she felt safe with Todd was that she'd witnessed his ability to control his anger. Now she also knew that Sam would never snap on her. There was no monster lurking beneath his calm exterior.

"Mom, you were depressed," he said in a composed voice. "I wanted you to be happy, but to not stop being a mother. It's important that you do things for yourself, but I didn't want you to throw us away. That's what hurts me."

"I never threw you kids away! I slave to put food in your mouths, a roof over your heads! While your jerk-off father pays only one hundred bucks a month for each of you! And when you break it down to the hours I'm forced to spend with you, I could make more sewing shoes in China!" Scarlet yelled, though she was swaying. "Throw you away? Ridiculous!"

"Yes, you did. You sacrificed us for yourself. And not even us." Sam glowered at Stevie, who was digging in his right ear with a two-inch-long fingernail. "Me! You sacrificed me! Stevie has been the priority. He's violent, and you're abusive. Mentally, verbally, and emotionally! And I'm sick of babysitting you both! I'm tired of being pitched into a volcano!"

"You're so stupid, Amanda." Stevie snorted. "If you got in a volcano, all your skin would melt off and you'd die. What'd they teach you at high school? I'm smarter than high school."

"Fuck you, Stevie!"

"Don't talk to your baby brother that way—"

"He's not my baby brother! He's a fat slob!"

"I'm not fat," the boy responded, seeming to be focused on his game. "I'm photosensitive. It's a disability. I can't go outside to exercise. A symptom is I'm husky. And husky as in big-boned, not the dogs." He chuckled. "Stupid bitch, have to waste my time explaining everything to you."

"You're not photosensitive! You're lazy!"

"I am so. I can't be in sunlight. I'll get ninth-degree burns."

"Then what the fuck are you doing outside at six o'clock?" Sam pointed at the sun, which was well above the mountain range. "That's not a street lamp! How are you out in the sun if you're photosensitive?"

Stevie looked around, as if noticing where he was for the first time. But he just shrugged.

"I'm wearing my hat. Sun can't get through hats, you dumb whore."

"You're an idiot, Stevie. A complete moron." He put his fingertips to his temples and rubbed them in slow circles. "Mom, you need to see a doctor. You look—"

"Don't call me stupid!"

Julie moved aside when Stevie threw his video game at Sam, his face twisted with rage. Sam reacted fast enough, so instead of being struck by the Game Boy, the device shattered on the asphalt. The boy looked from his ruined toy to his mother and roared.

"Mom! Amanda broke my game! She's always breaking my stuff! She owes me a new one! She owes me! She owes me!"

"Stevie, get in the car!" Scarlet braced a hand on the trunk after recovering from another coughing fit. "We're going home, baby. Momma doesn't feel well."

"But I want—"

"Go!"

Stevie took a step closer to them and Julie again saw pieces of Sullivan. The boy's eyes were black with nothing behind them. And he spoke in a cold, even tone. He'd dropped from intense fury to subzero temperatures. Like a light switch...

"Fine," he said. "But you owe me, Amanda. A new game *and* a new TV. I don't care that Mom bought a new one, you still owe me. You think it was funny cutting the plug off? Well, everything saved from the basement that was yours, I took it. And I destroyed it. Everything. Your books. Your clothes. Your pictures. Even the ones of you and Grandma. Did you take any of those on your DC trip? No? That's too bad isn't it? They're all gone now. And the scarf she crocheted for you? The blanket? The baby shawl? I shredded them and flushed the pieces down the toilet. Gone! Gone! All gone!"

Stevie tilted his head and, with his arms raised, bellowed a cackle. Julie had watched Sam's face during the manifesto. He was so similar to Todd that she detected the flash of pain before it vanished.

"You better get in the car before too much sunlight gets on you, Stevie. You don't want ninth-degree burns," he said.

"No, I don't. I'd rather be husky." Stevie nodded in triumph. He then put two fingers to the brim of his Confederate cap and turned first to Todd and then to Julie. "Good day to you, sir and madam." He made several flicking motions toward Sam. "And fuuuuuck you, Amanda."

And the photosensitive, husky soldier marches away. Jesus Christ.

The passenger door closed. "Listen, Amanda—" Scarlet began.

"Don't call me that, Mom."

"I'll call you whatever I want, young lady!" She gasped before swallowing. "You can come too. If you take off those clothes and promise to get Stevie's toys—"

"No."

"You can't be happy with your father and his fish-finger wife. I'll forgive how horrible you've been since I don't feel well. If you behave and start watching Stevie and—"

"I'd rather sleep in a gutter! It's more sanitary!"

Scarlet sucked in a breath and wadded her blood-soaked tissue before turning to Todd. "I apologize, Mr. Keegan, for the filth and disrespect that constantly spews from my daughter's mouth." She then looked at Julie. "Even to you, I apologize. As far as lesbians go, you could do much better."

"You can't drive like this," Sam said as she stumbled alongside her car. "You need a doctor."

"And with what funds would I do that?" Scarlet opened the door and slid in the driver's seat. "Child support from my first husband? No. Financial help from my second husband? No. And why not? I don't have one, thanks to you."

Scarlet started the car and edged from the spot. Before they drove off, the passenger window rolled down and Stevie's face appeared.

"You ruin lives everywhere you go, Amanda. I missed *The Jeffersons* and *Welcome Back, Kotter* for this. Those could've been new episodes." The boy threw the car's cigarette ashtray out the window at Sam. Having been unable to spend time outside in the sun unless wearing his Confederate cap, Stevie hadn't had much practice throwing, so he missed.

The car swerved away. Once it was gone, Julie and Todd moved from being at either side of Sam to face him. Julie was sure he'd kept a strong face in front of those miserable people, and now that they were gone, he'd break down.

But even her sharp eye couldn't decipher the slightest bit of upset.

"Admit it. You thought I was exaggerating." Sam smiled. "I know it doesn't seem they could be real, but they are."

"Are you sure you're okay?"

"Yes, Mr. K. I'm used to it. I don't know what's wrong that she didn't put on the fake persona for you, but that's my mother. I've dealt with it for eighteen years. Whatever damage her behavior was going to do, it's done. I'm so numb to it that it's nothing."

Julie knew that wasn't true, and from the look on his face, her brother was aware of the lie as well; however, the three of them continued walking toward the car. And though she was trying to be careful, Julie threw caution aside and laced her arm with Sam's.

"Your mom is sick. She needs to see a doctor," Todd said as he unlocked the car.

"You heard me tell her that multiple times. She won't go." Sam squeezed Julie's hand before releasing it to open the rear door for her.

"That's why I held you back. Whatever she has, it could be contagious."

"It'd be better if she died. Better for Stevie if he had to go with my dad. Or into foster care."

Todd had paused in buckling his seat belt and looked at him from the rearview mirror. Julie also turned in her seat beside Sam. He didn't display signs of it, but there was the possibility that he could be a light switch. Beneath the empathy, there could be a darkness incapable of genuine focus on anything aside from the most primal concerns. But it was Sam, and no Mr. Hyde had taken control. There were just his normal gray eyes looking at her.

"Do you really mean that?" her brother asked.

"Yes. She's been slowly killing herself for years, and there's nothing I can do. It may as well happen sooner, rather than later. Maybe Stevie could be rehabilitated. And you see how she treats me. Why would I care what happens to her?"

But you would care. You're kidding yourself when you say you wouldn't.

Julie moved to the middle seat and leaned her head against Sam's shoulder as Todd maneuvered out of the parking lot. He was going to drive home, and then the two of them were going to dinner alone. It'd be the first time in years that Julie would be more than a mile from her brother. But Sam's fingertips were caressing her hair, and she felt secure. He was neither of the two men who'd left permanent marks on her life. He was uniquely himself, which empowered her to be as well.

If something does happen to his mother, I hope it's after we're in New Orleans. It doesn't matter what you say you'll think or feel. You'll change your mind and won't go. You need to go. Not only for me, but for yourself.

The house had been sold, the closing on the week to follow. Sam's court date was days away. He'd also received the hormone replacement approval letter from his therapist and scheduled his doctor's visit. He'd get his first prescription filled, they'd move to New Orleans after the judge signed his name change papers, and he'd never have to see his horrible family again.

Please, God, if you can take time from boogie boarding or whatever you do, keep that awful woman in one piece until we've left this place.

TWENTY-ONE

SAM SAT ALONE in his mother's hospital room, waiting for her to wake up. He didn't have to be by himself—Julie had offered to stay for the conversation or keep him company until Scarlet woke. He'd declined, saying he needed time to think. Now though, he was wishing he hadn't sent Julie away.

There wasn't much to figure out. In his backpack was the name change petition and hormone replacement letter listing his diagnosis. He'd also brought the testosterone vial and was prepared to roll his sleeve and reveal the first injection site.

I want her to know it's serious, legitimate, and already in progress. That's how I'll tell her.

He'd made this decision a couple of days ago—now was the time, and this was the best approach to take. But since no additional epiphanies had come to him, he was sorry to be alone.

No, I'm sorry to be without Julie. Even if Mr. K was here, I'd be missing her. So, I'm still screwed, and the deck is still stacked.

Sam would give Scarlet every opportunity to make the right decision. He'd present indisputable medical and legal facts and do his best to keep emotion separate. It was what it was. Medical treatment being sought to correct a condition. Not exactly a disability, but a defect. It'd be painful for her, but she'd have to face reality.

Furthering his cause was the current mood she'd been in. Sam hadn't had contact with her in the two weeks separating his graduation and her hospitalization. But now he'd spent a solid week in the hospital caring for her. Where was "poor, sweet Stevie"? He couldn't miss *All in the Family*, and he didn't "do hospitals." Where was Gary? Sam had called him, but the man hadn't returned his calls. When the chips were down, he was the only one who'd stay. And Scarlet seemed grateful. There hadn't been fights or outbursts. She hadn't picked at him or accused him of ruining her life. And perhaps coming off Sam's unquestionable selflessness would predispose her to show a glimmer of acceptance.

That's all I'm looking for. I'm not demanding you approve of everything right now. I understand it'll be an adjustment for you. I just need to know you're willing to try. If you're not, I'll walk out and never return. But if you can give me a sign that you'll recognize me as your son, I'll stay. He took a breath. *In your life, and also in Idaho to take care of you.*

That was the real reason he'd told Julie she could go home. With her beside him, he was rigging the game against Scarlet. He wanted to go with her and Mr. K to New Orleans. He'd be much less inclined to see a good reaction from his mother with Julie present. The touch of her hand or scent of her perfume might cause him to discount something important.

You're a beautiful distraction, but I can't cloud my head with you. This needs to be a clear and unbiased decision.

"You *can't* make a clear and unbiased decision, Sam," Julie had said the night before.

He wasn't sure it could be counted as a fight. Fights were what happened between him and Scarlet, or him and Stevie. And in every adolescent relationship he'd been in, the subject of a "fight" was so menial he chose to not engage. It wasn't worth his time arguing over the best kind of toaster strudel or who had the hottest boyfriend.

Was Julie's pushback and attempt to persuade him considered fighting? She'd been upset, but so was he. Couldn't she understand he didn't *want* to stay here? He wanted to be with her. He'd been thinking about telling her the big *it*. But it sounded too dramatic. She'd laugh it off, or it'd scare her. That aside, he thought his intentions were clear. He *wanted* to be with her; he just felt *obligated* to take care of Scarlet.

"She didn't take care of you. You said it yourself—she's abusive."

"But she's my mom."

"That's exactly why you can't make an impartial choice." Julie had pulled her legs onto the couch and hugged her knees. "Womb tracks."

"Womb tracks?"

"You feel like you owe her something for room and board for nine months. And that's not true. You've repaid that a thousandfold. You aren't indebted to her for squeezing you out. *You* made your life what it is."

"You don't think it's right to respect and honor your parents?" Sam asked.

"Respect and honor should be earned like with every other person on the planet—they aren't a given. Having had a working reproductive system doesn't entitle a person to lifelong reverence or worship." She sighed. "I don't blame you. The pull of womb tracks is strong."

"I may have fallen for 'womb tracks' before, but I can make an objective decision now."

"You've already shown you can't, and here's why, Sam. Put aside how horribly she's treated you and that you're a forgiving person. Reduce it to the ultimate outcome."

"The ultimate outcome?"

"Yes. This is life and time only moves in one direction." Julie unfolded her legs and shifted closer to him. "Your mother is in her fifties and in poor health. Even if she treated you like gold, she won't make it another twenty years. Anyone you could have a long-term relationship with closer to your own age could be with you for fifty years."

"You're judging someone's significance based on their potential expiration date?"

"A balanced decision would have you choosing to devote your time and energy in the most advantageous way. Even if things don't work between us, you're better off pursuing someone who'll stick around, rather than clinging to a thing halfway in the grave. And again, that's discounting her treating you like garbage. If you were unclouded by womb tracks, you'd be packing for New Orleans."

Julie made rational sense. Besides a human, what other animal species had this parental-care compulsion? Not that he knew much about zoology, but didn't the parent give its offspring the boot at a certain point? Why did society expect a child to pay unending devotion and reverence to two people who'd managed successful copulation? It wasn't anything new, the human species having been around for the last 200,000 years. And it wasn't that complicated—even a toddler could stick a peg in a hole.

But Sam couldn't evict the hope of having both his mother and Julie. It wasn't like he'd never see Julie again if he stayed. After Scarlet was on her feet, he'd move.

"You'll put your life on hold for her?"

"No," he said. "I have everything aligned and I can pursue it while I'm taking care of her."

"You'll be able to stand being called that name? Having the bullshit thrown in your face? If you come with us, you'll never have to hear yourself called that again, Sam."

That's when he arrived at the compromise to throw the ball in Scarlet's court. He couldn't abide being called Amanda any longer or being referred to as a female. He wasn't willing to handle this behavior from Scarlet while she recuperated.

I'll only stay if she shows me it won't be like that. Otherwise, I'm gone. There's every reason for you to be agreeable. I've not only been at your bedside for a week, but it's because of me that you're even alive.

Sam reclined in the plush chair and tried to shuffle Julie from his mind as Scarlet snored.

It was much easier said than done, since for the past couple of months she'd played a prominent role in most memories he had. Even before he "rescued" her from Principal Smith and heard her story. The difficulty of *not* thinking about her began after her last outburst when he declared himself worth not hiding. The way she seemed touched by what he said had intrigued him. After all, he was only a high school student—adults didn't care what he had to say.

Yes, it was partially a stroke of my vanity. But also, even if the sentiment hadn't affected you, you overlooked my age and circumstance. You saw through and into me. The only person who'd done that before you was Mr. K.

Julie had been more talkative after that. She'd engaged with him, instead of only sitting beside Mr. Keegan looking anxious and confused. There was obviously something troubling to her, but she revealed her lighter side. She shared Mr. K's dry wit and seemed just as fearless about calling people out on their shit. He'd noticed other things too.

Her smile could go from shy to one hundred watts in an instant. Her eyes were blue, but they looked almost green when she wore a certain blouse. She didn't bother spending hours fixing her hair, so it had a gnarled, untamed look to it. When she was nervous, she'd take a piece of hair at her temple and twist it around her fingertips. If someone said something interesting, she'd tilt her head to the left. And—

Sam had been listing these things in his head while Mr. Keegan lectured on Rubinomics, and he stapled in the corner. When the thought struck him, he hit the stapler too hard and it clattered to the floor.

I'm crushing on her. He'd never crushed on anyone. Ever. He didn't have time, and no one was that intriguing.

"Careful back there." Mr. K had interrupted his lecture to give him a brief smile.

And not only is she a teacher, which is stupid and immature anyway. But it's Mrs. Keegan. He's my friend. To like his wife? If there's a hell, a special spot is reserved for me in it.

Sam became sure that his name was on the mailbox outside this fire hut, since as the weeks went by he was unable to stop his thoughts about her. He was faced with coveting someone he could never have in addition to the guilt of wanting to take her from his friend.

Of course, when Julie revealed that Mr. Keegan was her brother, the shame departed. But she'd remained unobtainable by virtue of not only being a teacher, but with him being what he was.

When she is amazing, why would she even consider a relationship with an awkward-looking eighteen-year-old? She's too perfect to settle.

Sam had been torn—his heart ached for her pain, but it was wonderful to hold her and indulge in the fantasy of her being his. It was with a sense of disappointment that he'd released her. He should've been relieved that she stopped crying, but hearing her breath near his ear, feeling her arms hugging him close, lightly petting the ends of her hair with his fingertips...

Looking at you is nice too though, even when you've been crying. This is how I know I'm in over my head—people usually look awful when they cry. But you're beautiful. What would you say if I told you that? A friend could hug a friend while they were upset, but what if I took a risk and touched your cheek? Moved a little closer and wiped aside a tear— Duty had interrupted the daring plans he probably wouldn't have acted on anyway. *Stop the stupid pandering bullshit, Sam. She needs you to think about* her. *Not about being with her.*

He tucked away his affection and reengaged with her feelings of imprisonment and stagnation he could relate to. He said what he wished someone had said to him: "Today you can't. But what you can do today has no bearing on what you're capable of doing tomorrow. What you *will* do tomorrow."

Acknowledgement of her struggle, but a genuine belief that she'd surmount the challenge. Perhaps this was what she'd been needing and waiting to hear. He saw a sort of changeover in her eyes. They'd been weighted with sadness, but the ropes had been cut. A dozen sandbags remained on the ground while a balloon rose into the sky. Julie had then bulldozed the structure on which he'd placed her and brought herself to his level by kissing him.

It was the best moment he'd ever had, though it sounded cheesy and stupid to think so.

I know I'm only eighteen, and it's early to call a moment "the best," but since when did anything ever unexpectedly fall into place for me? Good things have happened to me, including meeting her and Mr. K, but when has something I've wanted and had no way to obtain just appeared? Without me having to work for it. I can't think of a single thing.

Even if Julie had pulled away for a few days, he understood why. She hadn't changed her mind, and the kiss hadn't been an impulse she regretted. There was an attentive, warm way she looked at him, and when they were at home, she'd sometimes take his hand and give it a soft squeeze. So, it was okay, even if it made the days leading to graduation stretch.

Everything had to end though. School, the tedious sessions with his therapist, the wait for whoever to verify he wasn't a sex offender so he could change his name. To be honest, he'd been wavering about moving because of his mother before he knew she was sick. What if the basement flooded with sewage again? Or something happened to Stevie? If he was thousands of miles away, he couldn't pick up the pieces. She didn't treat him well or care about him, but he'd felt responsible for Scarlet. Until she had made that scene after his graduation. Then any reluctance he'd had to leave Idaho ended.

Between then and receiving the text message from Stevie, it'd been a pleasant few days without worry. Even his mother's health. She had "poor, sweet Stevie," right? She'd made Sam so angry that he let her condition roll and diverted his energy elsewhere.

He'd been thinking about Julie and saying "the big *it*" when the message came through. He was alone with her in the living room, as Mr. K had developed a pattern of disappearing. Usually he'd hole up in his library for hours to read, like he no longer wanted to be around Sam.

"No, he's tired of me," Julie had said. "He's glad to be rid of me."

"I'm sure that's not true."

"It is. I'm fine with it. He should be able to be alone and do what he wants. I have a new keeper. He's free."

"I'm not your keeper." Though her fragility and being needed were things Sam didn't dislike, he wasn't enamored of being anyone's "keeper." He was glad he made her feel comfortable, but he didn't want to own her, as that word implied. "You're your own keeper."

"It's getting better, but I prefer to have you around." She shrugged.

Sam supposed he could handle the attachment, as he preferred to have her around as well. That might also be why Mr. Keegan was suddenly making himself scarce—he knew he was no longer favored as he once was. Sam had felt guilty placing him aside, until he thought about what Mr. K would say were he to apologize for prioritizing Julie.

"I'd choose David McCullough over either of you any day. And when we're in New Orleans, the bars and nightclubs will drop your ranking further. I prefer a night on the town in my pink jacket to the pair of you. But since that's not possible in this..." He might've lowered his book for a second. "I guess God-saken place? Whatever you want to call this Puritan hole, I'm happier in my library than chaperoning you. That's not my job."

As long as everyone was content, which Sam definitely was. Julie had been lying on her side over his lap with her head on the couch's arm. He was curling his fingertips around her hair that'd recovered from the flat iron treatment. He'd been taken aback by how amazing she looked at his graduation. He had also been acutely aware of how pathetic he was in comparison, though that wasn't why he was glad her hair was thick and wild again, and that she was wearing her customary clothes.

As nice as she'd dressed, he missed the real her. Mr. K could be equally himself in a cocktail dress or a shirt and tie, but Julie was like most people. She didn't thrive when juggling two faces. She was herself when she conceded to what came naturally to her—wearing faded jeans and vintage band T-shirts. Throwing her hair in a messy ponytail so it wouldn't get in the way while she fixed machines in the garage. That was the authentic her, and he admired how she was displaying the courage to be herself.

He was thinking of interrupting what she was watching on TV, or if she was asleep, waking her. He'd say how he'd liked the light-green dress, but the real Julie was better. He didn't need her to be at her revised best to feel the same about her, and he was glad to have her back.

I could say "the big it." I could tell you that I love you. But you'd think I'm crazy. You might say, "You're eighteen. You don't know what love is." I guess that could be true. I've never "loved" anyone like this before. It could be something else.

I could be better off saying it in a less committed way. "I'm falling in love with you." But that's a stupid teenager thing to say. You'd definitely laugh at that. It'd be nice to get the idea in the open to see how you react. I should have the guts to admit it and deal with the consequences, whatever they might be. I've faced worse. Even though it felt like he hadn't. *Fine, we'll leave it to fate. If she's watching TV, I'll tell her. If she's asleep, I'll think more.*

"Julie?" He straightened his posture to see her face. "Are you—"

His cell phone buzzed.

Son of a bitch.

Julie turned her head to him. She looked drowsy and could've been asleep or awake.

It didn't buzz loud enough to wake her. The way she's lying though... Whatever. Goddamn it.

Sam shifted his position to dig the phone from his pocket. When he brought it out and the screen alerted him to a text from Stevie, he felt like the knob had been turned on a gas stove. Click, click, click. He prepared for the flames to rise as he opened the message.

—Mom won't move.

This could mean anything. Maybe Scarlet wouldn't move from his chair or leave the television. Sam's reply indicated he needed more information.

—Stayd home frm work. Now won't move. Poked with stick. Nadda.

The red flag was more that Scarlet hadn't gone to work, since he couldn't remember her ever having taken a sick day. He called Stevie. There was no answer.

"Who is it?" Julie yawned.

"My brother." Sam called again, but the phone kept ringing.

"Is something wrong?"

"I don't know." He tried to call a third time. Again there was no answer, but when he lowered the phone, a message came through.

—Stop caling. I dont do cals.

You fucking idiot. Stevie was convinced that cell phones were a conspiracy to give people brain cancer from radio waves, so he refused to put one to his head. Julie sat up as he dashed a message.

—Yeh. Brething. Just wont move. What to do.

"Call 9-1-1," Sam said aloud as he texted it. "You stupid jackass."

"Is your mom okay?" She pressed his arm.

"I don't know. He says she's not moving, but she's breathing."

He stood and turned on the light. Julie winced from the sudden brightness, and a pang struck him when their eyes met. "The big it" would have to wait.

Another text came in.

—Dont do cals.

"Well, you can't text an ambulance, dipshit!"

Sam stepped in. He paced the room while he called the paramedics and gave his mother's address. No, unfortunately he only had the information his brother gave him. His brother has a phobia about using phones; that's why he didn't call himself.

"Would you mind holding?" Sam took the phone from his ear and looked at the screen.

—Dont seem brething. What to do.

The operator he was speaking with directed him to ask Stevie if he knew CPR.

"This is ridiculous," Julie said as Sam texted the question to his brother.

—Gros. Germs.

"Ma'am, he doesn't know CPR," he relayed to the operator, who advised there wasn't more to do than wait for the ambulance. He passed this information to Stevie via text after ending the call. There was nothing further he could do either since he wasn't on the scene.

"I'll sound like an ass, but I'll say it anyway." Mr. Keegan now stood in the doorway, having been dragged out of his library by Julie. "Whatever has made her sick stands an exceptional chance of originating in that house. I'll drive you if you want, but I think you should wait to see where they transport her. Then we'll go to the hospital."

Who knew what Scarlet had, but with the state of that house and the cesspool basement it could be a number of things. He took the advice and waited for Stevie's next message, which came ten minutes later.

—Taking to hospitl. Say I shood go to. What to do.

Sam replied that his brother should go.

—Shows.

He answered that hospitals had televisions.

—*Germs.*

"You waded in shit for a week! Germs?" Sam texted Stevie that he should call their father.

As expected:

—*No cabl. Shows.*

"Don't bother with him anymore." Mr. K took his keys from the table by the door. "Let's go. If they're telling him he needs to leave, it must be bad."

It was bad.

"You know who gets typhoid fever? People in Sub-Saharan Africa." Sam had sunk into a hospital waiting room chair beside Julie. He put his hand to his forehead and closed his eyes. "Or people who lived a hundred years ago."

"Not true. Worldwide it's a common disease." Mr. Keegan closed his book and crossed his right leg over his left.

"*World*wide. In developed countries with sanitation this shouldn't happen," he said. "And if it does, it doesn't get to this extent! You go to the doctor! You get the antibiotics! You don't lie in your own waste until your intestines explode!"

The doctors told him Scarlet had been near to death. And yes, besides it being relatively uncommon in the United States, the disease was simple to treat and wasn't lethal. Unless, as in his mother's case, treatment wasn't sought. Then the serious complications leading to death piled on. The dehydration, abscesses, delirium, hemorrhaging. And septicemia caused by the intestinal perforation. Scarlet had to go straight into surgery for part of her bowel to be removed and to drain the hemorrhages. She'd been lucky to survive, but would need to recover in the hospital for a couple of weeks. Afterwards, she'd need care at home for a while.

That'd been when Sam told Julie he couldn't leave his mother. He'd taken care of everything and been at her bedside for a week. He handled the doctors, the paperwork, and took control of managing her care. He also kept things in motion at home—bills were paid, Stevie was staying with their father (even though he didn't have cable), and the hazmat crew came again, since Scarlet's basement had reflooded.

So, when Scarlet regained consciousness after surgery, she was only confronted with the task of getting well. Not thanks to Gary or "poor, sweet Stevie." She positively *had to* recognize that it was Sam to thank, and not only start treating him better, but accept him as her son. Hadn't he proven his love and loyalty? Granted, eighteen years hadn't shown it, but this event would. He shouldn't have to feel like he needed to earn her love, but that was the impression he always had. Hadn't he accomplished that now?

Julie was too emotionally involved to think objectively. She talked about "womb tracks" and "investing advantageously." But were it anyone else, would she have the same opinion? If *she* wasn't personally affected by the outcome, would she have taken the side she had? He wasn't sure. But there was one person he trusted to rise above partiality, whoever the person was. If Sam was full of shit, he wanted to know. And if Julie was, then Mr. Keegan could talk to her.

He'd explained everything to his friend. Didn't he think it was possible Scarlet could turn around? That when she realized what he'd done for her, she could change? He'd come to New Orleans eventually, but he'd see his mother recovered first, *and* he'd have gained her acceptance. How did this not make sense?

"You're expecting a lot from someone who doesn't deserve the benefit of the doubt," Mr. K had said.

"It's how a decent person would act."

"Says who?"

"Well, it's what I would do. It's what you would do. It's what most people would do, isn't it? Someone takes care of you, you feel grateful for it, and you're more disposed to accepting other things."

"Your mother isn't most people. You're in your own head too much, Sam. You preemptively give people credit for something *you* would do. But she's not you."

"You're saying I should go with you."

"I'm saying you're an adult person, and you're free to make your own decisions." Mr. Keegan shrugged. "If you choose to waste your time in a toxic relationship hoping things will change, that's your prerogative. Even if it's stupid."

"You don't think I should give her a chance?"

"Go ahead. I've never minded being proven right."

That's where things sat. Sam would give Scarlet one opportunity to show that she was willing to put aside her selfishness. He'd tell her he was transgendered, had started hormone replacement therapy, and the court date to change his name was next week. If she gave a hint of anything positive, he'd stay. If she shut him down, he was finished. And now she was waking up.

Sam straightened in his chair when Scarlet opened her eyes. She was groggy and didn't say anything as she fumbled for the bedside button to raise the mattress. She blinked a couple times before focusing on him.

"How are you feeling, Mom?"

"You're still here," she said. Her voice was monotone, and he couldn't tell if she was happy to see him or not.

"I haven't left."

"Did Stevie come by?"

"He doesn't do hospitals, remember?"

"Did Gary call?"

"No."

"I feel like crap." Scarlet leaned into her pillow.

"I'm sorry to hear that. Can I get you anything? Do you need your nurse? Are you in pain?"

"I don't want any more medication. I'm tired of feeling bubbleheaded. I may be miserable, but this is the first time I've been able to think clearly in days."

Which bodes well for me.

"Mom, do you feel up to discussing something important?" Sam tried to not rattle the documents he'd pulled from his backpack.

"You sound like you're getting a cold," she said.

The comment made him happy for two reasons. First, wasn't this a sign that she *did* care and had changed? She hadn't given a shit when he'd been prostrate with pneumonia, but now she was noting how he sounded hoarse. Second, his voice being thicker had nothing to do with catching a cold.

But then she added:

"Should you be around me if you're getting sick?"

"I'm not getting sick. I feel great. That's what I need to talk about."

"You need to tell me how well you're feeling? I've been delirious for days. I go through major surgery. I almost *die*. And you want to brag about how awesome you feel? Go ahead, Amanda." She crossed her arms. "Tell me how your girlfriend calls and texts you all day, but I haven't spoken to Gary in weeks. Rub that in while you're at it."

I should leave right now. He took a breath. *No, I'm going to stick by what I committed to do.*

"Mom, I'm not a lesbian."

"Ha, I knew you weren't." Scarlet's glare turned to a triumphant smile. "I don't know why you go to such great lengths for attention. I've never understood teenage 'phases.' You should be like Stevie. He is who he is. Even *you* weren't able to change him."

It was probably best to overlook all that as well.

"I'm straight." Sam swallowed. "But I'm a straight man. I'm not a woman."

"I changed your diapers, Amanda. I know what you are."

"You know what I look like on the outside, but no one knows me on the inside. I don't match. I've always felt like a boy, ever since I can remember."

"A boy who dated the quarterback and loved wearing makeup and pretty clothes." Scarlet rolled her eyes. "Since you're not getting enough attention from being a lesbian, you've invented something even more dramatic and stupid. Just so everyone will focus on you?" She held up her hands and wiggled her fingers. "Look at me! Look at me! That's all it is with you."

"I don't want attention. That's not why I'm doing this."

"Doing what? You're waltzing around in men's clothes and creating drama." She laughed again. "What will you do? Get a sex change like one of the freaks on Oprah?"

"That's exactly what I'm going to do!"

"Do it then! I dare you!"

"You *dare* me? Are you joking?"

"That's when I'll believe it. You can't 'change your mind,' like you can about being a lesbian. You can't get a sex change and then when you stop being the center of attention decide you're not a man and now you're a gopher. Go do it." Scarlet grinned.

Sam stood and took the two steps to her bed. He dropped the documents in her lap.

He watched her start to read through the papers. It was his hormone replacement letter first, and she read parts aloud.

"'Sam is an eighteen-year-old female-to-male transsexual. I've conducted an initial evaluation and also provided behavioral psychotherapy.' What the hell is this? Who is 'Sam'?" Scarlet lowered the paper.

He said nothing, but sat.

"'My evaluation of Sam Porter concludes that he has a history of gender identity disorder (302.85) starting from an early age. Sam also shows symptoms of posttraumatic stress disorder (309.81) from severe physical and emotional peer abuse. Sam was the victim of peer hate crimes that began after he came out in public as a male.' If this is supposedly you, you've never been involved in a hate crime!"

"When would you have noticed? What would you have said if I'd told you what they did to me? If I had shown you? I'll tell you what you would've said: 'It always has to be about you. You're ruining my life.' There wasn't purpose in telling you. You wouldn't have helped me."

"'I'm impressed with Sam's dedication to his gender transition, in spite of the persecution he has had to endure for individuation. It is my professional opinion that Sam meets the eligibility criteria for hormone therapy. He has shown a stable sense of mental health and well-being with steps I've witnessed him take toward gender transition.' You're not well, Amanda. 'Stable sense of mental health'?"

"You're an excellent judge, Mom. Much better than the certified sex therapist."

"What does this even mean?" Scarlet waved the paper.

Sam picked up the little cardboard box that contained his testosterone vial, and held it between two fingers. "I take this every ten days, and in a few months what people see when they look at me will be the same way I really am. That's why I sound like I'm getting a cold."

"You're shooting up drugs?"

"I'm taking prescribed hormones to correct a medical condition."

"This isn't a medical condition. This is bullshit. I know my child. What other garbage do you have?" She put the letter aside and looked at the other document. "'Order Changing Name.' You're changing your name? That's cute, Amanda. You know I can verify the legitimacy of this?"

"Go ahead. My court date is next week. Show up. I *dare* you."

"And what would the judge think about what your mother has to say?"

"He'd think I'm an adult, and what you think is irrelevant," he said. "I expect you'd sit behind the bar looking miserable, and he won't ask you. Why would he? I'm eighteen, and I have a medical diagnosis. I don't need your permission, and I'll do what I damn well want."

"Language!" Scarlet turned to the paper and read in silence before chuckling. "Why Sam?"

"For Grandma."

"All the names in the world, and you'd choose to honor that bitch? That's how I know you're doing this to get under my skin."

"That's the reason I do anything. It's my only motivation. The entire purpose to my life."

"To ruin mine? I honestly think it is. I deserve—"

"It isn't about deserving," Sam cut her off. "And it's even aside from me going through transition. It's how you've treated me for eighteen fucking years. It's taking ownership over the decision you made to have children. You made that choice and—"

"No, *you* made that choice. In the preexistence. You chose to be part of this family, Amanda. As usual, you're blaming me for things that are your own fault."

"Don't spout your Mormon ideological shit at me. You opted to have children when you should've kept your fucking legs closed because you can't even handle your own problems."

"Watch your language! I may not be the best mother; I should've pushed you and Stevie to go to church. But I know the church is true, and it's part of the plan of salvation to get married and raise children. It's not my fault your jackass father left us and—"

"Unfortunately, shit happened to you. That's life. But it doesn't change the fact that you brought children into this world who needed a mother, no matter how fucked her life was at any given moment. It's what *we* deserve, not you. That's why you're a poor excuse for a parent, and for a person." Sam stood and approached her bed. He retrieved the papers she'd discarded. "But you're right—*this* is about me. I'm doing what I need and putting me first. And there's nothing you can do. You can accept it, and I will be a part of your life. Or you can reject me. I'll walk out that door and never come back."

"No, you won't. I know you. And you'll be around when I need you. That's why you're here. You always come crawling, Amanda."

"Don't call me that. Ever again. My name is Sam, and I'm not your daughter. I'm your son."

Scarlet was silent a few seconds. She shifted her eyes, which gave him hope that she might be considering her next move. She may be taking into account the documents and everything he'd said—weighing these things against his actions over the past week and eighteen years. If not those, then perhaps she'd temper her response due to her need for care.

That's all I'm asking. For once, give me what I need. Please make me and my feelings a priority.

Her eyes snapped back to his. But they weren't warm—they were hollow, like Stevie's sometimes were.

"I will call you what *I* named you. I'm your mother and I know what you are. Even if you're intent on ruining my life, you are my daughter. Your name is Amanda. And I will never call you anything else, or see you as anything else no matter how much you mutilate yourself."

Though Sam had had a veneer of hope that it could be different, he'd expected this reaction.

When he turned from her bed and went to his chair in silence, he caught the smile on her face. She thought he'd sit back, they'd flip on the television, and life would resume. She thought she'd won. But a fork had been planted in the road, and he was splitting off for good.

He placed his papers and vial inside his backpack. While Scarlet's smile left, she only raised her eyebrow.

"You will never accept me for the man I am?"

"You're not a man. You're a mentally confused girl, *Amanda*."

"Then you can rot in this bed."

Sam left the room and shut the door.

In the hallway, some of the hurt reached the surface, and his chest tightened. He wasn't weakening or retreating. But even after eighteen years of abuse, when it sunk in that Scarlet would only have him as someone he wasn't, and she wasn't willing to even try to accept him...

I could be a good son if she'd let me. Sam cleared his throat. He was alone in the hospital elevator, descending to the lobby. He could let out a tear or two if he wanted; a couple would be more than reasonable. *But no, I won't think about this. There's an entire world of people who* will *love and accept me. I already have supporters.*

He unzipped the pocket of his backpack to retrieve his cell phone as the elevator doors opened.

I can't get over who I am. But while it might be hard, I will *get over you. I'm worth it. And you're just not. You can wallow miserable and alone in your shit hole. Not only do I have myself, who I know I can rely on, but I have Mr. Keegan. And I have—*

"Julie." Sam closed the phone.

There she was. Sitting on a bench in the lobby. Alone. How long had she been there? And how terrified must she have been, by herself on the bench with strangers walking in and out with him beyond earshot and her brother miles away? She'd explained how her anxiety could spiral. She looked pale and scared, her eyes ticking from person to person, and her hands curled tight under the bench.

Julie was so tense that she appeared startled when he approached her. Upon recognizing him, he saw the fear melt from her face, and she was able to declaw from the bench.

"Were you afraid to go home by yourself?" Sam asked. That week, they'd been working on her dropping him off at the hospital and then driving home alone.

"I was more scared to stay, but I did anyway."

"Why?"

"What did you expect me to do? Sit at home and wait? And wonder? If you can take a chance, I can too." Julie's smile faded. "I guess some don't pay off though?"

"They do. Things get better, just not always on their own and you have to *do* something. Even if it hurts at first."

Sam took his cell phone from his pocket as it buzzed with a text message. He looked at Julie before opening the phone.

"Please, don't go back there," she said.

He had no intention to. He considered not even opening the phone and tossing it in the garbage can. But there was the chance it wasn't Scarlet. In fact, he doubted it would be. She had too much pride to call him this soon. It could be anyone. He opened the phone.

—Mom text you leaf. Want come to hospitl. Dont do hospitl. Shows. Germs. What to do.

"Go. Fuck. Yourself," Sam said aloud as he tapped in the message. He sent it and smiled at Julie. "Let's go home and pack."

Before the phone could buzz again, Sam turned it off. He pushed it into the pocket of his jeans with his thumb and took Julie's hand. They exited the hospital together, and neither of them looked back.

About the Author

James Stryker is a Central Pennsylvania author who enjoys writing speculative and literary fiction. Themes in his work focus toward diversity in the LGBTQ spectrum and the voice of underrepresented or misunderstood viewpoints. His novel, *Boy: A Journey*, was released in 2016.

James shares a residence with a pack of pugs, who continue to disagree about the ratio of treats to writing. Despite his day job and writing projects, James is never too busy to connect with readers or other writers. He welcomes you to check out his website, follow him on social media, or drop a line to his email

Facebook: www.facebook.com/JamesScottStryker
Twitter: @JStryker21
Website: www.jamesstryker.com/
Email: jstryker21@gmail.com

ALSO BY JAMES STRYKER

Boy: A Journey

Recently Released from James Stryker

Boy: A Journey

Excerpt

LUKE DUCKED HIS chin into the jacket's high collar. "It's freezing, Tom. Fucking freezing. Don't you want to go inside?"

"Not really. I may not be this cold again until I'm dead."

"Most people would prefer it that way."

"I'm not most people."

Tom had doubted Beau would come, so he hadn't been too disappointed that Luke arrived alone. He hoped the boy had remembered the sonogram picture though. Maybe he had it in the book under his jacket. But since it was just the two of them, Tom wasn't inclined to relocate, despite Luke shivering like a madman.

Sometimes it's good to be uncomfortable. You have the rest of your life ahead of you, and I don't feel I should have to accommodate anyone. Not even you.

"Zip your jacket, spunky. Give it a few minutes, and you'll be fine."

"I *am* fine." Luke gritted his teeth and fidgeted on the cold metal of the chair.

"Put more conviction into your acting. Make me believe you're not freezing your ass off."

"That's hard to do when I'm freezing my ass off."

"Which may be why The Great White Way didn't work for you. Not that it wasn't always a one-in-a-million shot, but if you can't even pretend you're not cold for fifteen seconds, how can you make me believe that you could be anything else?"

Luke huddled around his coffee cup like a campfire until his body stopped shaking. Except his shoulders, which made Tom smile.

Jay was always cold in the shoulders too. You're so like him. You have his eyes, his hair, his posture. I could squint and swear you're him. It stunned me for a second when I stood face-to-face with you yesterday.

He deliberated telling Luke this, but decided not to. The boy had likely been reminded a hundred times during the viewing how much he resembled his father. And he'd hear the same thing a hundred more times today.

"Tell me about New York?" Tom offered, curious as to what lies Luke might create.

"Actually, I have questions I was hoping you could answer." Luke met his eyes.

"With pleasure."

He should've anticipated that Luke would have questions. Whatever Jay had told him, there must not have been time to address any confusion. And depending on what he wanted to know, Tom knew he was the only resource for certain details. As much as Jackie was aware, there were gaps that could be filled by Tom alone—he'd been there.

It was moderately entertaining when Luke unzipped his jacket and revealed the red plaid book. The boy pushed it forward on the table.

"This fucking thing?" Tom ran his hand across the cover—the motley Scottish terrier playing bagpipes under a gold-emblazoned year. "It's an ugly son of a bitch, isn't it?

"Yes," Luke replied.

Tom opened the book and flipped through the pages. As he turned them, he let the forgotten memories return. He hadn't seen this book in years. A copy was at home, alongside three other editions, but he hadn't taken it down since putting it on the shelf when he moved into the high-rise. And it'd been even longer since he'd gone through the photos. It seemed an old-man thing to do. Yet here he was at the end of his life, sifting through his youth and enjoying it more than he might've had he not been on cancer medication spiked with THC.

"There's me. Orchestra." Tom pointed to a photo of two dozen teenagers crowded onto three rows of bleachers. He was in the last row, the walnut-colored scroll of an instrument visible behind the shoulder in front of him. "I was first chair in violin my junior and senior year."

"Were you?" Luke leaned forward, moving his chair closer.

Tom nodded, continuing to comb through the pages. "It was good, but not great. I prefer the piano. I auditioned for both programs at Julliard to double my chances. But thank God I made it with piano. I don't think I would've been happy with anything else." He wondered if this might catch the boy's attention. Luke would be a special kind of idiot to not realize that Tom's connections in the music world might benefit him.

If you ask me, I'll do it. I can't guarantee you a place there, or wherever you want to go, but I can ensure you get a callback. Jay wanted you to make it of your own merit; but I don't have a problem giving you a leg up.

But that Luke didn't ask pleased Tom, and he knew would've satisfied Jay as well. Maybe he didn't want the help; he wanted to make it himself. It was an attitude Tom respected.

"Is my dad anywhere else in that book?"

"No." Tom pinched several sports pages together and passed over them. "Jay didn't do extracurriculars his senior year."

"What was he like?"

"What do you mean?"

"Well, what type of person was he?"

Tom looked up from the book as he was about to flip by the sophomore photos and into his own year. Luke fiddled with a red class ring that was as recognizable as the ugly yearbook.

No, he wouldn't have told you how it was for him. If he'd had an infinite amount of time, it was still a sensitive subject. But it's touching that you intuited how hard it was for him and want to know. Perhaps you're less selfish than everyone thinks.

"Before or after?" Tom returned to paging through faces. He wondered how many of his classmates were dead.

"Before or after what?"

"Before or after he came out. He was a different person before the spring of 2004, when he decided everyone could go fuck themselves, and he was going to concentrate on escaping alive. To most people, it was a complete changeover when he came clean and stopped being as the person everyone else thought he was." Tom located his junior photo and laughed again. "Was I ever this young?" He brought the book close to his face, tilting it to the side. "Or this awkward?"

"What do you mean he 'came out'? 'Came clean'?"

Tom's gut seized sharply as he lowered the yearbook. His stomach had that tight feeling it did when he'd been vomiting for hours.

For the love of God, please tell me you didn't, Jay. Or rather that you did—that you told him.

"Was my father gay? Is that what this is?"

"Not that I've been aware." Tom swiped through the first half of the senior class of 2005. When he reached the correct page, he read the elegantly scripted names in his head. He looked at each face on both pages. He turned the page and analyzed the faces behind it. And then he read all the names again.

"He's gone."

"You're not back far enough, Tom." Luke reached across and leafed four or five pages farther.

"That son of a bitch."

Somehow, there Jay was. In the same blue gown as the rest of the class. His name in the same font. In front of the same motherfucking slate background. How had he done it?

Tom moved the pages between his thumb and first finger. They were a different texture. It could be missed, but they were lighter, glossier. And the pages preceding and following Jay's page were of the same higher-quality paper. He turned the book on its spine and examined the binding. The yearbook was comprised of fifteen sections of folded paper, all professionally glued and stitched at their crease into the cover's spine. It was subtle, but the eighth section was out of alignment. Tom set the yearbook back on the table.

"I know it's fake." Luke's gaze slowly ping-ponged from him to the book, and his shoulders stopped shaking. "I want to know why."

Also Available from NineStar Press

WWW.NINESTARPRESS.COM

www.ingramcontent.com/pod-product-compliance
Lightning Source LLC
Chambersburg PA
CBHW050039180626
46810CB00002B/806